# A Change of Plan

They were silent for a while, listening to birdsong, watching the colors deepen over the mountains and the shadows swallow up the lawn. Then a sudden stream of lamplight poured into the dusky shadows of the porch as the front door opened, the screen door squeaked, and Lori burst out. "I've got it!" she exclaimed. "I've got the plan."

She bounced to a stop in front of them, a yellow legal pad in her hands, a very pleased expression on her face. "What we'll do," she declared, "is turn this house into a bed-and-breakfast."

Cici lifted an eyebrow. The other two sipped their wine and said nothing.

"I was talking to Ida Mae this afternoon," she went on. "Did you know this place used to be a boarding house for military wives in the forties?"

Cici said, surprised, "I didn't know that."

Lindsay and Bridget looked at Lori with new interest. "Is that right?" Bridget said.

And Lindsay added, "A boarding house?"

Lori nodded. "That's probably how we ended up with all those bathrooms. A house full of women . . ."

Cici grinned and lifted her glass to sip. "How about that? And sixty years later, it's still a house full of women."

*Also by Donna Ball*

A YEAR ON LADYBUG FARM

# At
# Home on
# Ladybug Farm

Donna Ball

BERKLEY BOOKS, NEW YORK

**THE BERKLEY PUBLISHING GROUP**
**Published by the Penguin Group**
**Penguin Group (USA) Inc.**
**375 Hudson Street, New York, New York 10014, USA**

Penguin Group (Canada), 90 Eglinton Avenue East, Suite 700, Toronto, Ontario M4P 2Y3, Canada
(a division of Pearson Penguin Canada Inc.)
Penguin Books Ltd., 80 Strand, London WC2R 0RL, England
Penguin Group Ireland, 25 St. Stephen's Green, Dublin 2, Ireland
(a division of Penguin Books Ltd.)
Penguin Group (Australia), 250 Camberwell Road, Camberwell, Victoria 3124, Australia
(a division of Pearson Australia Group Pty. Ltd.)
Penguin Books India Pvt. Ltd., 11 Community Centre, Panchsheel Park,
New Delhi—110 017, India
Penguin Group (NZ), 67 Apollo Drive, Rosedale, North Shore 0632, New Zealand
(a division of Pearson New Zealand Ltd.)
Penguin Books (South Africa) (Pty.) Ltd., 24 Sturdee Avenue, Rosebank, Johannesburg 2196,
South Africa

Penguin Books Ltd., Registered Offices: 80 Strand, London WC2R 0RL, England

This book is an original publication of the Berkley Publishing Group.

Copyright © 2009 by Donna Ball
Cover image of grapes by Bernardo Bucci/Corbis
Cover image of women planting by Mika/Zefa/Corbis
Cover design by Judith Lagerman
Text design by Tiffany Estreicher

First edition: October 2009

Library of Congress Cataloging-in-Publication Data

Ball, Donna.
    At home on Ladybug Farm / Donna Ball.— 1st ed.
        p.    cm.
    ISBN 978-0-425-22978-1
    1. Female friendship—Fiction.    2. Shenandoah River Valley (Va. and W. Va.)—Fiction.
  3. Farmhouses—Conservation and restoration—Fiction.    4. Domestic fiction.    I. Title.
    PS3552.A4545A95 2009
    813'.54—dc22                                                                        2009019127

PRINTED IN THE UNITED STATES OF AMERICA

10   9   8   7   6   5   4   3   2   1

# March Hares

*Homes really are no more than the people who live in them.*

—NANCY REAGAN

# 1

# Rushing the Season

Somewhere upon the small, blue, slowly rotating globe that over thirty billion people call home, a snowplow spewed dirty gray snow into banks on either side of the pavement. A housewife with chapped knuckles tugged frozen laundry off the line, and a fisherman cut a careful hole in the ice and dropped his hook. Children, wrapped in so many layers of winter clothing they could barely move, waddled like penguins toward the school bus stop, and windshield wipers beat a weary timpani against an icy rain while commuters dreamed of warm tropical destinations.

But in a place called Virginia, in a valley called Shenandoah, a rising sun melted the last puddle of snow. A crocus bloomed, and an easterly wind ruffled the unfurling blossoms of an apple tree. Spring had come to Ladybug Farm.

And not a moment too soon.

❧

Barely a year ago, Lindsay Wright, Cici Burke, and Bridget Tindale had turned their backs on their suburban lives in Baltimore,

Maryland, for the Shenandoah Mountains of Virginia. They had seen each other through divorce, widowhood, and child raising for over twenty-five years; they had traveled to Italy, Greece, France, Mexico, and the British Isles together; they had shared hopes, failures, and difficult truths with one another. But when they stumbled upon the one-hundred-year-old mansion during a routine vacation trip through the mountains, they knew their greatest adventure had just begun.

Their initial plan had been simple. Lindsay, who years earlier had abandoned her lifelong dream of becoming an artist for a much more practical role as an elementary school teacher, planned to turn the dairy barn into an art studio. Cici's passion for building was tailor-made for the myriad of projects that were just waiting to be tackled. And Bridget, a recent widow who once had dreamed of opening her own restaurant, was enraptured by the prospect of growing her own herbs and vegetables, creating her own recipes, and having someone to cook for again.

They had all, of course, underestimated what it took—both in terms of finances and energy—to restore a grand, hundred-year-old house. The sixteen acres of cultivated gardens, fruit trees, berry bushes, and grapevines, not to mention the sheds, outbuildings, reflecting pools, fishponds, and fountains, had seemed outrageously romantic and luxurious when they first toured the property. They envisioned restoring the blackened statues to gleaming alabaster, cleaning out the murky pools, setting the fountains to bubbling and splashing again, and lounging in beautifully painted Adirondack chairs in the rose garden, sipping wine and admiring the wonders of nature that surrounded them.

So far they had uncovered one stone path, and restored a two-foot-tall garden wall.

The sheer enormity of mowing, pruning, harvesting, and preserving all that was theirs was simply overwhelming. That was where Noah had come in. The sullen, unkempt teenager who had shown up one day to mow their lawn had been a godsend—even after they discovered he was camping on their property and living off what he could steal from their kitchen garden. He pruned bushes, he tied up vines, he cut and stacked firewood, he did heavy lifting; on one memorable occasion, he even helped kill a rattlesnake. Gradually, he had become part of the family.

Over the past year, the three women had discovered that neither their budget nor their master plan turned out to have any basis in reality. They worked harder in their retirement than they ever had at the jobs from which they had spent twenty years looking forward to retiring. They had started out with a beautiful old house and had ended up with a flock of sheep and a vicious sheepdog, a yearling deer who thought he was a house pet, a rebellious teenage boy, a cranky, ancient housekeeper—and Cici's twenty-year-old daughter Lori, who was herself a force of nature. The six-bedroom house, with maid's quarters, a wine cellar, a spacious attic, and multiple living areas, had shrunk to the size of a beach cabana over the winter, and the effort to blend such widely divergent personalities into some semblance of a functioning household had been, in Lindsay's words, "slightly more fun than spending the winter with the Donner party."

Repeated snowstorms had kept them housebound. Lindsay had tried to burn green wood in the fireplace and the resulting soot and black smoke had taken weeks to scrub off the wall.

Lori, whose youthful enthusiasm was matched only by her good intentions, kept trying to improve everything. Noah spent most of his time with the animals and, when he was forced to stay inside with the others, seemed to go out of his way to be miserable. The housekeeper, Ida Mae, and Bridget stirred up a familiar feud about the division of household chores. Cici, who spent the winter recovering from a fall from the roof, couldn't get to her workshop, and Lindsay's studio was so cold that her paints froze in the tubes. To date, things were not exactly working out as they had planned.

But spring was here. They had survived. Somehow, the old house had become home for all of them, and in truth, none of the women would have traded their lives on Ladybug Farm for those of anyone else on the planet.

On most days, anyway.

৵

"For the last time," Cici told her daughter, not bothering to try to disguise the impatience in her voice, "we are *not* getting a satellite dish."

"But for the low introductory price of $99 a month we can have 150 television channels *plus* high-speed Internet!" Lori flapped the sales brochure in front of her mother's face.

Since Cici was on her hands and knees at the moment, scooping out a shovelful of ashes from the fireplace, her daughter's gesture had the unfortunate result of sending a shower of white ash over the hearth, the floor, and Cici. Lori stepped back quickly, chagrined, and grabbed the broom. "What I mean is," she went on, undeterred, "you know how Aunt Bridget is always running back and forth to the library. If we had high-speed Internet, think how much gas she'd save!"

It was generally agreed among those who knew them that Lori got her looks and her charm from her father, and her obstinacy and determination from her mother. Cici, with her long legs, athletic build, and thick, honey-colored hair—not to mention the thousands of freckles, made even more prominent by a year of outdoor work—bore little physical resemblance to the petite, copper-haired Lori. But when the two women's eyes met in willful conviction over conflicting goals—which seemed to be the only kind of goals they had these days—they were mirror images of each other.

Cici glared at her daughter. "Do you know where they have really good high-speed Internet? At the University of Virginia dorms. Where, I believe we all agreed, you were supposed to be by now."

Lori returned a hurt look that was noticeably lacking in sincerity. "It wasn't my fault that my transcripts didn't get here from UCLA in time for me to be accepted for the spring."

"They didn't get here in time because you didn't send for them in time," Cici pointed out. "And I don't think I have to point out that a transfer acceptance is not the same as an enrollment."

Lori said, "I thought we agreed it would be good for me to take some time to think about the direction I wanted my life to take."

"And so you have."

"I'm just not convinced college is the right place for me right now."

"That makes one of us."

"It would be a lot easier for me to research my options," Lori pointed out single-mindedly, "if we had high-speed Internet."

Cici bit back a reply that she knew would be a waste of breath. After what Lori had termed a "less than satisfactory experience" at UCLA, it had not seemed unreasonable for her to take the winter off while she completed the paperwork for the transfer to UVA. But as more and more weeks passed, Lori grew less interested in returning to college at all. And while Cici loved having her daughter around, this was not a battle she intended to lose.

She simply knew better than to continue to fight it with words.

So she said instead, "I don't know what you're whining about high-speed Internet for, anyway. Your father is paying a fortune every month for that fancy Internet phone of yours."

Cici's ex-husband was a Los Angeles entertainment lawyer. He had greeted Lori's decision to drop out of UCLA and return to live with her mother in Virginia with a mixture of outrage and—as the responsibilities of fatherhood had never particularly suited him—thinly disguised relief. His way of dealing with emotions had always been through expensive gifts, and the phone was his way of saying "keep in touch."

Lori made a face. "Which only works when the moon is in Scorpio and the wind is out of the southwest."

Cici shrugged. One of the things she loved most about being surrounded by mountains was the limited access to technology. It slowed life down, and took out the background noise. "You can get perfectly good cell phone reception if you go to the top of the hill and face the antenna toward the east."

"A lot of fun when it's seventeen degrees outside, Mom."

"Do you know where they have really good cell phone reception?"

"The University of Virginia dorms, yeah, I know. Listen, I've been thinking—"

"Lord preserve us." Cici coughed and brushed ash out of her air as Lori's enthusiastic sweeping stirred up another cloud of dust. "Will you give me that broom? You're just making a mess."

Lori turned over the broom and dustpan without protest. "We should take a vote," she declared. "You're always saying we're a family, aren't you? And families decide important things together. I'll bet Aunt Bridget would love to have high-speed Internet. And where's that boy?"

Cici looked up from her sweeping with an exasperated look. "Will you stop calling him that? You've lived under the same roof for four months and his name is Noah, as you know perfectly well. And, as you also know perfectly well, today is his court date."

Lori rolled her eyes expressively. "Oh, right. You mean *juvenile* court. Trouble, that's what his name is."

"It's just a traffic ticket, Lori. There's no need to make it sound like he robbed a liquor store."

"If I had been cited for driving without a license when I was fifteen you would have made me *wish* I'd robbed a liquor store!" returned Lori smartly. "You all are way too easy on him, if you ask me—and I know, no one did. But maybe you should, now and then. I'm just trying to help."

Cici finished sweeping the ash into the dustpan with small deliberate movements, and straightened up, regarding her daughter with an exaggerated display of patience. "My beautiful girl," she said, "light of my life. It's been a long winter. We're all a little cranky. But you are standing in a six-thousand-square-foot, one-hundred-year-old house with walls that need to be painted, floors that need to be stripped, windows that need to be washed, and rugs that need to be cleaned, in the middle of a working farm with animals that have to be fed, stalls that must be be raked out, ground that needs to be turned, porches and walks that have to be swept, and gutters that need to be cleaned. And if you don't find something useful to do within the next thirty seconds I am going to strangle you."

Lori said meekly, "I think I'll help Aunt Bridget in the garden."

Replied Cici with a hard look, "Good plan."

Lori grabbed the sales brochure as she scurried out of the room.

She cut through the big stone and brick kitchen on her way to the backyard. The kitchen was filled with windows, and every windowsill was filled with flat plastic trays of seedlings that Bridget had been nurturing all winter. The room smelled like woodsmoke and vanilla, and, oddly, like vinegar. Lori wrinkled her nose and glanced around, and that was when she noticed Ida Mae half in and half out of one of the oversize industrial ovens. Her hands were clad in yellow rubber gloves up to the elbow, and she was scrubbing out the oven with a mixture of baking soda and vinegar.

"What is it about the first warm day that makes everyone want to clean something?" observed Lori, snagging a chocolate chip cookie from the jar on the counter.

Ida Mae craned her head around, swept her gaze over Lori's low-slung jeans and belly-skimming tank top, and scowled. "Put some clothes on, child. You're a disgrace."

Ida Mae was a square angular woman of undetermined age with blunt-cut iron gray hair and a habit of dressing in oddly matched layers. Today she wore a plaid wool shirtwaist dress over cotton dungarees and a purple turtleneck, topped by a pink cardigan and a gingham apron. Her face, etched with lines, rarely smiled, and her ears never missed a word that was said in the house—whether or not the words were meant to be heard.

Ida Mae had come with the house, and had been taking care of it, according to some accounts, almost since it was built. That gave her the right—in her own mind at least—to a great many opinions, and quite a few privileges. Lori, whose own grandparents were long gone, had been charmed by her immediately, although it was not entirely clear whether the sentiment was returned.

Lori hoisted herself lightly onto the soapstone countertop, which deepened Ida Mae's scowl of disapproval. Lori didn't notice. "Ida Mae, could I ask you something?" Taking silence as assent, she continued, "What's the deal with that kid Noah, anyway? Doesn't he have a family or anything?"

"Nope." Wringing her sponge out in the vinegar and baking soda solution, Ida Mae turned her attention to scrubbing the oven door. "His folks are dead."

"I know that. But I thought maybe aunts or cousins or something . . ." Lori eased open the lid of the cookie jar and slipped another cookie. "It's not like I haven't tried to be friends with him, but he's just weird. How did he end up here, anyway?"

"Same way you did," replied Ida Mae without looking up from her work. "He just showed up one day."

Lori bit into the cookie. "But I'm family. I mean, my mom owns the place. Partially, anyway."

"Then why don't you go bother her with your stupid questions?"

Lori sighed, examined the cookie for a moment, and took another bite. "I don't want her to think I disapprove."

Ida Mae looked up from her cleaning long enough to determine that the young woman was absolutely serious, and then, with a small shake of her head, stooped to wring out her sponge in the bucket again. She said gruffly, "You're a big-city girl. What you don't know about people would fill a book."

"Well, I don't mean to seem inhospitable or anything, but don't you think Mom and the others are a little old to be taking in foster children? And this isn't exactly a homeless shelter."

Ida Mae gave a grunt from inside the oven. "You just keep talking, Missy, about what your mama is too old for, and see what kind of shelter *you* end up in." She wiped down the oven door. "As for this place, it's been a lot worse than a homeless shelter, I can tell you that much. Back during the forties, it was a boarding house for war brides, and before that, in the Civil War, they turned it into a hospital—"

Lori interrupted curiously. "Civil War? I thought the house wasn't built until 1902."

"Rebuilt," corrected Ida Mae, glancing over her shoulder. "The first place burnt down. What I'm trying to say is—"

"No kidding? Was it burned by the Yankees? That's cool!"

Ida Mae scowled at her. "How should I know who burned it? It just burned. The point is—"

"Hospitality, I know," said Lori, hopping down from the counter as she finished off the cookie. "Thanks, Ida Mae, that was really interesting. Mom said I should find something useful to do. Do you want me to help you clean the oven?"

Ida Mae straightened up, bracing a gloved hand against her back, and her scowl only deepened. "The day I can't keep my own oven clean is the day they put me in the ground, young lady. Now get on out of here and pester somebody else. And put some clothes on."

Lori grinned at her as she scampered out of the kitchen. "The cookies are great!" she called.

Ida Mae muttered after her, just loudly enough to be heard, "You get fat off them cookies and you won't look so cute running around half naked."

Dodging the snapping, lunging attentions of Rebel, the sheepdog who spent most of his days lying under the porch and dreaming up ways to make the lives of the human inhabitants of the house miserable, Lori crossed the scrubby patch of winter lawn toward the back garden. A warm breeze tossed playful shadows across the ground and dappled her skin with a lacework of sunlight. The air smelled like baby grass and daffodils and the flock of sheep, grazing contentedly in the meadow that stretched beyond the house, looked like a painting. Bambi, the pet deer who had followed Lindsay home from a walk one day, grazed along the fence line with his rope harness trailing the ground, plucking up the juiciest blades of new spring grass.

Lori grinned happily and raised her arm in greeting as she approached the back garden spot where Bridget, wearing an oversize, long-sleeve chambray shirt and a big floppy hat, had stuck four sticks into the muddy ground about forty feet apart, and was carefully winding twine around them to form a large square.

With her short platinum bob, round, girlish face, and too-big clothes, Bridget looked more like Lori's sister than her aunt. In fact, she was not really Lori's aunt, and neither was Lindsay.

But the two women had been her mother's best friends since before Lori was born. Bridget's two children, Kevin and Kate, were adults now and Kate even had twin girls of her own, but Lori had grown up with them as though they were cousins or even siblings. Bridget and Lindsay had been part of all of Lori's holidays and every vacation; they had picked her up from school when her mother was sick and had made her lunch when her mother had to meet with a client. They had held her hands at her grandmother's funeral. They were better than aunts. They were, to Lori, second and third mothers.

When Cici, Bridget, and Lindsay had impulsively decided to give up their suburban Maryland lifestyle and buy a crumbling mansion in the Virginia countryside together, some people had been surprised. But not Lori. Some people had predicted that three women living together, especially in rural isolation, were doomed to ruin their friendship. Lori had not. From her twenty-year-old perspective, they had always been together, and quite simply always would.

"Hi, Aunt Bridget," Lori called as she approached. "Wouldn't you like to have—"

"Satellite television and high-speed Internet for the low introductory price of $99 a month?" replied Bridget, concentrating on the knot she was tying in the twine. "Can't. We don't have a clear view of the southern sky."

Lori stared at her, then at the brochure in her hand. Her face fell as she read the small print regarding the necessity for a clear view of the southern sky. "How did you know?" she asked.

"I saw the same flyer in today's paper. Besides, we checked out satellite Internet service when we first moved in. Come and hold this string for me, will you, sweetie, while I tie this?"

Lori stuffed the brochure in her back pocket and hurried to help. "What are you building? An addition to the house?"

"Our garden," replied Bridget, securing the twine and regarding with satisfaction her perfectly cordoned-off square of crabgrass, dandelions, and vetch weed.

"It's awfully big," replied Lori skeptically.

"We have a lot of mouths to feed."

"Um, supermarket?" suggested Lori.

"Excuse me? This from the girl who has been preaching to us all winter about carbon footprints and social consciousness? Don't you know that growing your own food is the most ecologically responsible thing you can do?"

"Well, that's true." Lori's expression brightened. "Good for you, Aunt Bridget."

"It's a lot of work, you know."

"Nobody said saving the planet was easy."

Bridget said, "As soon as you and Noah dig up the ground, I'll mark off the rows. These first two will be for sweet peas, and back up against the fence there we'll plant corn, beans, and cucumbers. Over there where we get strong afternoon sun, we'll plant the melons, and—"

"Wait a minute." Lori straightened up. "What do you mean, 'dig up the ground'?"

Bridget looked up at her, squinting a little in the sun. "Well, first you'll have to dig up all these weeds and grass. Then you'll take a hoe and chop up the ground and work in the fertilizer—"

"Fertilizer?"

"Dried manure from the pasture," explained Bridget—Lori made a face—"along with the compost we've been saving all year. You work it all together and let it sit so that the sun can warm it before we plant the seedlings. Otherwise, they'll go into shock."

"What I mean is—I thought that's what the yard boy was for. That's *his* job."

Bridget smiled sweetly. "It's everyone's job to bring food to the table. Besides, don't tell me you didn't enjoy the soups and stews and pies and pasta sauces and salsa and casseroles we had all winter. Where do you think they came from?"

"Last year's garden?"

Bridget hesitated. "Well, technically, they were from other people's last year's gardens, but this year we're self-sufficient. And everyone contributes."

"I understand that," Lori said. "I just don't understand why we have to dig up the garden by hand. What about Farley and his tractor?"

Their nearest neighbor, Farley, was also their plumber, electrician, and all-around handyman. During their time at Ladybug Farm, he had been called upon to help with everything from replacing shingles to pulling their lawn mower out of the ditch.

Bridget feigned shock. "What? And pollute the atmosphere with all those diesel fumes?"

Lori made a wry face. "Okay, I get it. Practice what you preach, right?"

"Right. Besides, Farley wouldn't be able to get the tractor back here without wrecking the flower beds."

"I think I'd rather help cook."

"That," Bridget told her firmly, "is precisely why you have to dig up the garden."

When Lori had first arrived at Ladybug Farm after Christmas, she had begged Ida Mae and Bridget to teach her how to cook. Despite Cici's warnings, they had agreed—with results so disastrous that Ida Mae had threatened to leave if Lori ever so much as came near the stove again.

Lori's expression fell. "Aunt Bridget," she said seriously, "we need to have a family meeting. I really think my talents are being underutilized here."

Bridget sighed and sank back on her heels. "My darling," she agreed, "I often think the same thing about myself."

ʚ

The tires crunched on the gravel as Lindsay swung her SUV around the circular drive and stopped, with an especially forceful application of the brakes, in front of the deep, columned front porch. She sat there for a moment, saying nothing, staring straight ahead.

She was dressed in a light gray wool suit with a pink blouse. Her rich auburn hair, usually pulled back into a playful ponytail, was carefully wound into a French twist and secured with a pearl-studded clasp. Her makeup—with the exception of the lipstick that had been chewed away on the drive home—could have passed muster with a department store model, and she even wore a strand of her mother's pearls around her neck. All of this on a Tuesday morning, and there wasn't even a meal involved.

"I don't see what you're so pissed about," Noah said. He had pulled off his clip-on tie and stuffed it into his pocket the moment they left the courthouse, and now he jerked open the top button of his blue Oxford cloth Sunday shirt. "We beat the rap, didn't we?"

With the greatest of effort, and a campaign that had taken three women two weeks to mount, Noah had been persuaded to cut his hair above his shoulders. The result was a perfect square that ended at the ears that he had styled himself with sewing scissors, with long dark chunks that still fell lankly over his face. He had been persuaded to wear a new pair of crisp dark jeans for the occasion, but nothing could get him out of the dirty sneakers. Lindsay turned upon him a glare that had frozen the hearts of much older—and wiser—men. "We did not," she told him, enunciating each word with great deliberation, "'beat the rap.' There was no rap to beat. This was a juvenile court hearing to determine, among other things, whether or not this temporary guardianship arrangement was a mistake. Not to mention the fact that I just paid out $175 for your fine!"

He scowled. "I'll pay you back."

"You'd better know you will."

"I don't know what you're so uptight about. It was just traffic court."

"We have a social worker coming here to inspect our home!"

He reached for the door handle. "I ain't afraid of no social worker."

Lindsay held out her hand, palm up. "Keys."

He gave her a look that tried hard to be innocent. "What keys?"

"To the motorcycle. And a five-page report on the French Revolution by tomorrow morning."

"You ain't my mama."

A beat. There had been a time not so long ago, when Lindsay would not have known how to respond to a remark like that.

He was an orphan. She had taken on a huge responsibility by assuming guardianship. And she saw his challenge for exactly what it was. She kept her tone pleasant. "Very true. If I were your mother you would have learned not to use that disrespectful tone with me as soon as you learned to talk. However, I *am* your teacher, so make that ten pages."

His brows shot together angrily. "That's not fair!"

"And the keys."

"We had a deal," he persisted. "You said I could keep it and ride it around here as long as I paid for the gas myself."

"We said you could ride the motorcycle as long as you didn't leave the property, and you broke that deal when you took it on a county road."

"I had to get gas, didn't I?"

"You almost sideswiped a police car!"

He slumped back in the seat, arms folded belligerently.

Lindsay took a breath. "Noah, are you happy here? Because if you're not, now would be a good time to tell me."

He refused to meet her gaze. "I like the animals," he admitted, somewhat sullenly. "And the drawing lessons." He hesitated, and with even more reluctance, added, "And I guess going to school here ain't as bad as going to regular school with all those little kids."

When Noah came to live with them after the death of his alcoholic father, Lindsay would have been grateful to get half as many words out of him. She understood how far he had come. She also understood how far he had yet to go, particularly when he burst out, "But I don't like living with a bunch of girls! I want my own place."

"Yeah, well good luck with that, Mr. Rockefeller."

"I was doing fine living in that little place of yours out in the woods last year. How come you had to bring me in and try to civilize me?"

The sentiment was so reminiscent of *The Adventures of Tom Sawyer*, to which Lindsay had introduced Noah over the winter, that she had to struggle to suppress a grin—and was not entirely successful in suppressing a surge of pride. A year ago, he had never read an entire book. Now he was practically quoting *Tom Sawyer*. That was okay. That was a reason to keep trying.

So she explained patiently, "Noah, you can't live in the woods. There's a social worker coming to determine whether our *house* is a suitable environment for you."

He slanted a glance toward her. "And what if she says it ain't?"

"Well . . . there's always Reverend Holland and his wife."

He scowled. "All she feeds me is grits. And they pray all the time."

Lindsay shrugged.

"It's just not right," he grumbled. "A guy in a house full of women. Who cares what that stupid social worker says, anyway? She don't have to live here."

Lindsay bit back sharp words. "Noah, you just spent the morning in juvenile court. You're not exactly in a position to be making demands."

"I don't see why—"

"Look," she said, losing her battle with patience, "you can't move to a gazebo in the woods, and that's final. There's no heat, no shower, no toilet, and not much of a roof. It's not going to happen. Get over it. And give me the key to the damn motor-cycle. Now."

He glared at her for a moment, then dug into his pocket and slapped a key in her hand. "It's not fair," he declared again as he jerked open the car door and stormed out.

"Make that fifteen pages on the French Revolution!" she shouted after him as he slammed the car door. Then she sank back against the seat and closed her eyes wearily. "I'm too old for this," she muttered. "Really."

But she smiled, faintly and secretly, when she said it.

## 2

# Family Meeting

For the first time in four months they had lunch on the porch—
and they discovered in the process that the white wicker furniture needed to be repainted, and that a mouse had chewed a
hole in the siding. But the blue gingham tablecloth and the vase
of bright yellow daffodils Lori had gathered added a festive aura
to the picnic of leftover chicken and Bridget's tricolored pasta
salad. Ida Mae made the first sweet tea of the season—the kind
in which sugar is melted in the hot tea before ice is added—and
seasoned it with early mint from the back door herb garden.
Everyone lingered over the platter of chocolate-chip cookies Ida
Mae brought out, and even Noah seemed to relax once the topic
of his court appearance had been discussed and abandoned.

"Gosh, it's good to be outside again," said Bridget, smiling
beneficently as she gazed out over the yard. The tree limbs were
still bare, and the lawn was littered with broken limbs and
dead leaves, but in the distance the sheep meadow was turning
emerald, and a jaunty row of daffodils lined the fence. "I don't
mind telling you, there have been a few days when I started to
lose faith that spring would ever get here."

"Can you believe we have temperatures in the seventies this early?" Lindsay commented. "Although I have to admit if I had to face one more freezing night I'm afraid you guys would have had to lock up the kitchen knives."

"Thank heaven for global warming," sighed Cici, sinking back in her chair contentedly.

"Mom!" Lori's tone was indignant. "Global warming is not a joke."

"I know, I know. The poor panda bears."

"*Polar* bears!"

"Right." Cici hid a smile behind her glass. "Polar."

"Ya'll just don't get too comfortable in your T-shirts," Ida Mae advised as she stacked the dishes. "We got ourselves a few cool evenings yet. I wouldn't've started cleaning out them fireplaces just now, if it was me."

"I couldn't stand it anymore," Cici said. "Everything smells like ashes."

"You're just going to have to dirty 'em up again."

"Then I'll clean them again."

Ida Mae sniffed as she marched into the kitchen with the dishes.

Noah bit into a cookie. "Yep," he offered, with every appearance of casualness, "it's the time of year makes a fella think about sleeping under the stars."

"Noah wants to move back to the folly," Lindsay explained to Cici and Bridget.

"Folly?" Lori said with interest. "What's a folly?"

"It's a building that serves no practical purpose," Cici explained. "They used to build them a lot in Europe."

Lori's eyes brightened with excitement. "And we have one? Where?"

"Well, it's not exactly a building anymore," Lindsay said. "It's more like a porch with a fireplace in the middle of the woods."

"No kidding!" She looked at Noah with new respect. "And you got to live there?"

Noah ignored her. "It could be a building again," he insisted. "All it needs is the walls shored up and some glass for the windows. I could run a 120 line right off the back of the house—"

Cici's eyes flew wide. "You'll do no such thing!"

"And it sits right on a spring for water. I'd bury the electric line," he assured Cici.

Lindsay said, "That's a great plan, but you're basically talking about building a whole new house. We can't afford any of it."

"Besides," added Bridget, "if that social worker comes out to find you living in a folly in the woods, she'll have us all put in jail. You don't want that, do you?"

Noah scowled and stood up. "I've got a report to write."

Lori got up, too. "Will you show me the folly?"

"Hold on a minute, both of you." Cici raised a hand to stay them. "Sit down. We're having a family meeting."

Noah looked suspicious. "What about?"

And Lori said hopefully, sliding back into her seat, "Is a satellite dish on the agenda?"

Cici beckoned to Ida Mae as she returned to the porch. "This concerns you too, Ida Mae. Have a seat."

"Ya'll go ahead and meet all you want," Ida Mae grumbled. "Don't make no difference to me what you decide anyhow." Nonetheless, she settled herself into a wicker rocker a few feet away, her jeaned legs crossed, hands thrust into the pockets of her flowered apron. They had all done this before.

Cici, Bridget, and Lindsay had known each other so long and so well that they could finish each other's sentences, but even they had understood from the beginning that the only way the joint living arrangement could work was if they had a plan and stuck to it. When Ida Mae, with her strong opinions and specific routines, had joined the mix, it was clear that they needed to establish some boundaries. But with the addition of the two young people, Lori and Noah, the regular family meeting was born. Because, as sincerely as they used the term *family*, they were, in fact, six unrelated people who shared a household and were doing the best they could to make it work. And sometimes even the best families needed to be run like a business.

Cici said, "Okay, here we all are. It's the beginning of a new season, and we have a lot we need to accomplish this year. Everyone is going to have to double up on chores if we're going to get it done. Lindsay, do you have the list?"

Lindsay obligingly pulled a small notebook out of the back pocket of her capris. Lori slid down in her chair and muttered, "Some family meeting. Why do I get the feeling the Executive Board has already met?"

Cici smiled at her sweetly. "That's life on a farm, dear. Isn't that what you told me you wanted? To get back to nature?"

Noah scowled. "Do I have to be here?"

"You most certainly do," responded Lindsay, "since the first item on the agenda is you."

He looked suspicious, and then uncomfortable as Lindsay went on, "Sometime this month—I'll let you know the exact date as soon as I do—a county social worker is coming by to do an assessment of Noah's living conditions. She'll probably want to interview each of us to find out whether or not this is a suitable environment for a teenage boy."

At this point Ida Mae grunted loudly and derisively. It was anyone's guess as to whether this was an expression of her contempt for any social worker who had the audacity to question the suitability of her home, or a gesture of relief that soon there would be one less mouth to feed.

"Personally," Lindsay went on, with a mild expression on her face, "I think Noah has done exceptionally well here and I'd hate to see anything change that. Next month he should be ready to take his tenth-grade equivalency exam, which will not only mean he's caught up with his peers, but will be almost a full quarter ahead of them."

Cici and Bridget broke into spontaneous applause, and Noah's cheeks turned bright red. "Anyone who's seen his work will agree he shows real promise as an artist and I think he deserves a lot of credit for keeping up with his schoolwork, his art lessons, and his chores around here."

"Hear, hear," said Bridget, smiling.

Noah shrunk deeper into his chair, looking miserable.

"So," said Cici, "I guess the only question is whether Noah wants to stay here as much as we want him to."

Noah looked around the table, scowling. "Bunch of women," he muttered, "ganging up on me."

Lori leaned toward him. "It's called manipulation," she said, with an air of confidentiality. "Don't fight it. They're masters."

"Noah," prompted Lindsay gently. "You know how it is in this family. If you're in, you're in. No breaking the rules, no bending the rules, no trying to get around the rules. We have to work together, all of us. And if we don't, the social worker is going to find another place for you to live."

"If that's what you want," added Bridget, though with a sorrowful look on her face, "we understand."

"But we hope it's not," said Cici, "because we've really gotten used to you, and we'd like you to stay."

"So what's it going to be?" asked Lindsay. "Are you in or are you out?"

Noah's eyes went from one to the other of them in a stormy circuit that was part challenge, part embarrassment, and finally simple resignation. "I didn't know this whole damn meeting was going to be about me," he said finally. And then, with an elaborate shrug, "I don't want you to get in trouble with the county. So I'm in. But after that social worker leaves, I still want my own place."

All three women smiled, and even Ida Mae, rocking a little faster, seemed to have a smug expression on her face. Lori just rolled her eyes.

"Excellent," said Lindsay, spreading her hands on the table as she leaned back in her chair. "Now let's talk about the division of labor."

Noah folded his arms across his chest. "I knew there was a catch."

"As long as you brought it up," Lindsay went on cheerfully, "Noah, you're in charge of mowing the lawn, pruning the shrubs, and cleaning out the orchard. Also, cultivating the ground for the vegetable garden and building a fence to keep Bambi out."

He considered that. "How much does it pay?"

Lori gave him a scathing look, and Lindsay replied evenly, "Room and board."

His brows knit sharply. "I thought Lincoln freed the slaves."

Lindsay smiled. "Extra credit on your final exam for knowing that."

Lori exclaimed, "Oh, come on!"

Bridget said, "Did you know forty percent of Americans think Jimmy Carter freed the slaves?"

Cici lifted an eyebrow. "Seriously?"

"I read it somewhere."

Noah said, still scowling, "Who's Jimmy Carter?"

And because no one could be sure whether he was joking, Lori just rolled her eyes again.

Lindsay said, "If you want to earn a little extra money, you can start cleaning out the loft in the dairy barn. I need the space to store my canvases. And you still owe me $175."

She checked her list again. "Lori, I've got you down to help Noah dig the garden and build the fence."

"Wait a minute," objected Noah.

Lori said at the same time, "I think we should talk about that."

Noah went on, "I don't need help from no girl."

"I'm really not much of an outdoor garden-digging kind of person," added Lori. "I think I'd be of more help in the kitchen."

"No one who actually works in the kitchen agrees," Cici said mildly. "Besides, you need the exercise and the vitamin D."

"I'll get sunburned. Too much sun is very hard on fair-skinned redheads, right, Aunt Lindsay?"

"Wear a hat," advised the fair-skinned, auburn-haired Lindsay. "Also, I really have my heart set on getting the reflecting pool and the fishponds restored this summer. That means they'll have to be drained and cleaned of debris, then bleached and sealed and maybe even resurfaced. Lori, I thought that would be a good project for you."

Lori's eyes went wide, and Noah tried not to grin. "What, are you kidding? All that black gunky water and weeds and bugs? Those pools are gross! Who knows what could be living at the bottom of them? There could be, like, snakes and stuff!"

The three women glanced at each other, and shared the very slightest of shrugs. "Probably not this time of year," Cici offered. "So I'd get started right away if I were you."

"But I don't know anything about building ponds! I wouldn't know where to begin!"

"None of us knew anything about restoring a hundred-year-old house when we started," Cici pointed out.

"Or raising sheep or preserving food," Bridget added.

"Or building garden walls or bringing back an antique rose garden or managing an orchard," Lindsay added. "The point is to learn by doing. This is your project." And she beamed at the younger woman. "We know you'll do a great job."

"But—"

"We'll also need you to help with the berry harvest this spring," Lindsay went on, "which means spreading nets over the bushes to keep the birds out as soon as the blossoms fall off. And we're all going to have to pitch in to get all of these windows washed, inside and out, not to mention scrubbing the soot stains off the walls."

"And I know you don't mind continuing to help me with the sheep," Bridget said, smiling, "especially with the baby lambs."

Lori looked slightly mollified. "Well, that's okay I guess. I like the babies. As long as I don't have to go tromping across that muddy meadow through the sheep manure in my Doc Martens."

"Of course not, sweetie," Bridget assured her. "We've got work boots just your size for that."

Lori looked suspiciously from Bridget to Lindsay to her mother to Ida Mae. "And what about you guys? What are you going to be doing?"

Bridget widened her eyes innocently. "Why, I was planning to go to Acapulco."

"And I was going to write a novel," offered Cici, leaning back in her chair as she sipped her iced tea.

"Damn," said Lindsay, "that's what *I* was going to do. No, wait, maybe I'll just read one."

"In fact," Cici said, with an air of determination that made even Lindsay and Bridget uneasy, "I thought this spate of warm weather might be the perfect time to start refinishing the floors."

Lindsay groaned out loud, and Bridget said, "I don't know what would make you think that." Noah suddenly became very interested in a cloud formation in the distant sky and Lori, for once, had the very good judgment to keep silent.

"Come on," Cici insisted, "we've been putting it off for a year. We don't want to wait until it gets too hot, and it's warm enough now to leave the windows open to air the place out. Jonesie said we could rent a sander from him, and the whole project could be finished in three days. Well, five," she modified, "before we can move the furniture back in."

One of the first things they had loved about the old house was the beautiful heart pine floors that covered the downstairs living areas. Unfortunately, years of neglect had left them in less than optimal shape. After painstakingly restoring the stair treads of the grand staircase to all their gleaming glory, however, their enthusiasm for further work on the floors had waned. They had spent an entire spring and summer thinking of reasons *not* to tackle the floor refinishing project. But they all knew Cici was right. They couldn't put it off forever.

"Well," Lindsay agreed reluctantly, "this is the perfect weather for a project like that."

"I saw some really pretty rugs in the JCPenney catalog," Bridget volunteered. "Couldn't we just . . ." But a look at Cici's expression persuaded her not to finish the sentence. "No, I guess not."

"Well, if ya'll are going to start tearing the house apart," grumbled Ida Mae, heaving herself up from the rocker, "I've got things that need to get done. Varnish ain't never going to dry if it rains, you know."

"Wait," Cici said. "There's news." She took a breath, set her glass down, and glanced around the table at them with a smile that barely concealed her excitement. "Derek and Paul called before lunch. They're driving down next weekend."

Exclamations of delight rippled around the table until Noah said, "What? Them queer guys from the city?"

Lindsay shot him a look. "That's not a polite term, Noah."

"Jeez, where were you raised, in a barn?" Lori added. "They're gay, okay?"

He shrugged. "Queer is queer."

Lori opened her mouth again and Cici cut her off with a warning. "Lori . . ."

Bridget said quickly, "Do they know something about the wine?"

In the 1960s and '70s, the farm—known then as Blackwell Farms—had operated a winery. Ida Mae had given the women the last bottle of Blackwell Farms wine from that era as a Christmas present, and it turned out to be quite valuable. Derek, an amateur wine connoisseur, had offered to help them place the wine for auction with a friend of his who specialized in such things. They had been waiting weeks to hear how much it would bring.

"I think so," Cici said, her eyes taking on a spark of excitement. "Derek said he wanted to talk to us about it in person."

"That could be really good," Lindsay said hopefully.

"Or really bad," Bridget ventured.

"I better start airing out the guest room," Ida Mae said with an air of martyrdom as she trudged back inside. "Like we didn't have nothing better to do."

"What I'd really like to do," Cici said, "is get the floors finished before they get here."

"They'll be our first real overnight company," Bridget said happily. "We'll have cheese blintzes with wild blueberry sauce for breakfast."

"You'll have to make scones," Lindsay added. "You know Paul will consider the trip wasted if you don't. And I think we need to spruce up the guest room a little if people are actually going to stay there. There's still some furniture left in the loft. "

"Maybe we could use the money from the wine to hire somebody to clean out the pools," Lori suggested hopefully. "You know, a professional."

"Wouldn't cost but a couple of hundred dollars to fix up that little ole place in the woods," added Noah.

"Sorry, guys, the money is already spent," Cici said. "On taxes."

Lori sighed. "Well, it'll be nice to see them again. To have a conversation with someone who, you know, remembers the Internet."

Noah said, "Is this meeting over? I've got to tune up the lawn mower."

"French Revolution," Lindsay reminded him. "Fifteen pages."

"It's in my head."

"It had better be on paper by nine o'clock tomorrow morning."

He returned a wave that might have been acknowledgment, agreement, or dismissal as he took the stairs with a leap and trotted across the lawn.

Bridget said fondly, "Recent difficulties aside, he really is a good boy."

"He's come a long way," agreed Lindsay.

"Thanks to you," Cici pointed out, and Lindsay shrugged modestly.

Lori said, "You know, there's a lot to be said for doing what you're good at."

"Oh-oh," murmured Cici, "I recognize that tone." Nonetheless, all three women turned their attention to Lori with a look of polite interest.

"Like Noah, for instance," Lori went on earnestly. "He's really good at lawn mowers and hoes and chain saws. You should go with your strengths. Do what you're good at."

Bridget inquired helpfully, "And what are you good at, Lori?"

"I've been thinking about that," Lori answered with enthusiasm. "And you know how much I love this place and want to contribute."

"Oh, yes," agreed Bridget.

"No doubt about it," added Lindsay.

"Absolutely," from Cici.

"But I'm a business major," Lori pointed out. She took a breath, her eyes brightening with expectation as she came at last to the pièce de résistance. "That's what I'm good at. So what I'd like to contribute is—a business plan!"

The three women were silent for a moment, appearing to consider this. Then Cici said, "True enough. You were a business major. But did you actually take any business courses?"

Lori looked momentarily at a loss. "Well, that doesn't mean I couldn't come up with a good business plan."

"Of course it doesn't," Bridget assured her. "I'm sure you'd be just great at it."

"But what would we do with it?" Lindsay inquired.

"Make money!" explained Lori happily. "Listen, I know how expensive this place is. I think I can find a way to make it pay for itself, and I think I can do it *without* going back to college."

Cici drew in a sharp breath, and Lindsay and Bridget immediately turned their attention to their glasses of iced tea.

Lori rushed on before Cici could speak, "Just hear me out, Mom. I know we've had this conversation before, but I've been giving this a lot of thought. The whole point of college is to find your calling, right?" Cici opened her mouth to reply but Lori didn't give her a chance. "Well, I think I've already found mine!" She made a sweeping gesture with her arm, her face lighting up. "This place, this house, living off the land and communing with nature . . . I have a chance to do what other people only *talk* about doing!"

The three women shared a quick and secret look. Hadn't they said almost the same words when they had decided to leap into this adventure? Wouldn't it be somewhat hypocritical—not to mention selfish—to deny the younger woman her chance at finding what they had found?

Sensing her advantage, Lori pressed on. "College isn't for everyone, you know. Look at you, Mom. You worked your whole life in real estate—"

"I went to college," Cici pointed out sharply.

"But you didn't have to," Lori said. "That's the point. And Aunt Bridget married a college professor; she didn't become one. And even if Aunt Lindsay was a teacher her whole life, now she's an artist, which is what she always wanted to be, and you don't have to go to college for that! All of you are doing what you always wanted to do. It just took twenty-five years—and *no* college education—for you to get around to it!"

Cici drew a breath, released it; looked to Lindsay for help, who shrugged; looked to Bridget for help, who suddenly discovered her shoelaces were untied; started to speak, and took a sip of her tea instead.

"This is what *I* want to do," Lori said passionately. "I want to restore old houses. And I don't want to spend twenty-five years working in the wrong job before I do it! I know I don't have your talent with a hammer and T square, Mom," she rushed on, "or yours in the kitchen, Aunt Bridget, or yours with paint and decor, Aunt Lindsay. But I *do* have something to offer. All I'm asking is a chance to prove it to you."

This time, when Cici looked at her friends, it was not for help, it was for confirmation—and, along with sympathetic resignation, she saw it in their eyes. There was only one reply she could legitimately make, and so she did.

"You've seen how much hard work is involved in this place," Cici pointed out, "and it's about to get harder."

"I know that," Lori insisted.

"You've got to keep up with your chores, and that includes restoring the pools."

Lori squared her shoulders. "I promise."

Once again, Cici passed a silent consultation to Lindsay and Bridget, and received barely perceptible nods in reply.

"Three months," she said. "You've got three months to come up with a viable business plan to make this place self-supporting, and it has got to be accepted by all three of us. If you can do that, that will be enough evidence to convince me you're mature enough to make your own decisions about your career. But if not..." Her tone darkened in warning. "You are going back to college, no questions asked, end of discussion. Fair deal?"

"Fair deal," agreed Lori, her eyes glowing. She sprang from her chair and threw her arms around Cici's neck. "I love you, Mom! You're going to be so proud of me."

"I'm already proud of you," Cici assured her, and she couldn't help smiling. "But that doesn't mean I'm going to go easy on you."

"Any of us," added Bridget.

"Remember, *all* your chores," added Lindsay.

"And we're the final judges," said Cici. "No arguing."

"I'm going to surprise you," Lori assured them gaily as she hurried off. "You just wait and see!"

Cici blew out a breath when she was gone. "Well," she said.

"Well," agreed Bridget.

Lindsay looked at Cici. "What if she actually does it?"

"That," replied Cici, and took a long gulp of tea, "is what worries me."

ᔔ

Evening. Even with two young people in the house, it was a sacrosanct time of day. The supper dishes were done. Ida Mae always went to bed in her downstairs suite immediately afterward. The sheep had been rounded up for the night by the ever vigilant sheepdog, who had been fed and was snoozing on a pile of hay in the barn. Bambi the deer was in his pen, safe from predators and hunters. Noah was in his room, working on his report. Lori was, presumably, watching DVDs or listening to her iPod—with headphones either way, which was the rule at Ladybug Farm. Lindsay, Cici, and Bridget gathered on the front porch to watch the sunset for the first time in four long, cold months. The expression on their faces as the setting sun cast hues of gold and pink across their skin was reminiscent of those of prisoners who had just walked outside the big gate and who stood dumbstruck, barely able to comprehend the glory of the freedom that was offered them.

"Six o'clock," murmured Lindsay contentedly, "and it's sixty-two degrees. I love this place."

"Days like this make you believe Nature has a master plan," agreed Bridget.

"Speaking of plans . . ." Cici slanted her a sly look. "Good job assigning Miss Lower-Your-Carbon-Footprint to garden duty. I suspect we'll hear a lot less out of her now that she's got a chance to practice what she preaches."

"And how about my contribution to the work schedule?"

Lindsay demanded archly. "Was that a stroke of genius or what?"

Cici almost choked on her wine. "I didn't think I could keep a straight face! Good heavens, Lindsay, you couldn't pay me to clean out those pools!"

"My solution was to fill them in and make a patio," admitted Bridget.

"Well, there you go," said Lindsay smugly. "You want something done, you ask someone with a little ambition." She sipped her wine. "I have a feeling fixing up an old house and living close to nature are going to seem a lot less romantic to Lori—and college dorm life a lot more appealing—before this summer is over."

There was a moment of silence in which they knew Cici was trying to convince herself Lindsay was right.

Then Cici said, "Should we be worried about the social worker's visit?"

Lindsay gave a half chuckle. "It's just Carrie from town. She's the one who came up with the idea for us to share guardianship with Reverend Holland in the first place, and she's already approved the living situation once. It's just a formality. But I wanted Noah to *think* we should be worried."

"I think Lori is right," Bridget said. "We are a little manipulative."

"It's one of those self-defense skills they teach you in Mother School," Cici said.

"What is this about wanting to move back out to the woods?" Bridget wanted to know. "He's not serious, is he? After we practically broke our necks last fall sneaking things down there to him to keep him from freezing—and starving—to death!"

Lindsay rocked thoughtfully for a moment. "I'm not sure. Part of it is just his Davy Crockett fantasy, I guess. But I think it might have more to do with the fact that he doesn't know how to be part of a family. It can't have been easy, all the adjustments he's had to make this year."

"Well, he's not moving back to the folly," Bridget declared.

"I think we can all agree on that," said Cici.

"I don't think we'll hear much more about those plans for a while," Lindsay said with a wry tilt of her head, "since it's going to take him most of the summer to pay off that traffic fine."

They were silent for a while, listening to birdsong, watching the colors deepen over the mountains and the shadows swallow up the lawn. Then a sudden stream of lamplight poured into the dusky shadows of the porch as the front door opened, the screen door squeaked, and Lori burst out. "I've got it!" she exclaimed. "I've got the plan."

She bounced to a stop in front of them, a yellow legal pad in her hands, a very pleased expression on her face. "What we'll do," she declared, "is turn this house into a bed-and-breakfast."

Cici lifted an eyebrow. The other two sipped their wine and said nothing.

"I was talking to Ida Mae this afternoon," she went on. "Did you know this place used to be a boarding house for military wives in the forties?"

Cici said, surprised, "I didn't know that."

Lindsay and Bridget looked at Lori with new interest. "Is that right?" Bridget said.

And Lindsay added, "A boarding house?"

Lori nodded. "That's probably how we ended up with all those bathrooms. A house full of women . . ."

Cici grinned and lifted her glass to sip. "How about that? And sixty years later, it's still a house full of women."

"With plenty of bathrooms," Bridget pointed out.

"So here's the thing." Excitedly, Lori leaned forward so that they could see the drawing she had made in the light that spilled from the open door. "This whole front part of the house—the living room, dining room, the bedrooms, of course, and the upstairs sitting room—would be public space. That little room off the living room could be the office. The kitchen is already outfitted for preparing big meals, and, Aunt Bridget, you know you've always wanted to run a restaurant."

Bridget gave a conciliatory nod of agreement.

"The back part of the house," Lori went on, "would be our living space. We could turn the sunroom into our family room, and we eat in the kitchen, anyway."

Cici inquired politely, "Where would we sleep?"

Lori turned a page. "This," she declared, "is a sketch of the cellar—as it could be. All it would take is a little remodeling, putting in some windows, a few walls . . . it'll be a snap."

"A snap," repeated Cici, careful to keep her expression neutral.

Lori went on, "A room in the average B&B rents for about $200 a night—more on weekends and in peak season. And with this location—the view, the homegrown food, the gardens—"

"The pools," added Lindsay.

Lori ignored her. "You could keep this place filled just about year around! That's twelve hundred dollars a day! That's eight thousand dollars a week! Thirty-six thousand dollars a—"

"We can do the math," Cici said.

And Bridget added gently, "Honey, running a B&B is hard

work. And there are licenses and codes and permits and regulations..."

"And it may be a tad bit optimistic to count on keeping all the rooms rented," Lindsay said. "In such a slow economy."

"Bottom line," Cici said simply, but firmly, "we are not pimping out our house. We've worked too hard and love it too much to have strangers tramping through it for money. And I am definitely not sleeping in the cellar."

"Ida Mae does," Lori pointed out defensively.

"Ida Mae has her own room with a bath and private entrance from the garden. That's the way it's always been and that's how she likes it. I, on the other hand, like my big sunny upstairs bedroom with its claw-foot tub and heart pine floors. I like it so much that I left everything I knew and went into enormous debt for it. So I think I'll just stay there, thanks."

"Me, too," said Bridget.

"Me, too," agreed Lindsay.

Lori blew out a breath that ruffled her bangs, and her face settled into lines of disappointment. "Well," she said, "I guess I had a feeling you might say that." And then she cheered. "But it was a pretty good plan for a first try, wasn't it?"

"Absolutely," agreed Cici.

"Couldn't ask for more."

"Brilliant," said Lindsay.

"Okay, then, it's back to the drawing board." She gave them a wave with her legal pad as she swung toward the door. "I'll be back!"

Bridget laughed softly as the door closed behind her and the porch faded to dusk again. "Do you know what I love about having Lori here?"

Cici slid a glance toward her. "Name one thing. I dare you."

"Every time I look at her I'm reminded that I never, ever have to be twenty years old again."

"Amen," said Lindsay.

And Cici agreed, "I'll drink to that."

They rocked forward in unison, clinked glasses, and drank.

Stillness fell as the sky was leached of the last of its color. The birds settled in their nests; the animals slept in their stalls. The mountains, framed by the stark silhouettes of knotty tree branches, swelled indigo against a neutral background. The earth, not yet accustomed to holding the sun's warmth, gave up a damp chill that smelled of decaying mulch and sweet budding grass. The women lingered, ignoring the prickling flesh on their arms, sipping their wine in companionable silence, wrapped in the contentment of the night.

"Spring," said Bridget softly, at last. "Welcome home."

# 3

# In Another Time

*Pearl, 1863*

When Pearl stood beside her Papa's grave with her hand wrapped in Mother's cold, cold one, she did not cry. She was only six, and she understood that Papa had been kicked in the head by Caesar, their big red stallion, and had gone to live with Jesus and wasn't coming back, but she didn't understand why Mother wept so, if Papa was with Jesus, except that maybe she missed him. Later that day Mother put a rifle in the hands of Ebenezer, the big black man who helped Papa take care of the horses, and then they buried Caesar in a big hole that took half a dozen field hands almost a day to dig. Pearl wanted to cry for Caesar, who Mother said with a mean look in her eye was not with Jesus, but in the end she did not.

She was eight when the soldiers in the gray coats came and drove away all their horses, and even though Mother stood screaming in the yard after them and when they were gone she fell to her knees and wept in the dirt, Pearl did not cry. It seemed to her that eight years old was too old to cry over horses, because Mama Madie said she was almost a young lady now, and because it scared her to see her own mama carrying on so.

When all the field hands ran off, and even Ebenezer and Lula in the kitchen and Old Luke, who was nearly blind but still carried in the firewood every morning, ran off, too, everyone except Mama Madie, who was a free black woman and owed no man in this world, Pearl wanted to cry for missing them. And when she had to carry water in a bucket that was almost too heavy to lift and dig potatoes and sometimes there was nothing but grits for supper, she wanted to cry because she was tired and hungry and cold. But then at night she could hear her mama weeping softly in the room next to hers, and Pearl would get up and slip into bed with Mother and hug her tight, and she figured it was probably best if both of them didn't cry at once.

When the soldiers in the blue coats came, Pearl wanted to cry, because she was so afraid remembering how the gray-coated soldiers had stolen their horses. But Mother had fetched up her rifle and walked right out on the veranda to meet those soldiers with a real hard look in her eye, and Mama Madie came out the door and stood right up close beside her with her head high and her shoulders back. Pearl felt it was her place to stand tall, too. So she came between her mama and Mama Madie and stood up straight, and Mama Madie put her big bony hands on Pearl's shoulders and squeezed so hard that she really *did* want to cry.

The soldiers' horses tore up their yard and their wagons rolled over the kitchen garden, and they kicked up dust and noise something terrible. One of them rode up to the veranda and got off his horse and started up the steps until Mother raised the rifle at him. Likely he did not know Old Luke had used up the last of the ammunition shooting at a fox that was after their last laying hen. He'd missed him, too, probably because he was nearly blind.

So the man just stood at the bottom of the porch and took off his hat and said his name was Captain Somebody, and that his men would be camping here for a time, and Mother had said this was a peaceful house with no man soldiering on either side, and they wanted no part of their war. He answered that that was good to hear, because he was a man of peace himself, a doctor and not a soldier, and he had with him a bunch of folks just trying to get home, but some of them were wounded and bad sickening, and he was in need of the house and the beds, thank you kindly. Then he looked at Mama Madie like the color of her skin made him wonder if Mother had lied about this being a peaceful house, and her fingers tightened so that Pearl thought the bones in her shoulders would break, and she said, real cool like, "I, sir, am a free woman and I owe no man in this world." And he said just the same would she mind pouring him a cool draft of water, and she told him where the well was and to get it himself. That made him smile, tiredly, but he did.

The soldiers started carrying their sick and their bleeding into the house, and Mother said to Pearl, "Be quick and gather up the valuables and take them to Mama Madie." There weren't too many valuables left, but Mama Madie stuffed a bag of coffee down her blouse and Mother gathered up her medicines and her Holy Bible, but it was Pearl who thought to rescue Mother's treasure box from its place on the table near her sewing chair. She hugged it to her chest and was hurrying across the yard when a big soldier with small ugly eyes and tobacco juice in his beard stepped in front of her and said, poking at the treasure box with a dirt-nailed finger, "Whatcha got there, tadpole?"

She hugged the box closer and took a step backward, but her heart was beating hard.

The man made to snatch the box from her and she ducked past him, head low, the box wrapped tightly in both arms. She thought she would run free but he caught her hair, which was braided in a pigtail, and jerked it hard, and she screamed out loud because it hurt, and also because she was so scared he would steal Mother's treasure box.

He had his hands on the box and would have twisted it away from her but at that moment the captain, who had come from nowhere, shouted, "Sergeant, attention!"

The man with the beard stepped back and stood straight as an arrow, but he took the treasure box with him. The captain strode forward and took the box from him, and as much as Pearl wanted to, even though her chest was heaving with the effort, she did not cry. The captain opened the box, and plucked casually through the contents. Then he closed the box and said to the big man, in an odd, bitter voice, "Try to remember, Sergeant, that we fight on the side of God. And we don't, as a general rule, steal sewing notions from children."

Then he returned the treasure box to Pearl with a tender look, but she did not linger to thank him. She ran away as fast as she could to Mama Madie's cabin, and she thought that God must be in bad trouble indeed if He needed the likes of the bearded man to fight His battles for Him.

❧

That night, Pearl and Mother moved into Mama Madie's cabin, which was small but warm, and smelled like the dried plants and flowers that hung from the ceiling. Mother was real pleased to have her treasure box safe, and she hugged Pearl hard when she learned of it. Then Mother said she thought it wouldn't be so bad, having the soldiers camped here, because there wasn't anything left to steal and at least they would keep the gray-coated soldiers away. But Mama Madie said she didn't trust nobody in a uniform, and good thing they'd buried the silver in the stream bed and turned the hogs and cows loose months ago.

They sat piecing together a quilt top and talking like that in tight, nervous voices, and Pearl, whose stitches were fine and even, helped a good bit. Mother said she felt bad for all the sick soldiers and maybe she'd take some willow bark and blackberry tea up to the house in the morning, and Mama Madie said angrily that it wasn't her place to go ministering to white trash that drove her out of her own house like that, and then Mother's eyes began to flash as she said that the captain seemed a decent Christian man and it was her boundin' duty to help the sick. Then Mama Madie said that no Christian man would wear the coat of a soldier and, because Pearl didn't like to hear them arguing, she said, "Tell me the story of this quilt, Mama Madie."

All of Mama Madie's quilts had stories hidden in their patterns. Some were stories of the Far Country, where the sun shone on dry rivers and the hunters carried spears and eyes hid in the tall grass, that her grandmother's mother had told to her. Others were stories of nearer times, and slaves that hid beneath the bridge at Four Corners on a night when the moon was full, awaiting rescue by something called the Underground Railroad, which did not run underground and which was not a railroad at all. Mama Madie said the only way her people had to tell their stories was through songs and women's work, because the white Master didn't pay attention to either one of them.

Mama Madie had been a slave once, and the man she loved who fathered her twin baby girls had been sold to Georgia, then the twin babies died and Mama Madie had come to raise Pearl's mother, whose papa had made her a free woman. Pearl knew all the stories of all the quilts. But when Pearl asked her the story of the newest quilt, Mama Madie got a strange, kind of sad look on her face and said, "Why, child, I don't rightly know just yet."

Pearl looked at her mama. "Maybe this quilt could be our story, Mother."

Mother smiled, but in a way that said she was thinking of something else, and agreed that maybe it could.

Pearl dragged Mother's treasure box out from under Mama Madie's low rope bed, and put it in Mother's lap. A soft look came over Mother's face as she opened up the lid. It smelled of cedar and dust and old, dear things. Inside were scraps and pieces of lives that had gone before—a snippet of lace from a wedding dress, a knitted baby sock, brass buttons off one of Papa's coats, a spool of delicately spun thread too fine to use for everyday work, a cluster of pressed dried violets pinned to a square of lavender silk, and, finally, the greatest treasure of them all: a square of strong dark wool, tattered now and a little frayed at the edges, embroidered with brightly colored silken threads in the shape of a flying horse against a red and gold shield, and over it a banner with words written in a language even Mother couldn't read.

As she traced it with her fingers Pearl said softly, "Tell me again, Mother. Tell me our story." And so Mother told again the story of the emissary of the king who had come to Virginia long ago with the flying horse embroidered on his wool cloak, so that everyone would know he was a nobleman from the king, and how he wrapped his newborn baby in the cloak and went off to fight the Indians, and was killed and never came back, and how for years and years the cloak had been passed down through Mother's family until it got so worn-out all that was left was the embroidered horse.

And she always ended the story by saying, "And one day you will pass this down to your daughter, little Pearl, so that she will never forget where she came from."

But Pearl worried that the scrap of cloth, which seemed to be getting smaller with each generation, would be too small to see by then, and the beautiful flying horse would be gone. So her heart leapt with joy when, as her mother finished the story this time, she looked thoughtfully at all the treasures in the box again, and said, "Do you know, sweet Pearl, I believe you may be right. These scraps and pieces are doing no good locked away in this box where the moths can get them. Let's make our own story quilt, and you can start the center square."

# 4

# Discoveries

"I don't know why I have to be the one to dig up the rocks," Lori said, poking at a knot of granite with the tip of her shovel.

Noah, who was chopping at the ground with a hoe a few yards ahead of her, favored her with a disparaging scowl over his shoulder. "If you're having trouble working that shovel, you can come up here and work this hoe. What kind of girl don't know how to dig a hole, anyway?"

"The kind who'd rather get her workout in a gym," Lori grumbled, but Noah either didn't hear or didn't care. He went back to swinging the hoe, breaking up the weeds and root-webbed ground, and Lori resignedly dug her shovel into the ground and turned up another rock.

They had been at the chore of clearing the garden spot for almost two hours, and Lori was dismayed by how little ground had actually been cleared. While Noah went ahead of her, turning over earth with the hoe, her job was to gather up the big clods of grass and weeds and carry them to the wheelbarrow, as well as dig up the rocks when the hoe struck one, and carry those to the wheelbarrow. When the wheelbarrow was full,

Noah would roll it to the edge of the woods and dump it. Even though it had sounded like a fair division of labor when Bridget had first spelled it out, Lori soon began to suspect she had gotten the worst of the job. Her short denim overalls, stylishly accented with rhinestones on the back pockets, were smeared with mud, her work boots were clogged with it, and her leather work gloves were grimy and damp. She wore a wide-brimmed straw garden hat over her long copper braid, which only made her sweat. Moreover, every time the hoe opened up a section of ground, it seemed as though another swarm of tiny insects clouded the air. It was miserable.

"This is why man invented the plow," she said, heaving the rock out of the ground and carrying it, double-handed, to the wheelbarrow.

"Will you stop your griping? It ain't that hard. Half the plot is already cleared from last year. If you'd shut up and work we'd have this done before noontime."

Now it was Lori's turn to scowl as she waved away a cluster of gnats. "What's your hurry? Have you got an appointment?"

"Gotta get your taters and peas in the ground before St. Paddy's Day, or you won't get a crop."

"Who told you that?"

He tossed a sneer over his shoulder. "Everybody knows that."

Lori carried more grass clumps to the wheelbarrow. "You know why she's making us do this, don't you? It's *The Little Red Hen* all over again."

"What hen?" He did not look around. "We ain't got no chickens."

She made a grimace of impatience. "You know, the story about the little red hen who was going to make bread and she went around asking all the farm animals to help her gather the wheat and grind the flour and bake the bread and everyone said, 'Not I!' but when she said 'Who will help me eat the bread?' everybody who couldn't be bothered to help make it lined up and said 'I will! I will!'"

Noah turned around, leaning on the hoe, and stared at her. Sweat dripped from his lank dark hair and left rivulets in the dust on his face. His eyes were narrowed and his lips were twisted with contempt and disbelief. He demanded, "Something wrong with your head, girl?"

"Don't tell me you never heard the story of the little red hen!"

"There ain't no such thing."

"Come on, didn't your mother ever read it to you when you were a kid?"

He turned back to the hoeing. "Ain't got no mother."

He said it with such casualness, such an utter lack of interest, that Lori was compelled to pursue the subject a wiser—and perhaps more sensitive—person would have dropped. She took a step to follow him. "Everyone's got a mother!"

"Not me. Ain't got no father, either."

"Well, I know they're dead," Lori said with a touch of impatience. "But that doesn't mean you were hatched. You have a mother and a father, and you need to claim them."

"What for?" He kept working. "They never did nothin' for me."

"Well . . ." Lori was momentarily taken aback. "Because they're part of who you are."

He gave a short harsh laugh, and didn't turn around. "My pa was a no-account drunk and my ma—who the hell knows what she was? That's what's part of me, all right."

Lori did not have the first idea how to respond to that.

Noah's hoe hit something with a clink, and Lori, feeling a little awkward, went forward to dig up another rock. But all her shovel turned over was a small, dirt-encrusted glass bottle. "Hey, look at this." She sat back on her haunches and rubbed some of the dirt away, revealing the pale celadon color of the glass.

Noah cast a glance over his shoulder. "Just an old piece of glass."

"Wait, there's writing here." She began to scrape off the dirt with her gloved thumb, revealing the raised letters imprinted in the glass. "R...m...e...d...i....s...Remedies!" She looked up at him, excited. "This is a medicine bottle!"

"So?"

"So, Ida Mae said this place was a hospital during the Civil War. This could be an antique!"

"So?" he repeated.

"So people pay a lot of money for antiques! This could be worth something."

He dropped the hoe and came over to her, his expression guarded. "Let me see that."

She handed him the bottle, and watched as he rubbed more dirt away with his T-shirt. "When was the Civil War?" he asked.

Lori rolled her eyes. "And Aunt Lindsay thinks you're smart." She thought a moment. "Eighteen sixty to eighteen sixty-five." A pause. "Or something like that."

He returned the bottle to her. "Well, if it wasn't 1896, this ain't from the Civil War."

She looked at the bottle, the raised writing now fully exposed to read: Dawson's Reliable Remedies, Richmond, Virginia, 1896.

"Well," she said, her tone only slightly disappointed, "it's still old. It might be worth something."

"Nobody's gonna pay for an old empty bottle."

"People will pay for anything," Lori assured him, and stuffed the bottle into her back pocket. "Besides, Aunt Lindsay likes to display the things that show the history of the place, so it's worth keeping."

He grunted and picked up the hoe again. "Not worth as much as that ole hen of yours."

She frowned. "What hen?"

"That red 'un. I knew a fella over in Boulder Creek that made a fortune raising red chickens."

"Do you mean he had a chicken farm?"

"Nah. Not like eggs and chicken houses and such. These here was show chickens. Cost a couple of grand a piece."

Lori stared at him. "They have shows for chickens?"

"You gonna dig up this rock, or what?"

Lori came forward and dug up the rock without complaint, her expression skeptical. "I never heard of chicken shows."

"Guess there's a lot you never heard of."

"I guess." She carried the rock to the wheelbarrow.

When she returned, he was still chopping at the ground with a hoe. Without turning around, he said, "You really think somebody would pay cash money for that ole bottle?"

"Sure. You see stuff like this in antique shops all the time."

"How much, do you think?"

"I don't know. Maybe fifty dollars."

The chopping slowed. "Fifty dollars?"

"Maybe."

He turned, looked at her, then gave a contemptuous shake of his head. "I never heard of such foolishness."

Lori replied complacently, "I guess there's a lot you never heard of."

He gave her a final glowering look, then turned back to his work without a reply. But the next time his blade clinked against a glass bottle he looked around quickly to make sure Lori hadn't noticed, then dug it up himself and put it in his pocket. Before the garden plot was finished, he had a dozen such specimens hoarded away, and was already counting his fortune.

❧

Lindsay said, "Here it is." She led the way across the floor of the loft of the dairy barn, gesturing toward the far corner. "I remember seeing it from when we were trying to get the house ready for Christmas and bringing down all the furniture that was stored up here."

Cici glanced around the dusty, cluttered space with interest. "Obviously, you didn't get all the furniture that was up here."

Cici, whose arm had been in a sling at the time, had been limited to standing at the bottom of the stairs and directing Farley as to where to place the pieces of furniture they had recovered. She had forgotten how much still remained in the loft.

"Well, some of it's no good. I'm going to pay Noah to start clearing this place out before it gets too hot. But this little vanity table would look great in that nook in the guest room, and I'd like to get it down before Paul and Derrick get here. I think we can handle it, don't you?"

They started lifting cardboard boxes off the canvas-covered

surface. "I can't believe we've been here a year and we still haven't cleaned out the attics," Cici said. She set one of the boxes on the floor and it rattled. "Or even inventoried everything we own."

"Well, we've been a little busy," Lindsay pointed out dryly, "what with tearing out wiring and putting in plumbing and moving walls and all." She pulled off the canvas sheet to reveal a pretty little cubbied vanity with a cherry finish that was only a little dulled with age. "Isn't this precious?" She tested its weight by lifting the two front legs off the ground. "I think we can get it up the stairs if we take the drawers out."

The loft was accessed via a ladder, but during the Great Christmas Furniture Exodus Farley had devised a method of lowering the heavier pieces to the ground via the large double loft doors on the west side of the building using a pulley and ropes. The only difficulty then had been carrying the furniture to the house and up the stairs to the bedrooms . . . which was another reason they had been in no hurry to clear out the loft over the winter.

Cici did her own weight test with one hand and agreed. "I wonder why they stored all their old furniture out here instead of in the house attic."

Lindsay shrugged and started removing drawers. "Ida Mae said there used to be a lot of servants. Maybe they used the house attic for sleeping space."

"Probably." Cici sank down on her haunches and began to poke around in one of the boxes. "What is all this stuff?"

Lindsay said, "Well, will you look at this?"

From one of the drawers she had pulled out a round

cardboard container that was decorated in a rose pattern. She carefully prized the lid off and sniffed inside, smiling. "Talcum powder."

Cici sniffed the box, too, and a similar pleasurable smile crossed her face. "It smells like my grandmother."

"Mine, too. Gosh, it must have been here for years."

"Well, they don't make artificial rose scent like they used to." Cici turned back to the box she had been sorting through. "Linds, look at this."

Lindsay recapped the box and put it aside, frowning in puzzlement at the tinted glass square Cici had removed from the box. "What is it?"

"Look." Cici turned the glass toward the light that poured in from the high windows opposite the loft, and an amber image became visible.

Lindsay gasped and dropped to her knees beside Cici. "Good heavens! That's a glass plate from one of the old shadow-box cameras." She took the plate in her hands reverently. "Look at that! This must be from the turn of the century—look how the woman is dressed. And—why, that's our house! Cici, this must be one of the first photographs taken after the house was built!"

The plate depicted a woman in a long pale dress with leg-o'-mutton sleeves, standing on a lawn beneath the limbs of a spreading oak. Her dark hair was pulled back into a poufy bun, and her features were fair. She looked to be in her midthirties but, by the standards of that day, she was almost certainly younger. There was a wicker chair beside her, and in the background stood a very familiar house.

"It has to be one of the Blackwell women," Lindsay said.

"Maybe it's her wedding picture," suggested Cici. "After all, she is wearing white."

"It's possible," agreed Lindsay. "Maybe it's part of a set."

"There are dozens of them in this box," Cici said, pulling out another.

Lindsay eagerly took it from her, while Cici resumed her study of the first picture by holding it up to the light.

"Gosh, I wish this were clearer!" Cici said. "I'd love to see the detail on the house. How it must have looked when it was first built."

"I wonder if there's any way to develop these things? Or whatever you have to do to them to print them on paper."

"There must be. This is the age of technology. You can do anything."

"You can't play a 45 record without a phonograph," pointed out Lindsay.

"And you can't play an eight-track on anything," Cici admitted.

"Still," Lindsay said, "what a piece of history this is! I'll get Noah to wrap them so they don't break, and carry them down for me. I can't wait to see the rest of them."

"One project at a time," Cici said, carefully returning the last of the plates to the box as she stood. "Come on, let's get this vanity out of here."

❧

Farley's familiar blue truck creaked to a stop in the circular drive in front of the house just as Cici and Lindsay had finished trundling the vanity across the yard, up the wide curving steps, and across the columned porch to the front door. They carefully lowered the furniture to the painted floorboards of the porch and straightened up, grateful for the break, as Farley got out of the truck.

He was a big, slow-moving man with a propensity for dressing in camouflage and cracked steel-toed boots. He always sported a two-day growth of stubbly beard, and carried a soda can, into which he periodically spit a stream of tobacco juice. He was a man of few words but apparently endless skills. He had repaired their water heater, replaced the tiles on their roof, rewired their house, rebuilt their porch railing when it was destroyed by a flock of sheep, and performed numerous other emergency services for them around the house. It had been he, in fact, who had supplied them with the sheepdog, who was now barking and circling the truck madly, occasionally lunging in to take a nip at the tires.

Ignoring the barking dog, Farley politely tipped the bill of his camo cap to the two ladies on the porch. "Mornin'," he said, and spat into the can.

"Good morning, Farley." Cici raised her voice to be heard above the din.

Lindsay shouted, "Rebel, quiet!" to no avail, and then smiled at Farley. "Hi, Farley."

"Doing deliveries for Jonesie," he said, and nodded toward the back of the pickup truck. "Got your sander here."

Jonesie and his wife—who was generally known as Mrs. Jonesie—were the proprietors of Family Hardware and Sundries, the biggest store in the tiny town of Blue Valley. From teaspoons to masonry saws, from dish towels to windowpanes, if they didn't have it, they could get it.

"Oh, good!" exclaimed Cici, coming down the steps.

"Great," added Lindsay with slightly less enthusiasm.

"Hi, Farley!" Lori called from across the yard, waving as she skipped toward them. Doing the requisite little dance that was necessary to avoid being bitten by the dog, Lori drew up to the truck, breathless. "Aunt Bridget said for you not to leave until she wraps up a pie for you. She baked an extra one this morning." She turned to her mother. "We finished hoeing the garden. It's going to be ready to sow next week."

Farley walked around to the back of the truck. "Your tiller broke?"

Lori turned an accusing gaze to her mother. "We have a tiller?"

"Oh . . . you mean that thing that attaches to the back of the lawn mower." Lindsay tried to sound vague, and avoided Lori's eyes.

"I'll fix it for you," volunteered Farley. "Ten dollar."

"Um, no, thanks. It's fine." Cici, too, avoided Lori's eyes. "Besides, Bridget is in charge of the garden. Let's get this thing out of the truck."

"Got to get your peas and taters in by St. Paddy's Day," observed Farley, and swung down the tailgate with a clatter. "Lot faster to use the tiller."

Lori's expression soured. "Why do I feel I've just been had?"

Bridget came out with a pie wrapped in aluminum foil as Cici and Farley reached the front porch with the sander. "It's apple and currant," she told him. "I'll put it in your truck."

Farley touched his cap brim. "Kind of you, ma'am."

"Aunt Bridget," Lori challenged darkly, "did you know we have a tiller?"

Bridget looked perfectly innocent. "Why no, dear. I don't believe I did."

Farley collected his soda can from the porch rail where he had left it, and spat again. "Supposed to make sure you know how to use it."

Cici smiled patiently. "I've used a floor sander before, Farley."

"Knew a man cut off his toe with one, once."

"I'll be sure to wear shoes."

He looked skeptical. "You got a long cord?"

"One hundred feet."

"Got to ground it."

"Grounded."

He gave a grunt that sounded neither convinced, nor happy. "Here's an extra belt, and some replacement pads." He handed them to her. "You know how to replace a belt?"

"I'll bet I can figure it out."

He grunted again, and then turned to Bridget as she came back up the steps from placing the pie in the front seat of his truck. "Supposed to tell you Burt Shaw is coming next month. You want to get on his list?"

"Who's Burt Shaw?" Bridget asked.

"Sheepshearer."

Lori, forsaking the matter of the tiller, exclaimed, "Are we going to shear the sheep?"

Bridget looked uncertain. "I suppose we have to. After all, it's been two years."

"Oughta have good fleece by now," observed Farley, gazing out over the meadow where the sheep nibbled the new spring grass. "Lotta money in fleece."

Lori was immediately interested. "Really? How much?"

"Heard about a girl out on Route Twelve that pays ten to fifteen dollar a pound."

Cici said, "How much does it cost to shear a sheep?"

He shrugged. "Fella charges by the head. Course if it was me, I'd do it myself."

"I don't know ..." Bridget still sounded uneasy.

"Is it hard?" Lori wanted to know.

"Nah. Just like skinning a cat."

All four women on the porch were silent at that, none of them wanting to ask just what, exactly, he knew about skinning a cat.

"Well," Bridget said after a moment, "I guess I'll let you know."

"Thanks for bringing out the sander," Cici said.

He spat politely into the can once again and held out his hand. "Ten dollar."

Lindsay dug into the back pocket of her jeans and found a ten-dollar bill, which he carefully arranged in his billfold alongside several others. The ladies had learned to ask for multiple tens whenever they went to the bank, and to keep them about their persons at all times, just in case they needed help from Farley.

Lori walked Farley to his truck. "Say, Farley," she inquired thoughtfully, "how many pounds of fleece would you say a sheep has?"

He lifted his hat, scratched his head, spat again into the can, and spent a moment gazing thoughtfully into the distance. "Dunno," he admitted at last.

"Oh."

Then she had another idea. "Do you know anything about cleaning out ponds?"

He followed her around the house, down a flagstone path now half obscured by brown leaves and dried mud, through a winter-ravaged flower garden, and to the largest of the two garden ponds. This one was a pool of about ten by ten feet and no more than two or three feet deep in its prime. Now, filled with uncounted years of rotted garden debris, leaves, broken branches, and who-knew-what-else, the oily black skim coat of fetid water was barely six inches deep. The pool was surrounded by a paving of smooth white stones—at least they might have once been white, and would have been smooth, had the mortar been restored—and a scar of ground where once there had been a statue. Lindsay and Cici had moved the statue to the center of the rose garden last year, where it would be more fully appreciated.

"Aunt Lindsay wants to bring the pools and fountains back into operating condition again," Lori said. "I offered to help her."

Farley grunted.

"The problem is," prompted Lori, "that I don't know where to start. I don't suppose you . . . ?"

She left the sentence unfinished, hoping he would volunteer for the job.

But she either overestimated her charm, or underestimated his good will. Because all he said was, "Need a pump."

She blinked. "What?"

"You're gonna need a pump," he explained, "to get the water out."

"Oh."

"I got one I can let you have for a day or two. Cost you ten dollar."

Lori smiled weakly. The one major disadvantage of leaving school, California, and—most importantly—her father's household was that she was always cash poor. "I don't suppose you take Am-Ex?"

Now it was his turn to stare.

"Never mind." Lori sighed, then cheered as she turned him back toward the front of the house. "Let's talk about sheep."

# 5

# History Lessons

On Day One of the floor refinishing project, everyone was recruited to move the furniture out of the living area and onto the front porch, where Ida Mae, barking instructions all the while, covered everything with canvas dustcloths. The grand piano, which was too big to fit through the front door without lifting and turning, had to be rolled on its squeaky wheels behind the staircase, down the wide corridor, and into the double-doored dining room. The only obstacle was the uneven threshold at the dining room, which kept catching the front wheel.

Cici crawled underneath the piano to survey the situation. "We're going to have to lift it," she called up.

Lindsay pushed her hair back from her face. "Who's got the forklift?"

Noah said, "Does anybody play this thing?"

"I used to," Bridget replied, stretching out a kink in her back. "But I haven't for a long time."

"Seriously, Aunt Bridget," Lori pitched, "there could be some real money in those sheep. I think we need to look into it. Farley says there might be ten or twelve pounds of fleece on each sheep by now—maybe more!"

Lindsay huffed, "I do believe Farley puts more words together for you in a single visit than he has for us in the entire time we've known him."

"That's because she's young and cute," replied Bridget with a grin, "and we're old and bitter."

"Speak for yourself," said Cici, pulling herself out from under the piano and dusting off her hands. "I'm not at all bitter . . . yet."

Noah grumbled, "What's the point in having one, then?"

Bridget looked at him curiously. "Having what, dear?"

He turned his gaze meaningfully toward the object between them in something that was very close to an eye roll. "A *piano*."

Cici said, "Okay, we've got to do this one leg at a time. Noah and Lori, you're the least likely to end up in traction, so you take the front. Everybody else, push."

Inch by inch, leg by leg, they rocked and eased the baby grand across the threshold and into the dining room. Lori scrambled ahead, moving chairs out of the way as they wedged the piano between the table and the buffet. Finally, they all straightened up, breathing hard and flexing their fingers.

Lindsay looked around. "Well, this is convenient."

"We can eat in the kitchen for a while," Cici offered.

"How're you gonna get there?" Noah asked.

They looked around. The piano occupied the aisle between the table and the buffet that led to the kitchen, and it blocked the double door through which they had pushed it. In turning and positioning the huge piece, everyone except Noah had ended up on the wrong side of that door.

Lori rolled her eyes. Cici shook her head in disbelief. Lindsay said, "Does anyone have a cell phone?"

Lori growled, "What difference does it make? It wouldn't work."

Bridget said, "I am *not* pushing this thing out again."

"If we pushed it a little farther, we could stand on top and reach the window," Cici offered.

Lori deftly grabbed the keyboard, swung herself underneath the piano, and crawled beneath it to join Noah on the other side of the door.

The three older women stared after her. "Or," said Cici, deadpan, "we could crawl under."

And so they did.

"You see, Aunt Bridget," Lori said earnestly as they walked back to the living room, "that's between a hundred and a hundred and fifty dollars per sheep. You've got twenty-five sheep, not counting the lambs! That's twenty-five thousand—"

"*Hundred*," corrected all three women at once.

"Right, twenty-five hundred dollars! That's nothing to be sneezed at."

"No," agreed Bridget, "it's certainly not. But that's not all profit, either. You have to pay the sheepshearer, for one thing. There's a lot of research to be done before we start counting that money."

"Maybe one of the things you could research is how a girl who spent a whole year and a half at UCLA doesn't know the difference between twenty-five hundred and twenty-five thousand dollars," Cici said.

"What I'm trying to say," insisted Lori, deliberately ignoring her mother, "is that this could be the start of a real business. You already have the setup, and a small flock. If you expanded ..."

"Well now, we'd *really* have to research that," Bridget said.

"We should get started right away. To get a good price, you want to be the first to the market."

"Well, I don't know about that ..."

Lindsay said, "Cici, are you sure you can handle that thing by yourself? It looks awfully big to me. We'll be glad to help."

"It's fully automated," Cici assured her. "Couldn't be simpler. I don't need any help." She leaned the big boxy machine back on its rollers and positioned it for action. It made a sound like a train clattering across a trestle in the empty room, even before it was turned on. "It's even got three speeds."

"But won't your arms get tired?" Bridget said. "Shouldn't we trade off turns?"

"Thanks," Cici said, and her smile tried to soften the hint of condescension in her voice, "but you can really do some damage if you don't know how to operate one of these things. Really, I don't need any help."

Ida Mae stood in the open doorway, her hair in a scarf, her hands on her hips, and a sour look on her face. "She don't have the first notion how to work that thing," she observed, as much to herself as to anyone.

Cici looked at her sternly. "There is really nothing to it," she assured her.

She pulled a sporty baseball cap over her own hair to protect it from the dust, arranged a paper respirator mask across her mouth and nose, and, taking a firm grip on the handle, flipped the power switch. Everyone backed away.

Nothing happened.

Frowning, Cici lowered her mask and toggled the switch off, then on again. "That's funny."

"Is it plugged in?" offered Bridget helpfully.

Cici checked the plug in the wall outlet, then came back and toggled the switch again.

"Maybe you have to put it in gear or something," suggested Lori.

"Or hold a button down," Lindsay said, "like with a weed whacker."

"Is there an instruction book?" Bridget wanted to know.

"Maybe it's broken," said Lori.

Cici bent down and played with the switch some more.

Then Noah crossed the room, found the end of the extension cord that was not plugged into the wall, and connected it to the cord from the sander. The big machine roared to life.

Cici sprang back just as the machine lurched forward, screeching across the floor with the fury of a turbocharged demon, leaving a ten-inch-wide gouge in its path. The sounds of their horrified cries were drowned out as it crashed into the opposite wall and fell sideways amidst a shower of plaster dust and broken lathing.

Noah rushed forward and pulled the plug. The silence resounded. Cici stood still in the middle of the room, her hands clasped to the side of her head, looking from the scar across the floor to the hole in the wall.

No one spoke for a very long time. Then Lindsay said, timidly, "I guess you don't want us to help, huh?"

Without turning, Cici shook her head.

"Maybe you'd like us to just get out of your way."

Again without turning, Cici nodded.

Lindsay beckoned to Noah with an expression that clearly indicated they should go while the going was good, and they hurried away

Bridget lifted a finger as though the idea had just occurred to her, and said, "Lori, how would you like to go to the library with me and do some research on sheep ranching?"

They left so quickly that Bridget had to return to the house by the back door to get her car keys.

ॐ

The stone dairy barn was one of the property's most charming features. With skylights, clerestory windows, a loft for storage, and easy-maintenance stone floors, Lindsay had quickly seen it as the perfect place for her art studio. There was room for twenty or thirty students, when she got her classes going, as well as space for her own work, an office, and even a gallery if she chose.

Like most of the women's ambitions for the place, Lindsay's plans had diminished in scope since they'd actually moved in. Noah had spent most of the autumn last year dragging out rotten timbers, squirrels' nests, and other accumulated debris, and Cici had patched windows and holes through which various forms of wildlife had been making their way in over the years. Eventually Lindsay had been able to scrub down the floors and windows, slap a coat of paint over the plank walls, and call it good. There were still randomly placed half walls throughout the building that indicated where stalls once had been.

The downside of having such an enormous space was that it was virtually impossible to heat, which made it unusable in the winter. Lindsay's grand plans for having a bathroom installed had fizzled when she discovered that the main water line that led to the building was broken, and instead of the twenty or thirty easels she had envisioned, accompanied by eager art students, there were two worktables: one for her, and one for Noah.

She believed in keeping regular classroom hours and a regular classroom space, even though Noah was only in school three hours a day. She had chosen the art studio because it was neutral territory, the place in which they were both comfortable. It smelled of linseed oil and pastel dust, and on its walls were drying paintings and charcoal sketches. Cici had made a moveable partition out of two-by-fours and plywood to enclose their classroom—and also to conserve heat during the winter—and that was covered with thumbtacked photographs and pages torn from magazines that represented potential subject matter for future art lessons. There was also a whiteboard, which Lindsay used instead of a blackboard, and a bookshelf that held texts. But no one walking into the space would suspect that its main function was as anything other than an art studio.

Noah slouched over his worktable, working algebra problems with a chewed-up pencil, and glancing a little too often at the clock—which was shaped like a color wheel with paintbrushes for hands—on the wall behind Lindsay. He had learned the rules the first day and, after one or two false starts, had learned to abide by them: The art materials did not come out until all of the day's assigned schoolwork had been completed to his teacher's satisfaction. At last he tore the sheet of math problems out of his notebook and stretched across the table to hand it to her, waiting impatiently until Lindsay checked it.

"Very nice," she said, after what seemed like a very long

time. "You transposed your variables here on number six. Try it again."

He erased, recalculated, and handed it back to her before she had resumed her seat. Lindsay lifted an eyebrow. "Learning comes easily for you, doesn't it?"

He shrugged. "Jonesie down at the Hardware says I can have a job when I get my GED. Pays nine dollars an hour."

"Good for you."

"Why can't I take that GED test now?"

"One, because you're not old enough. Two, because you don't know enough. You wouldn't pass." She handed the paper back to him with a *100%-Perfect* scrawled across the top.

He stuffed the paper in his notebook without looking at it and began to stack his schoolbooks out of the way to make room for the tabletop easel and paints.

"Hold it, hotshot," Lindsay said. She reached behind her to her own worktable and took up another stack of papers. "I read your report on the French Revolution." She turned up the first page, which was a sketch of a man in eighteenth-century costume with the caption "Robespierre was a jerk" and the second, which depicted a woman in jewels and powdered wig jumping out of a cake—"let them eat cake"—and the third, a drawing of the guillotine and the single line "Off with their heads."

"Very amusing," Lindsay said.

He grinned. "I thought you'd like it."

Lindsay gave him a stern look. "I should make you do the whole thing over."

His grin vanished. "Ah, come on—"

"Except for the fact that you've obviously read the material."

She shook the papers at him. "Otherwise you couldn't have made such a joke of it."

"It *is* a joke," he returned, scowling. "Who cares about a bunch of dudes who've been dead three hundred years already?"

"The French Revolution was a pivotal point in world history," she insisted. "It changed a nation's destiny and overthrew an entire tradition of government. It was important!"

"It's *over*," he replied, sounding bored. "Why do I have to study history anyhow? They're not going to ask me about Frenchies on the GED."

As always, Lindsay chose her battles. "We study history," she explained patiently, "because it tells us who we are. Because it gives us continuity from one point in time to the next. Because if we didn't know what the people who went before us had been through, we would have to do everything in the world all over again with each new generation. And because when we study history, we understand that we are all part of something much bigger than ourselves—a story that goes on and on."

"Are we gonna have a drawing lesson today or what?"

She hesitated, then said, "Come up in the loft with me."

Noah followed her up the ladder, and she dragged forward the box of photographic plates she and Cici had discovered earlier. Holding one up to the light, she said, "This is history."

He squinted at it, trying to make out the faded shapes. "Looks like this house."

"It is. It's this house, the way it used to be a long time ago, and the people who lived here. They're dead now, too, but without them we wouldn't be living in this place, having this conversation. Do you understand?"

He was rummaging through the box. "What are these things anyhow?"

"They're photographic plates from an old camera. I'm going to try to have them developed."

"They worth anything?"

"I wouldn't be surprised. People pay a lot of money for pieces of history. Why do you suppose that is?"

"Because they're dumb?"

She smiled patiently. "Your homework assignment is to answer that question with a five-hundred-word essay."

He groaned out loud.

"And, because I know how much you like to illustrate your work," she added, "we're going to start your art lesson by choosing one of these plates for inspiration. You'll be interpreting it in charcoal, monochrome oil, and multimedia using an acrylic base, so choose one you like."

Now he looked interested. "What's monochrome oil?"

She smiled and dusted off her hands as she stood. "And while you're choosing, you can wrap each one of those plates in newspaper so they don't break, and bring the box downstairs."

He was deeply absorbed in the task when she left him, pulling out the plates, holding them up to the light, wrapping them in newsprint, putting them back in the box. He kept out a few that he liked for drawing practice. And he kept out a few more, hiding them under his shirt, because she'd never miss them.

And who knew? They might be worth something.

∂❧

When Bridget walked into the Blue Valley Public Library, with its speckled linoleum floors and dark-paneled walls and curved oak circulation desk, she paused for a moment to breathe in the smell of old books and printer's ink. It smelled like home to her. Lori, on the other hand, headed straight for the Internet station.

Bridget's childhood had been spent in libraries like this one, and in such places she had discovered the world had no limits. She always liked to take the time to examine whatever was on display behind the glass case as she came in the door; this month it was a collection of artwork entitled "My Favorite Place" by fifth graders at the local school.

She had some books to return, and the librarian greeted her by name. She was a frequent patron, and besides, everyone knew the women who had bought the old Blackwell farm. "I found something for you the other day," the librarian said, looking pleased with herself. She was a plump, ponytailed woman in her forties who, Bridget was given to understand, had already been working in the library for twenty years. "It's a guide to landmarks and historic places from the 1960s." She pulled it out from under the desk. "Blackwell Farms is listed in it. I thought you might get a kick out of it."

Bridget's face lit up. "Really? Thanks!"

"And the new Stephen King book came in. I've been saving it for you."

"Terrific," Bridget said. Then she added, "Say, Katherine . . . I don't suppose you'd know anything about sheep fleece, would you?"

"I don't personally, but Ann Marie Lucas is an expert. She wrote an article for the paper one or two years ago . . ." As she spoke, she was tapping on the computer. "Here it is. Do you want me to pull it for you?"

"Thanks, that would be great. And anything else you can find."

By the time Bridget had finished browsing the latest bestsellers and making her selections, Katherine had a stack of periodicals waiting for her. Bridget settled down at a table to make notes, was referred to the "agriculture and husbandry" section of the shelves, and made several selections. She had just finished checking out her stack of books when Lori joined her, fairly bursting with self-satisfaction, and declared, "Our problems are solved." She brandished a collection of printed pages. "I found out everything we need to know."

"Did you now?" Bridget slid her books into a canvas tote bag. "And in a library, of all places!"

On the way to the car, Lori regaled her with all she had learned about sheep ranching, the most valuable fleece and the best time to harvest it, the amount of sheep an acre could support, sorted by breed, and the current market price in Australia for high-quality Cotswold wool.

"But we're not in Australia, and we don't have Cotswold sheep," Bridget pointed out.

"Well, that's just an example. But listen to this . . ." She continued to read from her notes as they stopped by the Dollar Store for paper towels and a new broom, and Family Hardware for the stain Cici had ordered for the floors—where Bridget assured Jonesie they hadn't had a bit of trouble with the sander, not at all, and expected the job to be finished by suppertime—and was distracted only when she spotted a cute vintage hat in the thrift store where Bridget stopped to donate a bag of clothes the ladies had put together over the winter. Lori paid a quarter for the purple felt fedora with the gold ribbon rose, plopped it atop her head—where of course it made her look as though she had just stepped off the cover of a fashion forward, funky-chic magazine—and continued her narrative where she had left off.

"The point is, there *is* money to be made, and we already have everything we need to get started. First we sell the wool, then we invest in some good breeders, let nature take its course, and voilà! Before you know it we're a certified member of the wool producing industry. All we need now," she added, sliding into the passenger seat of Bridget's SUV, "is the name of that woman Farley was talking about who buys fleece."

"Her name is Ann Marie Lucas," Bridget informed her, starting the engine, "and she's a local hand spinner. She weaves the yarn into shawls and capes and sweaters that sell for hundreds and hundreds of dollars—like wearable art."

Lori gave her an admiring look. "Wow, good work. How did you find that out?"

"The old-fashioned way." Bridget couldn't prevent a smirk. "I read it in a newspaper."

"Well, what are we waiting for? Let's call her."

"There's a problem," Bridget said. "She only buys the finest quality wool, and our sheep are—well, they're a mess. They've been wandering around in the pasture for two years. They're filthy and matted ..."

"We can wash them," Lori insisted.

Bridget shot her a look. "Wash sheep?"

"How else are you going to get their wool clean?"

Bridget thought about that. "Well, I guess I've done crazier things. But before they can be washed, they have to be dipped to get rid of parasites ..."

"You can buy sheep dip at the hardware store."

"And there's no point in doing any of it until right before we have them sheared, because they'll just get dirty again. And the sheepshearer doesn't come until April."

Lori shook her head adamantly. "No, no, no, don't you see? If we wait until then—until everyone else has fleece—we've lost our home field advantage! We have a flock of sheep with two years' growth of wool on them in a market where no one else has any wool at all. We have to strike while the iron is hot."

Bridget cast her a puzzled look. "I don't know how we're going to get them sheared any sooner."

Lori sat back and folded her arms across her chest with a self-satisfied smile as she pronounced, "By doing it ourselves."

❧

Some people might have put a temporary patch over the hole in the wall, and proceeded with sanding the floors. But Cici believed in doing things right, and since the floor molding had to be taken off before the stain could be applied to the floors, anyway, and since repairing the hole in the wall was bound to make a mess, she put the sander away and gathered her tools for the repair job.

By the time Ida Mae came in from the kitchen to ask if she wanted lunch, Cici had the floor molding off and had trimmed away the broken edges of the cracked wall to a six by eight rectangle. She had also made a rather intriguing discovery.

"Ida Mae," she said, turning away from her examination of the inside of the hole, "this wall is hollow! Did you know that?"

Ida Mae returned a scowl. "How do you suppose I'd know that? I wasn't born here, you know. You want soup or what?"

"You don't remember there being a closet or anything here?"

Ida Mae gave her a look that suggested there were no words to express the stupidity of that question. "There ain't no closets in this house except the ones you built."

"That's right," murmured Cici thoughtfully, "there aren't. I'm going to get a flashlight."

"You're eating soup for lunch."

By the time Lindsay came in, Cici had widened the hole enough to insert her hand, with the flashlight, and part of her head. "There's a whole big space back here!" she exclaimed. "Lindsay, come look at this!"

Lindsay hung back. "Um, spiders?"

Cici scooted back out of the hole, brushing the plaster dust off her cheeks. "Seriously, it's like someone walled over a whole room. Why would anyone do that?"

Lindsay looked uneasy. "I read a story once about a nun who was walled up inside a convent. Some questions are better left unasked."

But by the time Bridget and Lori returned, Cici had enlarged the hole with her reciprocating saw to a two foot square, and Lindsay, who was smaller about the shoulders and torso than Cici, was halfway in, halfway out of the wall.

"Well?" demanded Cici anxiously, hovering over her.

"There's something in here," came Lindsay's muffled voice in reply.

Bridget came forward hesitantly, tugging Lori with her. "A body?" she suggested.

Cici glanced at her. "Do you and Lindsay read the same books?"

Lindsay wriggled out, the flashlight in one hand, and a length of lavender ribbon, dull with grime, in the other. Her hair was mussed and her cheeks were smudged and she sneezed, twice, from the dust. Proudly she held up her find.

"Wow," said Cici, taking it. "Look at that. How do you suppose it got there? "

Bridget examined it curiously. "Grosgrain," she pronounced.

"Mom," Lori said, "you cut a hole in our wall for a *ribbon*?"

"There's some more junk back there," Lindsay said, "but this was all I could reach. It looks like it's been closed up forever. There must be six inches of dust on the floor."

"What kind of junk?" Cici wanted to know.

"I couldn't tell."

"Did anything look like it might be a chest full of money?" prompted Bridget.

"How far back does it go?" Cici asked.

"Not as big as a room. Maybe a foot. But it's long."

Cici looked around thoughtfully. "Lori," she decided, "wiggle in there and take a look."

Lori's eyes flew wide. "Me? Are you kidding?"

Cici plucked the new purple hat off Lori's head and pushed her gently toward the opening. "That's what you get for being a size two. You're the only one who can fit."

"But—there could be mice!"

Cici turned to Lindsay. "Did you see any mice?"

Lindsay shook her head.

"Go," she told Lori.

Five minutes later a very disgruntled Lori wriggled back out of the hole, covered with grime, and with nothing to show for her effort but a rusty tool of some sort, a wooden block, and a broken iron chain. "These jeans will never be clean again," she declared, brushing at them furiously, "and all for an ice pick, a chain, and a piece of wood!"

"It's not an ice pick," Cici replied, disappointed, "It's an awl. You use them for punching holes in things."

"I guess whoever built the wall dropped it while he was working," suggested Bridget.

"I guess," Cici agreed. "I wonder why they built the wall in the first place."

"And what about the ribbon?" wondered Lori.

Cici looked at the space thoughtfully. "You know what?" she said. "I'm going to open it back up."

"The wall?" Bridget sounded alarmed. "That's an awfully big job."

"Not really. It will be easier than fixing the hole, actually. And I'm thinking some built-in bookshelves would be perfect there."

"But what about the floors?"

Cici shook her head. "No point in starting the floors until we get the wall torn down."

"We?" Lori said. "Did you say *we*?"

"I'll get the sledgehammer," Lindsay said.

"I'll get the wheelbarrow," Bridget volunteered.

As they departed, Cici looked at her daughter. "Didn't you say something about wanting to learn how to restore old houses?"

Lori looked at her fingernails, which she had painstakingly French-manicured herself only last night. "I kind of pictured myself on the management end."

"I kind of pictured you learning from the ground up."

Lori looked at her mother's determined expression, spared a

last regretful look at her manicure, and said, "Guess I'd better go find my work gloves."

❧

Four hours and twelve wheelbarrows of debris later, Lori couldn't stop saying, "Oh my God. Oh my *God*."

What they had uncovered was a tall arched alcove, framed in white decorative trim, of the kind often found in the grand old houses of Europe. Inside the alcove was a painted mural that depicted a pastoral scene. The more they scrubbed away the accumulated dust and grime, the more they came to recognize the scene as a portrayal of their own sheep meadow, with the mountains behind.

"Durndest thing I ever did see," commented Noah, who had been recruited to do the sledgehammer work after their arms grew tired. "Why'd anybody want to paint a picture on a wall?"

"Murals have been very popular at various times in history," replied Lindsay absently, studying the painting. "Like the Sistine Chapel, remember?"

"Oh, yeah. That dude that painted on the ceiling."

Bridget gave the bottom corner a final once-over with her sponge, and stepped back with her bucket of soapy water. "There's no signature," she pointed out.

"Traveling muralists were commissioned, just like any other craftsperson," Lindsay said. "They rarely signed their work."

"Wow," said Lori reverently. "A real work of art, right on our walls. It's like one of those stories you hear about people finding Picassos in their attics. Should we have it appraised?"

Lindsay had to smile. "Hate to disappoint you, sweetie, but

without a signature it's not worth much. Besides, even if it were valuable, how would we get it off the wall?"

Lori's sigh was wistful. "It just makes you wonder, though, doesn't it? About who painted it, and when, and why?"

"And why anyone would cover up something so beautiful," added Bridget.

"There's something odd about it," Cici said, scrutinizing the painting from the opposite doorway. "It looks out of place, somehow." She shrugged. "Maybe that's why they covered it up. Ida Mae, are you certain you don't remember this alcove ever being here?"

Ida Mae, whose curiosity over all the racket had finally gotten the best of her, had come to watch the final stages of the unveiling and remained to polish away the soap and water with a collection of old towels. She straightened stiffly from gathering the last of the towels and pointed out irritably, "I can't be expected to know everything, can I? Used to be paintings and whatnot all over these walls. Years pass, things change." And that appeared to be all she was going to say on the matter.

"That must mean it was walled over before . . ." Here Cici paused delicately. No one had ever been able to persuade Ida Mae to reveal her age, or even to pin her down on when she had first come to work in the house. And when Ida Mae made no sign of clarifying the point now, Cici merely concluded, "Well, not long after it was painted."

"Peoples' tastes change," Bridget pointed out. "Maybe someone brought in a new bride, and she didn't like murals on the walls."

"Or alcoves," Lindsay agreed.

"I still say it looks odd," Cici said. "Off center or something. Maybe it's because it's opposite the windows. It's like an optical illusion."

"I see what you mean," Lindsay agreed hesitantly. "It's a little disorienting."

"Which is probably why they covered it up," Bridget said.

"But we're not going to, are we Mom?" Lori insisted. "I mean, this is just the coolest thing ever!"

"It is kind of cool," agreed Cici, grinning. The other women chimed in, "Of course we're keeping it!" and "We'll never cover it up!"

Lori darted forward and hugged her mother impulsively. "I really understand why you love this place now! Every day is like a treasure hunt. Why wouldn't everybody want to do this?"

Cici hugged her back, but her smile faded into a shrug of helpless resignation as she looked over Lori's shoulder at her two best friends.

ॐ

As dusk fell, all three women peeled back the dust covers on their living room furniture, sitting out on the porch, and settled themselves in to watch the sun set. Cici inched between two wing chairs and an armoire to find a place on the sofa, swinging her feet up to rest on an end table. Lindsay sprawled on a cushy hassock with her feet resting on the arm of the sofa, and Bridget curled up in one of the armchairs.

"Ida Mae is going to have a fit if we leave this furniture out here another night," Bridget commented.

"I thought she was going to start moving it back in, stick by stick, all by herself."

"Oh, I don't know," Cici said, stretching back. "I kind of like the furniture out here. It's so ..."

"Trashy?"

"I was going to say 'rustic.' Anyway, she'll have to get used to it. I can finish the sanding in the morning, and we should be able to get the stain on tomorrow if everyone pitches in. But it's going to take three days for the finish to dry hard enough to put furniture back."

"Just as long as everything is in place in time for company," Bridget said.

"Not a problem," Cici assured her. "Once we get started, it's just a matter of waiting for it to dry."

Somewhere in the distance, a bird began a funny little song. A pink glow outlined a cloud behind the mountaintops, giving it the illusion of being surreally white, lit from within. They turned as one to appreciate the sight, and Lindsay murmured, "This may be my favorite time of year. Right before the leaves come out to clutter up the view with all that green, the light is so *vivid*. The colors are so pure."

Bridget replied, "I don't know. There's nothing prettier than apple blossom time."

"Face it," Cici said, "we live in the most beautiful place in the world, no matter what time of year it is."

No one could argue with that.

Then Lindsay said, "I'm afraid we lost a little ground today in the battle to deromanticize this place for Lori."

Cici gave a half-smothered grunt of laughter. "I'm not sure it's possible to deromanticize anything for a twenty-year-old girl."

"Be warned," Bridget said. "Another business plan is in the air."

"Sheep?" inquired Lindsay.

"Sheep." Bridget was thoughtful for a moment. "The thing is, it's not a bad idea . . . if we were thirty years younger."

"Neither is the bed-and-breakfast," Cici said, "if we had the time, money, and energy to spend developing it."

"I just don't want to spend my declining years dipping sheep and carding wool."

"The lanolin is really good for your hands," Lindsay pointed out.

"But the very thought of having to learn a whole new set of skills," Cici objected, masking a small shudder, "an entirely new *trade* . . . what is 'carding wool,' anyway, and why would I want to learn how to do it? I don't use half the things I know as it is. Why do I have to know more?"

"Hear, hear." Bridget sighed. "The older I get, the more I'm convinced life is a game for the young."

"What I hate," said Cici, "is being constantly reminded how much smarter they are than I am."

"They're not smarter," Lindsay protested. "They can just think faster."

"Think faster and learn better," qualified Bridget. "I used up my last brain cell learning how to operate my microwave oven."

"I can't even program my voice mail," admitted Lindsay.

"But show me one techno-geek who can recite the periodic table *and* knit a cable stitch sweater."

"At the same time."

"Yeah, and I'd like to meet one person under twenty-five who knows how to operate the Dewey Decimal System."

Cici looked at Bridget. "Do they still use that?"

Lindsay said, "Actually, I don't think kids are really smarter *or* faster than we are. We just have a lot more stuff in our brains to sort through before we come up with the right answer. If you're under thirty, all you have to know these days to do almost anything in life is how to push a button."

"Yeah."

"Yeah."

Lindsay slanted a glance toward Cici. "But you *could* have checked to make sure the sander was plugged in."

"Wasn't it you who wanted to call 911 to help us get out of the dining room when all we had to do was crawl under the piano?"

"I think Lindsay is right," Bridget said. "We'd all be a lot smarter if we didn't have so much on our minds."

Her pronouncement was met with stares. "I mean, I read somewhere that we've actually lost something like two percent of our brainpower over the past century. We can't solve problems because we're used to technology solving them for us. And the very technology that was supposed to make life easier has actually made it more complicated. The average caveman used to spend four hours a week providing food and shelter for his family. The average American spends over a hundred hours a week doing the same thing. How has life gotten easier?"

They thought about that for a moment. "Clearly, that caveman did not live in a hundred-year-old house with an adolescent boy and a college-age girl," Cici said.

"Which is just one more way in which his life was simpler."

They sat in silence for a moment, listening to the distant bird, watching the sky turn ever-deepening shades of cobalt.

Lindsay said, "We should make a display case or something for the things we find here."

"Like a piece of old chain?"

"Well, maybe not that. But someone used that tool one time, to work on this house. I think he should be remembered. And maybe someone wore that ribbon in her hair, a long time ago, or hung a brooch on it, or used it to tie up a bouquet of flowers. It would be nice if it had a home again."

"You," said Cici, with a small shake of her head, "are the most romantic person I know."

"There's not a thing wrong with that," Bridget pointed out mildly.

When the front door opened, and the screen door creaked, no one was surprised to see Lori standing there. "Mom," she said excitedly, "I've got it! I've figured it out!"

Cici pretended polite interest. "A new business plan?"

"No." She shook her head impatiently. "The alcove—the painting. I know what's wrong with it. Come inside, I'll show you."

Curious, the three women threaded their way through the furniture to join Lori inside the main living area. "Look," she said, gesturing grandly to the opposite wall, as though the answer should be obvious.

The only light, since all the lamps had been removed from the room, came from the grand chandelier over the staircase, and the smaller one in the foyer. The fireplace wall, with its recently uncovered muraled alcove, was in shadows. Even if it had been obvious, they could not have seen the answer in the dark.

"Don't you see?" Lori prompted. "It's uneven! There's got to be another one—one on either side of the fireplace! So," she added happily, "I measured the same distance from the fireplace on the other wall, and sure enough—it's hollow. Do you want me to go get the sledgehammer? Can we open it up tonight?"

Cici looked at Lori, then at Bridget and Lindsay. The other

two women shrugged. Cici went forward to the place Lori had indicated, and rapped the wall with her knuckles. Sure enough, it sounded hollow.

"Damn," she said, straightening up. Hands on hips, she surveyed the wall. "Why didn't I think of that?"

"We're going to open it, aren't we?" Lori insisted. "Don't you want to get started?"

"We are not going to start swinging sledgehammers this time of night," her mother said firmly.

"But it's not even dark!" Lori protested.

Cici's tone brooked no argument. "Morning is soon enough."

Lori's disappointment was replaced almost immediately with a grin. "Well, I guess I can wait. See Mom, I *told* you I'd be good at this! This is just the best job in the world!"

When she had skipped back up the stairs again, Cici drew in a long breath and released it through pursed lips.

"Too much energy," Bridget said.

"Too little impulse control," added Lindsay.

"Too damn smart," Cici concluded with a final mournful shake of her head.

# 6

# In Another Time

*Pearl, 1863*

The next day Mother did go to the house with teas and medicines, and she went the day after that and the day after that, which made Mama Madie mad. They whispered about it in low harsh voices whenever Mother came back to the cabin at night, all pale and worn-out looking, but in the end Mama Madie would make Mother sit down and drink some broth and she'd wrap Mother's feet in warm flannel. And then Mother would ask Pearl to show her how the quilt was coming, but sometimes she would fall asleep before Pearl could unfold the portion of the square she had finished that day.

Pearl worked on the quilt all day, because she was not allowed to leave the cabin while the soldiers were there, and after a time she came to understand that was why Mother thought the quilt was such a good idea, so that Pearl would have something to occupy her days while she sat in the cabin waiting for the soldiers to leave. Pearl did not mind staying in Mama Madie's warm cabin, because outside was an ugly, scary place. All the chickens were gone, eaten by the soldiers. Once she heard a heart-stopping sound, like a woman screaming, and she rushed to the door to see a pig—Mama Madie later said it had had the bad sense to wander up near the house looking for scraps—running crazily around the yard with a sword sticking out of its neck and blood flooding everywhere. Later that day the smell of roasting pork was so sweet it made Pearl's stomach hurt, and her mother brought back a big hunk of it wrapped in a napkin, plus a slab of bacon big enough to last more than a week. Pearl couldn't eat very much of it though, because she kept seeing that pig running around screaming with the sword in its neck.

Mostly the smells that drifted across that yard and down the little trail that led to the cabin weren't so sweet as cooking pork though. They were outhouse smells and horse corral smells, and another, a sickly rotting smell that Mother whispered was because there weren't enough men left with the strength to dig graves. Every day they carried uniforms, and sometimes Mother's good bedsheets and feather pillows, out of the house and lit a bonfire with them. They made a choking black smoke. Pearl was glad to stay inside and sew and sew.

Then one night as Mama Madie was dishing up dried-pea stew made with an onion she'd found growing under the house and the last of the fatty bacon, the captain came knocking politely on the door of the little cabin. Madie went to the door with a formidable look on her face and her hand on the hilt of the sewing scissors she kept in her apron pocket, and he said a few quiet words to her which Pearl couldn't hear. But she did hear Mama Madie scream at him, "May God Almighty above curse your black and murderous soul to the fires of hell!"

She slammed the door with a terrible look on her face and

opened her arms wide to Pearl, crushing her to her bosom. "We got to pray, child, we got pray," she said. "Your mama's took the fever, and we got to pray."

So they did. During the daylight Pearl sewed and prayed, and at night when she came back from tending Mother, Mama Madie got down on her knees and prayed, swaying with the rhythm of her prayers. But in the end it was to no avail. The captain came knocking one pink dawn with a face as long as the grave, and all he said was, "I'm sorry."

Mama Madie started to wail, and Pearl clung to her skirts, wrapping herself in them as if she were a little girl again. And then the captain grabbed Mama Madie's arm and held it sternly and said with a grim face, "Ma'am, you need to take that child and go. It's the cholera, and it will kill us all if we don't burn everything it's touched."

Mama Madie gave him a look of purest hatred, and she jerked her arm away and spat on his boots. She slammed the door shut, and started bundling up cook pots and dried beans and cornmeal in a blanket that she knotted at four corners and slung over her shoulder, and Pearl rolled up her threads and her needles and her sewing scissors in the quilt square with the flying horse in the center, and she tied it around her waist under her dress. Mama Madie grabbed hold of her hand and they left the cabin for a murky gray dawn that smelled thickly of smoke.

But it wasn't until Pearl looked back and saw the only home she'd ever known collapsing to the ground in a shower of orange sparks and crackling flames that she began to cry.

# 7

# Sheepshearing

Lori was right, of course, about the second alcove's location on the opposite side of the fireplace from the first. It, too, contained a mural that depicted the sheep meadow, only this version was framed by bare winter branches rather than blossom-covered ones, and the rolling pastureland was covered in snow. A cardinal, rather than a blue bird, was perched on the fence post.

When the last of the dust was swept away and the buckets of dirty water were emptied, everyone gathered around to examine what had been uncovered.

"The technique itself isn't bad," Lindsay said, appraising both paintings, "but the approach is pretty generic."

"Kind of like a greeting card," supplied Lori helpfully, and Lindsay gave her an annoyed look.

"Some of the illustrative art used for greeting cards is quite good," she pointed out. "And a lot of successful commercial artists sell to greeting card companies." She struggled briefly to erase the scowl from her face. "The point I was trying to make," she said, rather stiffly, "is that I don't see anything here to make me think these were painted by an artist of note. The homeowner probably told him exactly what to paint and paid him by the hour."

"Is there any way you can tell how old it is?" Cici asked.

Lindsay shook her head regretfully. "I can't. Maybe an expert in antiques could, or an art restorer. The colors look custom mixed, but a lot of artists mix their own pigments, even today. If the paintings were less generic—if the artist had included something we could date, like a car or a wagon or even a person—it would be different."

"What about the barn?" Noah asked.

Lindsay looked at him. "There's no barn in the paintings."

"Right," he said.

"Oh!" Bridget exclaimed suddenly. "But you can see the barn—or a part of it—in this view of the sheep pasture today!"

"Which means these must have been painted before the barn was built." Cici turned to Ida Mae, who was wiping down the arched frame of the alcove with a damp cloth. "Ida Mae, do you know when—"

Ida Mae spoke before she could finish. "You're gonna have to repaint this trim."

Lindsay said, "The artist might have left it out for aesthetic purposes."

"I'll paint it back in for you," Noah volunteered. "Wouldn't charge you more than fifty dollars. For each one, of course."

Cici said quickly, "Thank you, Noah, but I think we'd better leave it the way it is."

And Lindsay added, "After all, you wouldn't want someone else to come behind you and add something to one of your paintings, would you?"

He shrugged. "I wouldn't mind. Especially if I was dead. Twenty-five," he offered. "Apiece."

"Thank you, Noah," Bridget said firmly, "but no. Besides, you were going to finish planting the potato eyes this morning."

He shrugged. "Suit yourself. But if the painting ain't worth nothing, stands to reason I can't mess it up."

"Potatoes?" insisted Bridget.

Hands in pockets, he ambled off.

"And we've got sheep to shear," Lori declared, rubbing her hands together in anticipation. "Today's the day!"

Lori had determined, from all her reading, that the Ladybug Farm sheep were Irish in origin, and so declared there could be no more appropriate day to begin Project Sheep Shear than St. Patrick's Day. And even though Bridget was not quite as excited to begin what she suspected would be a dirty and exhausting task, she had to admit that having the patron saint of their flock's homeland on their side was not a bad idea.

~

"It's too early to be shearin' sheep," Ida Mae warned dourly. "You might as well go ahead and use the mutton for your Irish stew, if that's what you've a mind on."

"Maybe it wouldn't hurt to wait a few weeks."

"Aunt Bridget," Lori insisted, barely suppressing an eye roll. "The *market*."

"Right," Bridget said. "Apparently March is a hot market for wool around here," she explained to the others. "April, not so much."

"So let's go!" Lori said, heading for the door.

Cici caught Bridget's arm as she turned to go, a hint of alarm in her eyes. "You're not really going to let Lori near those sheep with a pair of shears, are you?"

"Of course not," she assured her, with a small smile. "Farley's coming to help."

☙

Lori had seen a program on the Discovery Channel in which a sheepdog lined up an entire flock of sheep outside a dipping shed, then herded the queue into the shed, up a ramp, and into an automated harness device, which clamped each sheep between its jaws and dipped it in a vat of insecticide. The sheep then scampered up another ramp and down the other side, out into the freedom of the sunny pasture to dry off.

Bridget assured her that Ladybug Farm was very far removed from the Discovery Channel, and while Rebel was in fact a competent sheepdog who had no trouble moving the sheep from pasture to pasture, he was unlikely to be able to persuade twenty-five sheep to climb single file up a ramp and into a vat of sheep dip.

They had spent a good deal of time discussing the pros and cons of the sheep-dipping process, and finally decided upon a more organic approach. Chemicals were dangerous, and smelly, and would cling to the wool for days, even weeks. They couldn't sell wool that reeked of pesticides. Besides, what was better for cleaning *and* disinfecting than good old-fashioned soap and water?

To obtain the optimal softness and fluffiness from the wool, they decided on baby shampoo. Bridget bought a half dozen bottles of it at the Dollar Store.

The plan was simple. They spread out a ten-by-ten tarp on the ground outside the barn door, where each sheep would be shampooed and then turned loose in the barn to await shearing. They hooked up the garden hose to the outside faucet and Bridget went to collect the first animal.

Rebel had been eyeing them suspiciously all morning, and when Bridget opened the gate to the meadow, he went into action. He streaked across the grass like an optical illusion, so swift and silent that the peacefully grazing sheep didn't even see him coming until he nipped one of them on the ankle. The flock bleated and trotted restlessly in a dozen different directions and the dog dropped to his belly, his mesmeric gaze stopping the animals in their tracks. He began to circle and the sheep began to bunch. As though contained inside an invisible circle, the herd trotted toward the opposite fence line.

Bridget had learned quickly that all she had to do to get Rebel to herd the sheep toward the west was to *pretend* she wanted them herded toward the east. So when she started waving a towel at the flock, urging it on in the direction it was going, Rebel immediately turned the flock around and moved it the opposite way. Bridget kept screaming at him and waving the towel, and Rebel kept ignoring her, trotting the flock toward the open gate of the sheep pen just outside the barn. There Lori stood, ready to close the gate as soon as the last sheep was herded inside.

"Good job!" she called as Bridget came jogging up a few dozen yards behind the sheep. "Not a single straggler!"

"All it takes is a little reverse psychology," Bridget called back with a grin.

Rebel, his job complete, streaked off to do whatever it was

he did when he was not circling the sheep or trying to attack members of the household.

Lori planted her hands on her blue-jeaned hips and looked over with satisfaction at the shuffling mob of securely contained sheep. "And you thought it was going to be hard," she chided Bridget. "I told you we could do this. And think of the money we're saving."

"We haven't even started the hard part yet," Bridget reminded her.

"Still . . ." Lori raised her palm for a high five. "Not too bad for a couple of city girls."

Her optimism was contagious. Bridget laughed and slapped her palm in agreement.

Fortunately the sheep were a relatively docile bunch, and Bridget had no trouble getting a loop around the neck of a ewe and leading her out of the pen to the tarp, where Lori stood ready with the garden hose and the baby shampoo.

"Okay, you just hold him there—"

"Her," corrected Bridget.

"Right. You hold her and I'll do the shampooing."

"She's a sweet girl," Bridget cooed, stroking the sheep's woolly head. "She's going to like her bath. She's not going to be any trouble at all."

And so, for a time, it seemed she wouldn't be. Lori soaked the woolly sheep with water from the garden hose—which was surprisingly cold on her hands—and poured on a generous amount of shampoo. She added more water to work up a lather, and more shampoo, scrubbing up to her elbows. Rivers of brown suds were sluiced away with the final rinse from the garden hose, and with Bridget tugging and Lori chasing, they finally maneuvered the ewe into the barn.

Two blow-dryers had been attached to long extension cords that were plugged into the barn's single outlet. They used old towels to rub away the worst of the water and, with Lori on one side and Bridget on the other, began to blow-dry the sheep.

Half an hour later, Lori stepped back to survey the fluffy, white, and rather annoyed-looking result of their efforts. "Well," she said, though with slightly less enthusiasm than before. "One down, twenty-four to go."

Bridget groaned out loud. "There has *got* to be a better way."

ॐ

Lindsay carefully spread newspapers out on the newly sanded floor and pried the lid off the gallon of wood stain with a screwdriver. "I'll start in this corner and you start in that one," she suggested, "and we'll meet at the staircase."

Cici looked up from the section of floor she was scrubbing with a mixture of turpentine and mineral spirits. All of the doors and windows were open, but the air was still sharp with the odor of chemicals and the ghost of dust from the sander.

"How are we going to get out?"

Lindsay looked momentarily nonplussed. "Oh. Okay, you start in that corner and I'll start in this one and we'll meet at the door."

"Better plan."

Cici sat back on her heels and stared in exasperation at the spot she had been scrubbing for the past twenty minutes. "Well, I give up. I've tried everything I know—sanding, bleaching, steel wool, and mineral spirits . . . whatever this is, it's not coming out."

Abandoning the stain, Lindsay came over to examine the spot. It was an irregular dark splotch a couple of feet wide, surrounded by smaller, coin-shaped blotches of the same color. "Maybe it's a defect in the wood," she suggested.

Cici shook her head. "It's more like some kind of spill."

"Maybe the wood stain will cover it."

"I doubt it. It's too dark. But I don't know what else to do, short of replacing the floorboards."

"Uh, veto that idea. We've got to get this finished today, remember? Besides, that's antique wood. Where are you going to find matching boards?"

Cici sighed. "I suppose. It just seems a shame."

Ida Mae stood at the doorway. "Don't look like ya'll are makin' much progress," she commented. "Them men just drove up."

Lindsay blinked. "What men?"

"About the sheep. Thought you'd want to know who was in your yard."

"Oh," Cici said, still preoccupied with the blot on the floor. "Not really. I don't suppose you have any secret recipes for removing stains from wood floors, do you? I've tried everything, and I just can't get this stain out."

"Nope," replied Ida Mae flatly. "And you ain't gonna get it out either."

Cici looked at her curiously. "Why not?"

"Because," said Ida Mae. "It's blood."

They were blow-drying their fifth sheep when Bridget looked up to see Farley standing at the door with a man they did not know. Her jeans and sweatshirt were splotched with wet patches, her platinum bob was tangled, her makeup had worn off, and her face was feathered with scraps of curly fleece. Every muscle ached with stiffness and she was as exhausted as she looked. Nonetheless, when she saw company had arrived, she automatically ran a hand over her hair and made an effort to smile.

"Hi, Farley," she said. She turned off her blow-dryer and nudged Lori, who was using a dog brush to comb out the wool around the sheep's ears.

Neither man spoke for a moment; they simply stared. The stranger bore a faint though noticeable resemblance to Farley that stopped at his head, which, rather than the perpetual camo cap Farley wore, was covered by a tattered straw hat. He chewed thoughtfully on a matchstick, which he removed from his mouth before speaking.

"Damn," he said. "I reckon I've seen it all now. A beauty parlor for sheep."

Farley, deadpan, spat into his soda can. "My cousin Zeb. He does sheep."

Bridget came forward, first wiping her hand on her damp jeans, then extending it. "Nice to meet you, Zeb. Thank you for coming, but"—she glanced helplessly over her shoulder at Lori—"we're really not ready yet. We didn't know it was going to take this long."

Zeb walked forward, his expression thoughtful as he examined the sheep Lori was working on, and looked over the stall door at the four fluffy white specimens who were stored there. He ventured, "Ya'll taking these sheep to a party?"

Lori, who was at least as tired as Bridget and far past the point of humor, bristled. "Well, you can't shear wet sheep, can you? We had to dry them somehow."

He sniffed the air. "They smell funny."

"Baby shampoo," Bridget explained, plucking an almost invisible strand of wool from her lips.

Zeb looked at her for a long moment. He looked at Farley. He lifted his straw hat and scratched his bald pate. "You washed the sheep?"

Lori pushed a handful of her straggling hair out of her face and replied, with just the smallest note of condescension, "We can't sell dirty fleece, can we?"

He said, "How come you didn't wait till they was sheared and then just wash the fleece?"

For a moment neither Bridget nor Lori reacted. Then their eyes met in a moment of mutual recognition for the futility of the past three hours' backbreaking work.

Bridget said, very distinctly, "We didn't have to wash the sheep."

And Lori agreed in a small voice, "I guess not."

"We could have just washed the fleece."

Lori tried to smile. "Guess we should have thought of that."

Bridget drew a breath as though to say more, stopped herself, and then turned back to Zeb with a smile so stiff it looked as though it might crack.

"Well then," she said in a voice that was high and tight and far too cheerful. "Shall we get started?"

❧

"What do you mean, blood?" Cici asked.

"Whose blood?" Lindsay demanded, alarmed.

Ida Mae gave her an exasperated glance. "How'm I supposed to know whose blood? Somebody's, is all."

Lindsay took a step back from the splotch on the floor, her nose wrinkling in distaste. "But . . . blood. On our floor!"

Cici insisted, "Then how do you know it's blood? Who told you that?"

Ida Mae shrugged. "Just always knew it, that's all."

Cici's frown was skeptical as she gazed down at the stain. "If you know it's blood, you must know how it got there."

"Never said I didn't."

Both Lindsay and Cici looked at her expectantly. Ida Mae took a dustcloth from her apron pocket and ran it across the mantelpiece.

"Honestly, Ida Mae, getting information from you is like pulling teeth," Cici exclaimed. "Well? How did it get here?"

Ida Mae tucked her dustcloth back into her pocket. "Seems like there was some story about somebody shootin' a Yankee that tried to come in that window yonder."

Lindsay caught her breath, her eyes going wide. "No kidding? A Yankee?"

Cici cast her a dry look. "Yes, kidding. Unless somebody was still fighting the war at the turn of the century, which was when this house was built."

Lindsay looked disappointed, but Ida Mae returned smugly, "As much as you know, Miss Smarty-Pants. Like I told that pesky child of yours, there's been a house here since before Civil War times. Part of it burnt down, but they built it up again. "

Now Cici looked interested. "Really? What part?"

It was Ida Mae's turn to look annoyed. "I wasn't around then," she told her, "and I got to go take my nap. Ya'll finished making all that racket up here?"

Cici assured her that they were, and Ida Mae moved off toward her downstairs sanctuary.

Lindsay regarded the stain on the floor with new respect. "Well, at least now we don't have to worry about getting rid of it. You don't get rid of a piece of history."

"I'm not sure how I feel about preserving the kind of history where people are shot in your living room," Cici said uneasily.

Lindsay shrugged. "Times were different back then."

"I don't know why you say that. Blood is blood. And dead is dead."

"And we can't do anything about what happened here a hundred years ago."

"You're right about that." Cici cheered marginally. "Besides, it is a good story, isn't it?"

"No one I know has a better one."

"Okay." Cici took up a pair of rubber gloves and slapped another into Lindsay's open palm. "Let's get started then."

❧

After a dozen sheep were sheared—which was accomplished in approximately half the time it had taken the two of them to wash even one sheep, exclusive of the blow-drying—even Lori had to admit the advantages of hiring a professional far outweighed those of doing it themselves. Farley looped a hobble around each sheep's hooves to keep them from struggling, and with a pair of electric shears, Zeb peeled off the thick, furry fleece in a single piece. As the fleece dropped to a clean tarp on the barn floor, Farley released its former owner and a naked sheep trotted away.

"It's just like unzipping a jacket," Lori said admiringly. "I don't suppose you'd let me try it once, would you?"

Zeb replied simply, "Nope."

"Lori," Bridget pointed out as she led another sheep into the shearing pen, "we're paying this man by the hour. Aren't you supposed to be turning the sheared sheep out to pasture?"

"Right," Lori said, and hurried after the newly released animal with a rope. "Where's that dog, anyway?"

Bridget hesitated, looking around. "I don't know." She sounded uneasy. "He's awfully quiet." That was never a good sign.

Noah came into the barn behind Bridget, with Bambi following close at his heels. "Noah, get that deer out of here! Can't you see we're busy?"

"I need the posthole diggers if you want me to start on that fence." But his attention was on Farley, who was wrestling the sheep to the ground, and he looked interested enough in the proceedings to take his time finding the posthole diggers.

"Well, they're not in here."

Farley flipped the sheep over to pin its hooves together, as he always did, the sheep bleated in protest, as it always did, and Bridget objected, as she always did, "Do you have to be so rough?"

Bambi wandered forward, neck stretched out to investigate, and that was the beginning of the perfect storm. The sheep Farley was restraining suddenly noticed the deer looming over him and began to struggle and bleat loudly just as Zeb fired up the electric shears. Lori, seeing her opportunity to get involved in the actual process, abandoned the already sheared sheep she had been leading out the back door to the meadow and rushed forward to help. Farley lost his grip on the sheep he was holding, and as it flung off its hobble and lurched to its feet, Rebel, who had been watching from a silent crouch in a shadowed corner, lunged forward in a frenzy of wild barking.

Bambi sprang over Zeb's crouching back and flew out the door. Zeb dropped the shears in astonishment. Bridget screamed at Rebel, who chased the sheared sheep out the back door and around the barn. The unsheared sheep, having escaped from Farley, charged after its flock mate in blind agitation, knocking Lori to the ground as it passed.

Bridget rushed to help Lori up. Noah, with a shout, took off after Rebel, who had Bambi in his sights. Farley retrieved his soda can from the post on which he had stored it, and spat. Zeb took off his hat and shook his head.

Lindsay was on her hands and knees at the open door to the porch, having just stroked golden stain on the last floorboard on her side of the room, when she heard the roar of barking and the thunder of hooves. She didn't even have time to gasp as Bambi sailed over the canvas-covered sofa on the porch and careened through the doorway, followed closely by Rebel. The deer's hooves splayed on the wet floor and he went skidding. Rebel's claws, scrambling for traction, left long crooked lines in the newly applied stain.

There was a voice: "Don't worry, I got 'im!" And Noah scrambled over the sofa in hot pursuit.

Lindsay cried, "Noah, don't—"

But too late. Noah's feet hit the wet floor and went out from under him; he slid halfway across the room before righting himself and grabbing the rope that trailed from Bambi's neck. He turned to Lindsay, covered in sticky brown stain, and grinned. "Told you I got him."

Rebel, hopping on first one foot and then the other, trying to shake off the floor stain that covered his paws, made his way to the door just as Bridget arrived. She gasped as she surveyed the scene of destruction, her hands going to her face.

"Oh my goodness! What happened?"

Cici, poised in a half crouch with her paintbrush in hand, mouth open, eyes stunned, looked slowly from Noah to Lindsay to Bridget. "I have no idea," she said.

Noah led the deer, slipping and sliding, out of the house and down the front steps, with Bridget following behind, frantically trying to wipe up the little crescents his hooves left on the painted porch floorboards. Lori ran toward them, breathlessly announcing, "We got the sheep back! Everything's okay. What's the matter with Rebel?" She stopped short, looking at Noah, looking at Bambi, looking at her mother and Lindsay standing on the front porch with their arms folded and their faces tight. What she could not see, her imagination supplied. "Oh," she said.

Zeb came up behind her, and addressed Bridget politely. "I'm ready to finish up, ma'am, whenever you are," he said.

Bridget looked around, flustered. "Well, yes, I suppose we'd better . . ."

"There's just one thing."

Zeb looked at Noah and the deer, then at the women on the cluttered front porch, and Lori and Bridget, flushed and sweaty and covered with wool, and he shook his head sadly. "I sure do hate to bring you trouble, when it's plain to see you already got plenty. But the fact of the matter is"—he reached in his back pocket and took out a small leather case, of the kind used to hold identification—"in my other job, I'm the game warden around these parts, and it's against the law to keep a wild animal without a permit. I'm afraid I'm going to have to write you a citation."

❧

They all sat on the porch that evening, paper plates balanced on their laps as they sprawled across the disarranged furniture, picking at the tuna sandwiches Ida Mae had made them for supper. They were too tired to eat, and almost too tired to move. It had taken every available hand to repair the damage done to the floor before the stain dried, so Ida Mae had been recruited to handle the sheep. She had of course complained about it nonstop, but there was a touch of satisfaction on her face as she joined them on the porch with a glass of iced tea.

"Something wrong with them sandwiches?" she demanded. "It's a sin to waste food."

They all murmured protests, insisting the sandwiches were fine, and Lindsay even took a bite.

"I had me a nice Irish stew planned," Ida Mae went on, "with old-fashioned soda bread and apple pie. But that was before you decided to let wild animals run loose in the house while you was painting the floors."

"Sounds wonderful, Ida Mae," Lindsay murmured, half asleep. "We'll have it later."

Ida Mae snorted.

"It was nice of Zeb to only charge us half price for the sheep," Bridget said, rousing herself to speak.

"That's still half our profit," Lori said morosely.

Noah said, "He ain't taking that deer."

"Oh, I don't think he'll do that . . ." Bridget looked helplessly to Cici. "Do you?"

Cici, too tired to even shrug, merely waggled her eyebrows.

Lindsay said morosely, "For fifty years I'd never even seen the inside of a courtroom. Not so much as a traffic ticket. Now I'm standing before a judge twice in one year."

"Next thing you know, your mug shot will be on *America's Most Wanted*," Lori said, peeling the crust off her sandwich. "Of course, without a satellite dish, we'll never see it."

"We only have to pay the fine if we don't either release him into the wild or find a suitable facility to take him before the court date," Cici pointed out.

"How much do you think the fine will be?"

Cici sighed. "More than we can afford."

"It ain't right, coming in a man's house, telling him what to do, threatening his property," Noah said angrily. "Ain't that against the Constitution?"

Lindsay focused with difficulty through her fatigue. "Umm . . . illegal search and seizure. Yes. That sounds like a good research project."

"I ain't writin' no report," Noah warned darkly. "And he ain't takin' that deer."

Bridget's tone was troubled. "It's my fault. I never should have asked Farley for help. But who knew he'd bring his cousin?"

Lori said, "It's okay, Aunt Bridget. You did right. We never would have gotten the job done by ourselves. I guess maybe sheep ranching is not as easy as I thought."

"Nothing ever is, sweetie," Cici said tiredly, and put aside her plate. "But next time, please, I'm begging you, just think it through, okay?"

Ida Mae said dourly, "You're all crazy as March hares, if you ask me. Letting wild animals run loose in your front parlor, moving your parlor onto the porch . . . And I'm telling you, it's too early to be shearing sheep."

"But at least we have the fleece," Lori said, cheering a little. "And we know someone who'll buy it. That's something."

Bridget reached across and patted her knee. "That's a lot, honey. You've worked hard and you did a good job."

"But," Cici pointed out, "I don't think there's much point in your writing this idea up into a business plan."

"Yeah," Lori agreed sadly. "Figured that one out."

They were quiet as the night settled in, bringing with it the clean sweet smell of new grass and turned earth. A night bird chirped and its mate answered. Something whirred in front of Lori's face and she swatted at it.

"Well, look at that," she said. "A ladybug."

Lindsay smiled faintly. "That must mean spring is really here."

"By the way," Noah said, "got your peas and taters in the ground."

"Now *that* means spring is here," Bridget said. She barely suppressed a yawn. "Good day's work, everyone."

Cici rose stiffly, muffling a groan. "And I, for one, am ready for it to be over."

A murmur of agreement went around the group and, one by one, they rose to follow her inside.

# April Showers

*A man travels the world over in search of what he needs and returns home to find it.*

—GEORGE A. MOORE

# 8

# Blackberry Winter

The floors finally dried, a post and wire fence was erected around the vegetable garden, and Lori and Bridget netted three hundred dollars for the fleece.

"It's not exactly what I expected," Lori admitted, trying hard to hide her disappointment. "But there weren't quite as many pounds of fleece as I had counted on, by the time we cut out all the damaged parts, and apparently the price-per-pound figure is for retail, not wholesale, and I guess our sheep aren't the highest quality wool producers..."

"Don't feel bad," Bridget tried to console her. "We had to shear the sheep, anyway, and three hundred dollars will go a long way toward paying for their hay this winter."

"Besides," Cici said, giving her daughter a bracing squeeze on her shoulder. "A determined entrepreneur doesn't look at losses. She takes her profit—however small—and reinvests it, right?"

"Right," Lori said, her expression brightening. She hugged her mother quickly. "Thanks, Mom!"

When she was gone, Cici shook her head and muttered, "I can't believe I'm encouraging her."

"Well, she did work awfully hard. And"—Bridget folded the bills and tucked them into her back pocket—"three hundred dollars is three hundred dollars."

They moved the furniture back onto the gleaming golden heart pine floors, carefully arranging the piano over the blotch near the window. The newly cleaned draperies were rehung over sparkling, freshly washed windows. Cici carefully applied a coat of white gloss paint over the arched trim around each alcove, and then decided that what the alcoves really needed was portrait lighting to spotlight the paintings. While she went to the hardware store for the necessary supplies, Lindsay put the finishing touches on the guest room. Paul and Derrick were arriving the next day.

The four-poster mahogany bed had been found in the dairy loft before Christmas, along with the ivory velvet-upholstered scroll bench at its foot. The velvet—originally an ugly wine color—had been moth-eaten and worn, but was easily replaced. The bed was dressed in a fluffy feather mattress and an ivory and sage brocade duvet cover that reflected, but did not match, the pale sage curtains that were drawn back from the sunny windows. The cherry vanity Cici had helped her get down from the loft looked perfect in the corner, particularly when topped with a lace doily and an overflowing vase of yellow daffodils. Two tapestry wing chairs, which Lindsay had spent the winter reupholstering, were drawn up before the dainty marble fireplace, and between them was a fluted pie table that held a china tea service, a selection of teas, and a basket, which, as soon as Bridget finished baking them, would be filled with blueberry scones.

Lindsay stood back and surveyed her efforts with satisfaction. "We really could run a B&B," she murmured to herself, and went forward to run her dustcloth, one last time, over the marble mantelpiece. That was when she noticed the crack in the wall.

Most of the bedrooms were covered with wallpaper; some of it, Lindsay imagined, as old as the house. But this room had apparently been redecorated within living memory, because the plank walls had been painted an inoffensive off-white, and the framed paneled wainscoting below it a glossier version of the same color.

The crack she noticed was really more like a seam that had been painted over, and when she applied gentle pressure with her hand, she felt the panel sway inward. "Good heavens," she exclaimed softly. "How many secret rooms does this house have, anyway?"

But it was not a secret room, or even another painted alcove. It was, as Ida Mae explained when she came up with a stack of freshly laundered towels for the guests, merely a covered wood storage bin.

"This was Miss Emily's room," she explained, "and when she got the notion to paint it all white, she thought the wood stacked up by the fireplace in the winter ruint the look of the room, and it did, too. Not to mention all the dirt it spread around on her white carpets. So she had them build a door to hide the firewood."

Ida Mae set the folded towels on the bed and gave the dust ruffle a critical little adjustment. "Miss Emily," she pointed out, "used to roll up the guest towels in a basket and put the basket at the foot of the tub. You want me to do that?"

"Sounds great," Lindsay said, her voice partially muffled by her explorations of the bin. "Oh, look! There's a pair of old andirons in here!"

She dragged one of the heavy, blackened objects out and examined it closely. "Is this brass?" She pulled out the other one. "I think it is! They'll have to be cleaned up, but wouldn't they look great in the fireplace?"

"They'll only get all sooted up again."

"Then we'll polish them again. Say, look at this." Using her fingertips she prized up what turned out to be a filthy piece of scrap carpeting, obviously put there to protect the wood floor beneath from the damaging effects of the firewood. As she pulled the carpet out of the cubby most of the detritus it had been placed there to hold spilled onto the floor.

"Broom's in the pantry," Ida Mae told her with a humorless look, and left to arrange the towels artfully in a basket for the bathroom.

Lindsay swept up two dustpans filled with shredded bark, dried leaves, and just plain dirt, before she noticed several sheets of newspaper, which apparently once had been used as fire starter, lodged at the back of the bin. She pulled them out, but they weren't very interesting—classifieds from 1962—and she tossed them in the trash bag. The last piece of paper was smaller, and half caught between the floor and the baseboard molding. She almost tore it tugging it out, but she could tell immediately it was not newsprint.

The paper itself was heavy, like stationery or even sketch paper, and it was yellowed at the corners with age. At first she thought it was blank, but when she turned it over she saw a crudely executed sketch—some kind of four-legged animal with wings in the center, a banner on top, and the whole surrounded by a pointed oval with one half shaded and what appeared to be feathers springing from the top. As she looked closer, Lindsay realized the animal was a horse. Lindsay smiled in puzzlement and started to crumple the paper into the trash, then hesitated.

This playful product of a child's imagination might have been drawn twenty years ago, or fifty. Perhaps it was even older. As she smoothed out the wrinkles in the paper, Lindsay could not help imagining some long-ago budding artist, rushing to show his mother his latest masterpiece, his mother faithfully tacking it up among the dozens of other similar works of art she couldn't throw away. This drawing, like the long-forgotten ribbon in the alcove, was a part of the history of the house, and it deserved a place of honor.

Lindsay found a dime-store frame in her studio, and was hanging the drawing on the tall narrow wall in the entry hall that was dedicated to personal art when Cici came in. On the same wall was a charcoal sketch Noah had done of the house, and a framed invitation to a party held at the house in 1920, which a neighbor had given them for Christmas. There was also a collage of newspaper scraps and receipts from the turn of the century that Lindsay had found while taking down the wallpaper in her own room.

"Look," she said as Cici came in with a bag from the hardware store. "I found another treasure." She stepped back to admire the drawing.

Cici tried to look appreciative. "What is it?"

Lindsay shrugged. "But it's old. It was in the cubby behind the wall in the guest room where they used to store firewood. I also found a cool pair of brass andirons."

"Good." Cici dropped the package on the sofa. "Because we're going to need them. I heard on the radio coming back that the temperature is really going to drop tonight. It's going to stay cold all weekend, too. Wouldn't you know? Just when we promised Paul and Derrick a lovely spring weekend in the mountains. I'm going to start bringing in some firewood."

Lindsay followed her through the house to the kitchen. "How cold is it going to get?"

"In the twenties tonight, the teens tomorrow."

Bridget was just taking the scones out of the oven and the kitchen was filled with the aroma of creamy vanilla and blueberries. She turned when Cici spoke, holding the baking sheet in her mittened hands. "*What* did you say?"

Lindsay went straight to the refrigerator and took out the butter dish. Cici filled the kettle and put it on to boil. "A cold front is moving in this afternoon. It's not going to get above freezing all weekend."

Bridget's eyes went in disbelief to the window, where an emerald meadow, unfurling green leaves, and snowy blossoms testified to the fact that this was definitely spring. "But . . . everything is in bloom! The fruit trees, the berries, the flowers . . . they'll all freeze!"

Lindsay, who was impatiently plucking the hot scones from Bridget's baking sheet into a napkin-lined basket, paused. "Oh-oh," she said. "I didn't think about that. My roses are starting to bud, too. I'll have to cover them."

"We can cover the blueberries and the hydrangea bushes," Bridget said. "But we'll have to cut all the flowers and bring them inside."

"You don't cover blueberries," Ida Mae said, coming into the kitchen from the pantry. "They need the cold to make. Same with blackberries and raspberries. You just leave 'em alone. Mother Nature has a plan."

"What about the cherry trees and the pears?" Cici said. "They're just starting to bloom. Does Mother Nature have a plan for them, too?"

Ida Mae shrugged. "They'll either live, or die. I told you it was too dang early to be shearing sheep."

The kettle started to shriek and Cici lifted it from the stove, pouring hot water over the tea bags in three cups. Lindsay put the basket of scones on the table and Bridget put away the baking pan, and for a moment the significance of Ida Mae's last words were lost on them. It was as one that the three of them turned again toward the window, and the view of twenty-five naked sheep peacefully scattered over the meadow.

"Oh, my," moaned Lindsay.

"The sheep," gasped Bridget.

"What about the sheep?" Lori, who could be counted upon to respond to the scent of baked goods from anywhere on the property, came in from the back porch and helped herself to a scone.

"Those are for company," Cici said. She took one for herself and sat down, reaching for the butter knife.

Bridget looked worried as she told Lori, "It's going to get cold tonight."

Lori said, "We'll bring the sheep into the barn. It's a mess to clean up in the morning, but we've done it before. "

"But," Bridget said, "that was when they had wool." She

sat down and pulled her cup of tea toward her, her forehead furrowed as she absently dunked the tea bag.

Lindsay took a scone and slathered it with butter. Steam rose from the crevices as the pale sweet butter turned to liquid, and Lindsay bit into it, smothering a moan of delight. "Oh, I hope you made more of these."

But Lori, with her own scone poised before her lips, hesitated. "What do you mean?"

"She means," interjected Ida Mae, setting a glass of milk in front of Lori with a thud, "that unless you figure out a way to get heat in that barn, them sheep is going to be dropping like icicles off a roof."

Lori stared at her. "You mean—they could freeze?"

"Dead," confirmed Ida Mae.

Lori turned a frantic look on Cici, who was buttering her second scone. "We can't heat a barn!" she objected before Lori could speak. "And even if we could, it wouldn't help. The temperature is not going to get above freezing until Tuesday at the earliest, and the sheep have got to get out and graze."

"This might be why the *real* sheep shearer don't come till April," Ida Mae pointed out, a trifle smugly.

Lori put her scone down on the tabletop, looking as though she might cry. Lindsay, feeling guilty for the pleasure she was taking in her own scone, placed it on her saucer and reached across the table to touch Lori's hand.

"We'll think of something," she told her.

And Bridget added, "Don't worry, we're not going to let a whole flock of sheep freeze."

"Couldn't we bring them in the house?" Lori pleaded, and almost before she finished speaking all three women responded.

"No!"

"But people in Europe used to bring their sheep in the house at night," Lori insisted. "The sheep would sleep downstairs, near the fire, and the people would sleep upstairs."

"People in Europe lived in barns!"

"In the Middle Ages!"

"It's not happening, Lori," Cici said firmly.

Bridget suggested, "Electric heaters?"

Cici shook her head. "Too dangerous. Besides, that doesn't solve the problem of getting them outside to graze."

Lori plucked morosely at her scone, leaving a pile of crumbs on the tabletop.

Ida Mae said, "Too bad you can't get back that wool you sold."

Cici looked at her sternly. "Thank you, Ida Mae. I think Lori feels bad enough."

Suddenly Lori sprang up from the table. "Mom, can I borrow the car?"

And even as Cici was saying, "Sure, but—" Lori turned to Bridget with her hand held out and her voice excited.

"I need some money," she said.

Bridget dug into her back pocket. "But, Lori, your mother's right. Heaters won't help."

"It's not for heaters," she said, snatching up the twenty as she dashed for the door. "It's for coats!"

❧

A bitter cold wind rattled tree branches and chafed their faces as twilight fell that evening, and still they lingered outside the barn, looking in, jacket hoods pulled over their heads, fringed scarves flapping in the wind, mittened hands shoved deep into their pockets. The hydrangeas and rosebushes were wrapped in cotton sheets and the vegetable garden was covered with mulch. Firewood was stacked beside each fireplace. And all of their sheep were wearing coats.

To be accurate, some were wearing fleece-lined UVA sweatshirts, others were wearing wool turtlenecks, some were wearing trimmed-down thermal long johns. Lori had raided every thrift store, Goodwill mission, and secondhand shop in the county, and she, Noah, and Bridget had spent the afternoon wrestling the sheep into the garments and then driving them into the barn.

"I've never seen anything like it in my life," Lindsay said, for perhaps the third time.

"Actually, I didn't think of it by myself," Lori admitted. "I saw it on a Nickelodeon cartoon one time . . . back when I used to have TV."

"Dumbest thing I ever did see," Noah pronounced, hunching his shoulders against a blast of arctic wind. "Them sheep's embarrassed, if you ask me."

"Well, they may be embarrassed," Bridget retorted, "but at least they're alive. Good job, Lori."

"I just hope it works," Lori worried.

"I don't know why it shouldn't," Cici said. "It may not be as good as their own wool, but it's the next best thing. They'll be able to generate enough heat bunched up together like this in the barn to keep warm at night, and during the day the coats will keep them from losing heat while they walk around to graze." She grinned at her daughter. "You're a pretty smart kid, if I do say so myself."

"I still say it's the dumbest thing I ever saw," Noah grumbled.

"Come on," Lindsay said, giving both young people a playful shove on the shoulder, "let's go in and get warm. We've got company coming tomorrow!"

# 9

# Company

The silver blue Prius glided to a stop in front of the worn brick facade of Ladybug Farm and its driver got out cautiously, keeping one foot on the floor mat and the door only half open, as though he were still debating whether to exit. He was a tall, pale, sharp-nosed man of about forty with a thick mane of perfectly coiffed chestnut hair and Italian shoes. He looked around cautiously.

The white-columned porch appeared to have suffered some from the mud of winter, and nothing but the sagging frozen stems of daffodils remained of the whiskey-barrel plantings on either side of the wide front steps. Somewhere in the distance—hopefully behind solidly locked doors—a dog barked furiously, and a deer with a rope around its neck was meandering toward the car.

"Well, well," Paul murmured to his companion. "The sheep are wearing coats and the shrubs are wearing bedsheets. We must be in the right place."

At that moment the front door opened and four women rushed down the steps, arms opened wide. Lindsay reached him first, flinging herself into his arms and burying her face in his camel wool coat. "Oh my God, you smell expensive!" she exclaimed

He assured her, tweaking her cheek, "My dear, I *am* expensive."

Cici grabbed the other door as it was opening and tugged Derrick out. "Look at you! Look at you both! How dare you look so good when I'm turning into a hag?"

Derrick, with his prematurely silver hair, bright blue eyes, and salon-perfect tan, preened under her praise. "Clean living and good hair products," he told her, grinning broadly as he kissed her cheek. "And who's turning into a hag? You never looked better! Your skin is positively radiant. Is that what fresh air and sunshine does to you? I might be tempted to try it after all."

"I'm so glad you came!" Bridget exclaimed, claiming her hug. "We haven't seen anyone from the old neighborhood in forever!"

And Lori pushed her way forward eagerly. "At last, someone from the civilized world! You've got to tell me, what's happening on *American Idol*?"

Paul gave her a look of disdain. "Like we would ever watch that trash." But as he tucked her arm through his and leaned in close he murmured, "You won't believe what Cowell is up to now. Tell you later."

"Inside, inside," Cici commanded, hugging her arms in the brisk air. "Before we all freeze to death. Noah will get your luggage."

"Yes, and could we speak with you about that gorgeous spring weather you promised, with daffodils in bloom and cocktails on the porch . . . Well, will you look at this?" Paul interrupted himself to stop and gaze in admiration around the foyer. "Will you just look?"

The grand, sweeping staircase gleamed beneath the prisms of the huge chandelier overhead, mirroring the golden glow of the newly refinished floors. Every surface held a vase of fresh flowers—mounds of buttery daffodils, jewel-colored tulips, stately sprays of forsythia and pink weigela. A fire crackled and danced in the fireplace, scenting the room with the aroma of hickory, and sunlight poured through the tall windows, forming inviting pools of warmth on the floors and tabletops. Derrick exclaimed over the painted tin ceiling and the stained glass window, and Paul went immediately to the draperies, the fabric for which he had helped Bridget track down over the Internet.

"Gorgeous!" he exclaimed, fingering the pleats. "Just gorgeous." He went quickly to one of the Queen Anne chairs that formed part of a group in front of the fireplace. "Don't tell me you found this in the attic! And what is this?" He had discovered the muraled alcoves.

Derrick said, "Well, I can certainly see why you were enchanted. This place is unbelievable. How old did you say it was?"

Several conversations were going on at once, as Cici told the story of uncovering the alcoves, and Bridget related the history of the house, and Lindsay interrupted with her discovery of the hidden firewood bin, and Lori piped in with her contributions to unearthing the hidden treasure of the house. The walls rang with the sound of voices and laughter, soprano and baritone, and inside the house it felt like home.

"I know you want the grand tour, so I'm going to duck out

and see about lunch," Bridget said. "I thought today would be a good day for Brunswick stew." She knew it was Paul's favorite.

"You are a queen!" Paul exclaimed. "Tell me you made beaten biscuits. Do I pay you now or later?"

Beaming, Bridget turned toward the kitchen and saw Noah lurking near the stairs. "Oh, Noah," she said, pulling him forward. "Come meet our company. Paul, this is Noah. We've spoken about him."

Paul extended his hand gravely. "A pleasure to meet you, young man."

Noah regarded him suspiciously, but did not shake his hand. "What kind of car is that?" he demanded.

Paul retrieved his hand graciously. "It's a hybrid."

He looked skeptical. "It didn't make no noise when you drove up."

"That's because it runs on battery power."

Noah grunted. "Couldn't afford a real car, huh?"

Paul's eyebrows shot up.

Lindsay said quickly, "Noah, come meet Derrick. Derrick owns an art gallery in Baltimore."

Noah regarded him with interest. "Oh yeah? Any money in that?"

Derrick replied, deadpan, "I do all right."

Noah jerked his head toward Paul. "Maybe you could buy your friend a real car."

By now Cici was beginning to catch on to Noah's sense of humor. "Very cute," she said. "Now, if you don't mind, would you bring the luggage in from the car? And you can let Rebel out of the barn, too."

"Okay." But he looked at Derrick curiously. "You got any of her paintings hanging in your gallery?"

Derrick looked at Lindsay in astonishment. "Are you producing? For display? You never said a word!"

"No, not really," she protested. "I'm a long way from having anything to show. Come on, let's see the rest of the house. Noah, the luggage?"

᠑

Before lunch, Paul and Derrick endeared themselves to everyone by distributing gifts. For Cici, Bridget, and Lindsay, spa baskets from Nordstrom. For Ida Mae, perfume, and even though she grumbled that she didn't "have no use for such nonsense" she could not quite hide her embarrassed pleasure over the gift, and she smelled suspiciously sweet at lunch. For Lori they brought a Prada bag—which Paul, as the author of the popular syndicated "In Style" column for the *Washington Post*, had received gratis ("'Swag,' as it's known in the business, sweetie," he explained)—and it made Lori squeal with delight. They presented Noah with an iPod Shuffle, preloaded with what the sales clerk assured them were the most popular tunes downloaded by teenage boys. And though Noah tried to be cool about it, it was clear the two of them had earned a place in his esteem very few others would ever approach.

Lindsay slipped her arm through Paul's and said softly, "That was sweet of you guys."

Paul patted her hand. "We know how hard it is for you to get nice things here at the ends of the earth."

And Derrick, smiling as he watched Lori trying to show Noah

how to work the player, added, "Besides, we missed Christmas, didn't we?"

They sat at the dining room table, at Ida Mae's insistence, which was dressed with crisp white linen and ironed napkins. A fire crackled in the fireplace and spring blossoms decorated the table. "This reminds me of that B&B in Vermont we stopped at in ninety-two, remember?" Derrick said to Paul. "On our way to Lake Placid?"

"Except the food wasn't as good," Paul said as Ida Mae set a steaming bowl of stew before him.

"Ida Mae, please, you don't have to wait on us," Bridget insisted.

And Lori said triumphantly, "See I *told* you a B&B was a good idea."

"We usually only eat lunch in the dining room on Sundays," Noah interjected. "Wouldn't want you to think we lived this fancy every day."

"I'm sure there's no danger of that," Cici assured him, passing the bread basket. "But it's nice to be a little fancy for company."

"And I want you to know we do appreciate it," Paul said, and raised his glass. "To our lovely hostesses."

"Hear, hear," agreed Paul and saluted them with his glass of iced tea.

"Sorry there's no wine," Lori said, sotto voce, glancing over her shoulder. "But Ida Mae doesn't approve of drinking before five o'clock. She barely approves of it after five o'clock."

Derrick cleared his throat. "Speaking of wine . . ."

Cici raised her hand to interrupt. "Let's enjoy our lunch. There's plenty of time for business afterward."

Derrick obligingly changed the subject. "Well, then. What is this you were saying about a B&B?"

Lori relayed her idea of turning the old manor into a bed-and-breakfast, and Paul and Derrick returned so much attentive enthusiasm that Cici finally had to beg, "Please, you two! Don't encourage her."

"Well, all I know is that if you served meals like this to your guests you'd have a virtual gold mine." Derrick spread thick purple jam on yet another buttered biscuit. "Bridget, what *is* this jam? It tastes like . . ." Derrick bit into the biscuit. "Wait, I've got it . . . Pinot noir! That's what it tastes like."

Bridget laughed as she got up to help Ida Mae with dessert. "Maybe it is. I made it out of the grapes from the vineyard out back."

"Pinot noir jam," mused Derrick. "Now *there's* something you could bottle and sell."

Lori's eyes took on a speculative light. "Say, that's right. All those little specialty shops in Washington and Baltimore are just filled with gourmet delicacies like that. They get ten or twelve dollars a jar!" She twisted in her chair. "Aunt Bridget! Have you ever thought about that?"

Paul murmured to Cici, "These children are consumed with high finance, aren't they?"

And Cici sighed in return, "Aren't we all?"

Bridget returned from the kitchen with a bubbling peach cobbler made from the peaches they had frozen last year from their own trees. Ida Mae followed with the coffeepot. "No, I haven't thought about that, Lori," she said. "But if you're willing to do the kind of work it would take to get those grapevines under control, we can certainly give it a try."

"We could make cabernet jam and chardonnay jam and pinot grigio jam . . ."

"Only if you have cabernet and chardonnay and pinot grapes," Derrick pointed out.

"Of course," Bridget went on, dishing up the cobbler, "you'll have to be careful of snakes—they love to hide out in grape-vines—and remember the wasps last year, girls?"

Lori said cautiously, "Snakes?"

"Besides," Cici added, "I think we'd have to harvest a lot more grapes than we have to turn jam making into a commercial venture."

"They used to make wine here," Lori pointed out. "How can there be enough grapes for wine and not for jam?"

Paul said, "I had no idea the vineyard was still here."

"If you could call it that," Bridget said.

"It's a mess," Lindsay admitted, "just like the orchard. When we first moved in, I planned to have all the gardens and the orchard *and* the vineyard cleared out and trimmed back and looking like a picture postcard by now. But it's a lot of land, and a lot of work."

"But you can still get grapes," Lori pointed out, "from tangled vines."

Paul smiled and toasted her with a jam-spread biscuit. "True enough, princess. Maybe after lunch you'll take me on a tour and we'll see just how much jam is left on those vines."

Derrick, glancing around the table, cleared his throat. "And now that the subject has turned, inevitably, once again, to wine . . ." He looked questioningly at Cici.

She smiled. "Okay, Derrick, let's have it. Noah . . ." She reached across the table to tap his arm. "It's impolite to listen to head-phones at the table. Ida Mae, wait. This concerns you, too."

Ida Mae, looking impatient, stood by the swinging door to

the kitchen with her arms folded. Noah, equally impatient, removed the earphones and dug into his peach cobbler. Paul looked longingly at his own cobbler, but gave his partner his attention. Derrick cleared his throat.

"The good news is," he said, "the broker was able to sell your wine."

The three ladies shared a hopeful look.

"The bad news is," Derrick went on, "it wasn't for as much as we'd hoped." He reached into his vest pocket. "I have your check." He removed an envelope, hesitated a moment, and passed it to Cici.

"The wine itself is still collectible," Derrick went on quickly. "And the fact that this was the last bottle of a popular vintage makes it even more so. Still . . . the eight thousand dollars that was paid for the other bottle was a fluke, I'm afraid."

Cici looked inside the envelope, smiled, and passed the envelope to Lindsay.

"How much?" Lindsay asked before she looked inside.

"Two hundred and fifty dollars," Cici said.

"That's minus the broker's fee, of course," Derrick said.

"Well," Lindsay admitted, "thousands would have been better. But that's still not bad for a bottle of wine." She passed the envelope to Bridget.

"That you didn't even pay for," Ida Mae pointed out.

Bridget said, "That's right, Ida Mae. If it hadn't been for your generous Christmas gift, we wouldn't have this money at all." She tucked the check into her pocket. "I'll get this to the bank first thing Monday. Thank you, Derrick. It will be put to good use."

Paul looked confused. "You're certainly taking this awfully

well. I know you were expecting a lot more—we all were. Aren't you disappointed?"

"Of course we are," Cici said, picking up her spoon. "We're just not surprised."

"We know you too well," Lindsay said. "You gave yourselves away with the expensive presents."

"I felt bad," Derrick said. "I should never have gotten your hopes up."

"Don't be silly," Bridget said. "We knew it was never a sure thing."

Lori dug into her cobbler with the enthusiasm of one who has never had to worry about calories a day in her life. "I don't get it. How can one bottle sell for eight thousand dollars and another just like it sell for two fifty?"

"Actually," Derrick said, relaxing a little as he picked up his spoon, "that was the problem. They weren't exactly alike." He tasted the cobbler. "Exquisite. What is that flavor?"

"Amaretto," Bridget said, pleased. "It is nice, isn't it?"

Ida Mae sniffed. "Plain old vanilla flavoring was always good enough for me."

Cici said, "What was different about this bottle?"

"The label," Paul supplied, tasting the cobbler. "Marvelous, Bridge. Forget manufacturing jam. You should open a bakery."

"Apparently," Derrick continued, "the first bottle—the one that sold for so much—was rare because it had a label that was discontinued in midrun. The new label—the one your bottle has—was picked up that same year and continued all the way till 1986, when the winery shut down. Clearly, not so rare."

"Do you mean it was the label that was valuable, not the wine?"

"In a way. That's the way it is with collectibles. The rarer the item, the more valuable, and when the wine is gone, the collector will still have a piece of art in the label."

Cici turned to Ida Mae. "Ida Mae . . ."

The older woman's brows drew together. "I told you, I don't have no more wine."

"I was going to ask," Cici said patiently, "why the winery closed down."

"How should I know? Weren't none of my business, anyhow. Long as I got my paycheck, what did I care? Ya'll want me to put on another pot?"

Bridget said, "Yes, thank you. We'll take our coffee into the living room."

"And now," Paul said, scraping the last bit of cobbler from the bottom of his dish, "if we've covered the subject of the wine . . ." He looked around the table. "Who's going to tell me why your sheep are wearing sweaters?"

❧

Derrick's footsteps clacked on the stone floor of the dairy as he walked around, hands clasped behind his back, gazing appreciatively at the space. Occasionally he would stop at one of the paintings that was hung to dry, or study a charcoal sketch thoughtfully before moving on. Noah, with his earphones in place, pretended disinterest as he leaned against the doorway, but his eyes narrowed whenever Derrick stopped before one of his pieces.

Finally, Derrick completed the circuit of the room. He stopped a few feet in front of Noah and simply waited until Noah, scowling, finally removed his earphones.

"Thank you for showing me the studio," he said. "You're very lucky to have a place like this in which to work."

Noah shrugged. "I guess." And then he added, casually, "So how good does a person have to be to get you to sell his stuff?"

Derrick tried unsuccessfully to suppress a smile. "*Good* is a relative term, Noah. "

"Oh yeah? Then who decides what's *good*?"

"If you are in the business of selling works of art, the market does."

"You mean whoever's got the money."

"More or less."

"Then what use are you?"

"I often ask myself the same thing."

Noah looked at him speculatively for a moment. "I ain't no dummy, you know."

Derrick lifted an eyebrow. "I never imagined you were."

"Lindsay could've showed you this place by herself, instead of telling me to."

"True enough. Why do you suppose she didn't?"

He shrugged. "So's you could look at my stuff and tell me if it's any good."

"Don't you imagine she could tell you that herself?"

"She tells me it's good all the time."

"Don't you believe her?"

"She's my teacher. She's supposed to say I'm good."

"I wish I'd had teachers like that when I was in school. I recall several essays that were returned with comments that were very far from good."

Noah said, "You know what I mean. She's supposed to encourage me. That's her job."

Derrick nodded. "Whereas I am supposed to be an objective expert."

"So?" Noah demanded. "What do you think? Do you like my drawings or not?"

Derrick turned and took his time studying the charcoals that were displayed, the pastels, a few experiments in oil.

"I like this one," he said at last, choosing a charcoal of the border collie in an attack crouch, teeth bared, fur wild. "And this one." He pointed to a pastel of the sheep meadow, patchy with snow, and a lone muddy sheep standing in a far corner. "But this is by far your best."

He indicated the eight-by-ten oil on art board that Noah had just completed as part of a class assignment using the glass plates Lindsay had found in the loft. This was a monochrome detail of one of the plates featuring a fountain in the rose garden. He had added, in the background, a deer wandering down the garden path, daintily nibbling on rose blossoms.

Noah said with interest, "Oh yeah? You want to buy it?"

Derrick replied, "No."

Noah's first surprise was quickly replaced with a belligerent scowl. "Why not?"

"Because your first question should have been, 'What do you like about it?' instead of 'What is it worth?' An artist has to be sensitive to what the viewer sees."

"That's bullshit." Shoving the earbuds back into his ears, Noah turned toward the door.

Derrick said, "Maybe. But I'm the expert."

Noah jerked open the door, took one step through it, and then turned around. He came back inside, closing the door with perhaps a bit too much force, and jerked the headphones out of his ears. "Okay. So what do you like about it?"

Derrick turned back to the painting and spent a careful moment in contemplation before he answered. "It's alive. It has depth and emotion, just like the sketch of the dog, and the pastel of the meadow with the one muddy sheep in the corner. It tells a story, and draws me in."

Noah, hands shoved deep into his pockets, affected indifference. But Derrick cast a sidelong glance at him without turning, and gauged the intensity of his interest. "I shouldn't be a bit surprised to see your work hanging in my gallery one day . . . if we could come to terms, of course."

Noah gave up the effort to disguise his interest. "Oh yeah? Then what're you wasting time for? Why not now?"

Derrick turned to face him soberly. "Man to man?"

Clearly, no one had ever addressed Noah in such a fashion. His shoulders squared a little, almost unconsciously, even as his expression grew more guarded. "Yeah, okay."

"Your work is unfinished," Derrick told him. "*You* are unfinished as an artist. To show a work before it's ready deeply undervalues it."

Noah thought about this for a moment. "You mean if I hold off my stuff is going to be worth more than if I sold it now?"

"That's exactly what I mean."

Noah grunted. "You think I could be an artist then?"

"I think you are already an artist. Don't you?"

He shrugged. "Lindsay is an artist and it don't make no never mind to her. I want to be the kind of artist that makes money."

"I'm sure you're not the first person to ever say that."

Noah regarded him speculatively for a moment, then seemed

to come to a decision. "Okay," he invited expansively, "talk to me. What do I need to do to get you to buy my paintings?"

Derrick gestured toward the door, smiling. "First, let's find a fire to sit in front of, and maybe a cup of tea with some of Bridget's shortbread cookies. Then we're going to have a long chat about the art business."

~U~

"Actually," Paul said, bending back a twiggy offshoot of a vine, "these vines aren't in bad shape. You're lucky they hadn't started to bud before the freeze hit, though."

"They go on forever," Lori said, stepping high over the crunchy brown grass and knotty roots that made the ground uneven. "But it gets a little thick back there close to the woods."

"I can certainly see what Lindsay meant by the amount of work it would take to clean this place up." Paul paused and looked around, eyes narrowed in the bright sun. "Still, if these are the original vines—or remnants of them, anyway—it might be worth it. You might even be able to salvage the original vinifera."

"What's that?"

"It takes a special kind of vine," Paul explained, "called vitis vinifera, to make wine. But the problem with letting a vineyard go wild like this is that the vinifera are constantly in danger of being contaminated—through pollination by bees and other sources—with more pedestrian grapes. Before long, they're no longer the original cabernet or shiraz or merlot, but something else altogether."

Lori said, "But the good ones are the vinif—whatever you said."

"Right. But only if you want to make wine. If you want to make jam ... well." He spread his hands expansively. "All it takes is grapes."

He added, "It seems a shame, though. It takes years to establish a productive vineyard, and here it is laid to ruin. Thomas Jefferson actually brought the first vitis vinifera to Virginia, did you know that? He thought Virginia could be one of the finest wine-producing regions in the world."

"How did you learn so much about grapes?"

"My dear, you live with a wine expert for ten years and you're bound to pick up a thing or two. And all those tours of Napa didn't hurt."

Lori bent to pick up a stick, switching it back and forth in the high grass as they walked. "Not that it matters," she said, a little dispiritedly. "It was a stupid idea, anyway."

"What was?"

"Making jam out of wine grapes."

"I don't see anything stupid about it," objected Paul. "A trifle ambitious, perhaps, especially from Bridget's point of view, since she's the one who would have to be in charge of manufacturing, but as an overall concept it seems perfectly sound."

"That's just the problem," Lori said. "Everything I come up with sounds good in theory, but when it comes to execution ... let's face it, I'm a total screwup."

Paul shot her a quick incredulous glance. "What are you talking about? Aren't you the one who came up with the idea that saved the sheep from freezing to death?"

Lori grimaced. "I'm also the one who came up with the brilliant idea to shear them in the first place."

"So, one little mistake."

"It's more than that." Lori focused rather grimly on slashing through a feathery stand of wheatgrass with her stick, and then she cast Paul a hesitant, uncertain look. "Can I tell you something?"

"I shouldn't be a bit surprised."

"But you have to swear not to tell my mother."

He chuckled. "When I was your age there was a saying—'You can't trust anyone over thirty.' Now that I *am* over thirty I'm here to tell you with absolute certainty that the axiom is absolutely true. We're all terrible finks, and you can't trust a one of us. I won't keep secrets from your mother," he told her, "especially the important ones." Then, sliding his hand into the stylish slit pockets of his camel coat, he added, "Of course, I don't tell her everything I know, either." He looked at her tenderly. "What is it, princess?"

She stopped, chewing her underlip, and for a moment she wouldn't meet his eye. Then she said, "The thing is . . . I don't think I'm very smart." And then, as though she were afraid he would dismiss her, she rushed on, "It's not that I don't try, and it's not that I don't *want* to get things right . . . it's just that every-thing somehow gets all muddled up in the end. It's like college. I told mom it was boring, and I wasn't learning anything, but that's not really it . . . I mean it is, but the real thing is that it was *hard*, a lot harder than I ever thought, and I just couldn't keep up with the work. I tried, but I kept flunking everything, and nobody likes to flunk *everything*. So I thought maybe I'm just not cut out for college. I mean, not everyone is, right? And maybe if I could just show my mom that I'm good at something else, anything else, it would be okay." She released a long, slow breath that puffed on the frosty air. "The trouble with that plan is that I'm just not good at anything."

They walked in silence for a while, and it seemed that Paul would not reply at all. And then he said, reasonably, "How do you know?"

She looked at him. "What?"

"How do you know you're not good at anything?" he repeated. "Have you tried everything?"

Her frown was dismissive. "Well, not everything. But—"

"But nothing. Oh, I could tell you all kinds of inspirational stories about how many books John Grisham had rejected before he sold his first manuscript and how Vermeer died a pauper and how Coco Chanel—well, forget Coco. The point is that if you keep trying, you're bound to get it right sooner or later."

She slid a glance toward him. "But Vermeer died a pauper."

"Only because he didn't live long enough," replied Paul promptly. "He's terribly famous now."

Lori couldn't restrain a giggle. "Uncle Paul, that's the worst inspirational speech I've ever heard."

He grinned and flung an arm around her shoulder. "That may be, my dear, but my heart's in the right place. Come along, let's get out of the wind."

They started back toward the house, and his tone grew serious. "You know, I'm a huge fan of your mom's."

Lori sighed. "So am I."

"She can run a business, a table saw, a sewing machine; build houses, drive a tractor, plan the perfect Zurich vacation, and throw the most exquisite parties I've ever been privileged to attend, and just when you think she can't top herself she does something utterly outrageous like moving into a century-old mansion in the middle of nowhere and deciding to restore the place brick by brick ... The lady casts one long shadow, that's for certain."

Again Lori sighed. "Tell me about it."

"She's a smart, ambitious, determined woman who made a lot of success for herself," Paul agreed. Then he stopped, and stepped in front of Lori, and rested both hands on her shoulders somberly. "But," he said, "the most incredible thing she has ever made is you. And don't you ever forget it."

Lori buried her face in his chest and hugged him hard. "Now that," she said, sounding a little misty, "was a great speech."

"Which only proves my point." He patted her back briskly. "If you keep trying, you're bound to get it right."

Lori laughed, scrubbed the moisture from her eyes, and stepped away from him. And with their arms around each other's waists, they made their way back to the house.

༜

They stayed up late that night, tossing logs on the fire when it started to die down, opening a second bottle of wine, reminiscing and catching up, laughing and musing. Lori and Noah stayed up late, too, though not as late as the adults, popping corn over the open fire and drinking hot chocolate and quizzing Paul and Derrick endlessly about the places they had been and the things they had done. The gentlemen told stories about artists' receptions and book signings, weekends in New York, and vacations in Brussels. The ladies told stories about drying apples and canning peaches, stripping furniture and reglazing bathtubs.

When Noah went upstairs to listen to his iPod and Lori, dozing before the fire, was reluctantly persuaded to say goodnight, Cici put another log on the fire. Lindsay took Lori's place on the sofa, stretching out with a glass of wine and swinging her wool-clad feet across Paul's knees. "Gosh, I've missed you guys," she sighed.

"Mutual, my darling," Paul returned, massaging her toes. "The old neighborhood just isn't the same."

Derrick refilled Lindsay's glass, and Paul's, and then raised the bottle to the others, who shook their heads. "I must say, I wouldn't have believed it if I hadn't seen it with my own eyes. Sheep farming, wood chopping, forest creatures and wild dogs and teenage boys roaming at will . . . a far cry from sailing on the bay and dining in Georgetown. And the most astonishing thing is that you all seem perfectly at home here."

"It grows on you," Cici agreed, contentedly stretching her own feet toward the fire.

"Tell the truth," Paul insisted. "Don't you miss it? Life in the real world?"

They laughed as one. "Of course I do!" Cici said. "I haven't seen a movie in a year."

"Or a manicurist," added Bridget.

"Or a shopping mall," sighed Lindsay.

"But . . ." Cici gestured to include the lamplit room, the glowing fire, the deep and velvety stillness of the night beyond the windows. "I would miss this even more."

"Oddly enough," said Derrick, "I can see that. And as much as I hate to admit I might actually have been wrong, I must say I think the move has been good for you."

He glanced at Paul for confirmation, who nodded. "It's the Zen of bucolic life," he agreed. "It's why agricultural peoples live an average of ten years longer than members of urban societies."

"Of course," mused Derrick, "one has to wonder what good ten extra years would be without Bergdorf's."

"Or Broadway," added Paul.

"Or lamb chops marinated in truffle oil and served on a bed of baby asparagus."

"Okay, now you're just depressing us," Bridget said, and everyone laughed.

"It was nice of you to take Noah under your wing," Lindsay said to Derrick. "I hope he's not being too much of a pest."

"I rather like the scamp, actually," Derrick admitted. "And you're right—he has a good deal of raw talent, with which you've done wonders, by the way. We might talk about his doing an internship with me at the gallery in a couple of years."

Lindsay's face lit up. "Really? That would be fabulous!"

Derrick held up a finger. "I said 'talk.' He'd have to be cleaned up and smoothed out a good deal before then."

"Not a problem." Lindsay sipped her wine and grinned. "You've just given me something to bribe him with for at least another year."

"And now let's talk about you," Derrick said. "I couldn't help but notice there wasn't a single one of *your* paintings on display in *your* studio."

Lindsay tried to look cavalier. "I think I'm a better teacher than an artist. You know what they say: 'Those who can, do, those who can't—'"

"Nonsense. Those who don't have the courage, perhaps."

Lindsay frowned.

"Besides," Bridget pointed out, "you've done some wonderful paintings of Bambi, and what about that portrait of Rebel you gave me for Christmas? Derrick liked that, didn't you, Derrick?"

"I thought all it needed was a spray of pine and a red bow

and it would be perfect for the cover of the holiday L.L. Bean catalog."

Lindsay lifted her foot as though to kick him and he leaned away with a grin.

"What?" demanded Cici. "Isn't that a compliment?"

"You're better than that," Derrick told Lindsay. "You just haven't found your passion yet."

"Well, when I do," Lindsay assured him, "you'll be the last to know."

Derrick chuckled, and Paul raised his glass. "A toast," he said. "To the lovely ladies of Ladybug Farm, who never cease to amaze me. May your lives always be as full as they are now."

Cici raised a cautionary finger. "But not any fuller."

# 10

# More Company

The next morning dawned cold and cloudy and, nestled under mounds of quilts, everyone slept late. It was the raucous barking of the sheepdog that shattered the silence.

Bridget, groaning, pulled a pillow over her head and waited for it to stop. But the barking went on and on, growing more furious and higher pitched with each moment, until finally she flung back the covers and reached for her robe.

She met Cici on the stairs, her hair tousled and her face puffy, belting her robe over flannel pajamas. "What in the world is wrong with that dog?" she said, and that's when they both noticed Ida Mae, turning away from the front window.

"Ya'll expecting more company?" she asked, looking annoyed.

Bridget and Cici joined her at the window, puzzling over the burgundy sedan that Rebel repeatedly charged, teeth bared and legs stiff, as though his life depended upon keeping the sedan at bay. Through the car's foggy windows they could make out the shapes of two cringing women.

"I wonder who they are," Cici said.

"Jehovah's Witnesses?" suggested Bridget.

"Somebody ought to do something," declared Ida Mae.

"I'll get 'im." This from Noah, who had come down the stairs bare-chested and barefooted, and headed straight for the front door.

"For heaven's sake," Lindsay called from the landing behind him. "It's freezing out there! Put on some clothes!"

But Noah, flinging open the front door, roared, "*Rebel!*" and dashed down the steps and across the frosty lawn to grab the dog's collar and drag him away.

"Well, I guess that woke everyone up," Bridget said. She smothered a yawn. "What time is it, anyway?"

Before Ida Mae could answer that, Lindsay joined them at the window, tying her French terry robe and peeling back the curtain for a better look. "What's going on? Who is that? I can't believe that boy went out in his bare feet!"

Noah, hopping on first one foot and then the other as the frozen grass cut into his soles, dragged the reluctant dog toward the barn, as the driver opened the door of the sedan. Lindsay gasped and sank back from the window.

"Oh my God," she said, her hand at her throat. "That's Carrie Lincoln. From the Department of Family and Children's Services."

Bridget peeked out the window again. "Who's that with her?"

"I don't know." Lindsay groaned. "I guess I can understand a surprise visit, but why did it have to be *today*?"

Bridget repeated. "What time is it?"

There was a knock on the door, and Lindsay tried rather desperately to smooth her tangled hair as she went to answer it.

"Carrie." She greeted her warmly and opened the door wide. "How nice to see you. Sorry about the dog. He really should be locked up. Come in. Goodness, it's cold this morning, isn't it?"

Carrie, a thirtyish woman with a pixie haircut and a quick—although at the moment rather strained—smile, stepped inside, accompanied by an older, stouter woman in a puffy quilted car coat. Carrie toted a messenger bag-type briefcase; the other woman carried a clipboard.

Carrie said, in her honey-thick New Orleans accent, "Lindsay, this is my supervisor, Marjorie Boynton. Marjorie, this is Lindsay Wright . . ." She turned to the other two, who did the best they could to straighten their hair and their bathrobes as they came forward. "Bridget Tindale and Cici Burke."

Marjorie's handshake was firm, cold, and no-nonsense. Her smile was nonexistent, her colorless gray eyes stern. She said, flatly, "Your sheep are wearing coats."

Lindsay suppressed another groan, and tried to disguise it with a weak smile. "I guess Noah let the sheep out of the barn when he put Rebel up."

Carrie said, a little uncertainly, "I hope we didn't wake you. But it *is* almost ten o'clock."

"Oh, good God," Cici said, turning to stare at the grandfather clock in the living room. And then she apologized, "We never sleep this late, really, but we have company and we were up half the night—"

It was at that moment that Paul appeared at the top of the stairs in his paisley silk robe and leather slippers, and called down cheerfully, "Good morning, my beauties. Loved the wake-up call. Now, if you'd only offer room service..."

And Derrick, similarly attired, appeared behind him. "Is that coffee I smell? We'll be down in a jiff."

Lori emerged behind them, wrapped in a quilt and looking grumpy and rumpled,. "Mooommm," she complained, "there's no heat in my room again and it's *freezing*. There's ice in the toilet!"

At the same time Noah blew in from the kitchen, rubbing his hands briskly over his goosefleshed arms and wiping one bare foot and then the other against the leg of his jeans to warm them. "Man, it's colder than a witch's—"

"Noah," Lindsay interrupted, perhaps a bit too loudly, "you remember Mrs. Lincoln from Social Services? And say hello to Mrs. Boynton."

Noah stopped, his affable expression immediately turning suspicious. He scowled at them. "What do you want?"

"Mom!" Lori insisted.

Cici said, "Excuse me, we're a little disorganized this morning." She flashed the visitors a reassuring smile as she hurried toward the stairs. "There isn't really ice in the toilet." Then, "For heaven's sake, Lori, use my bathroom!"

Mrs. Boynton said severely, "Your sheep are wearing coats while your children are freezing. Young man, do you have a coat? Or shoes?"

To which Noah returned sulkily, "What's it to you?"

"Noah!" Lindsay said sharply. She took a breath. "Go get dressed. And don't be late for breakfast," she added, loudly, as he turned away. She offered a weak apologetic smile to the social workers. "Teenagers," she said.

Carrie cleared her throat. "I can see we've come at a bad time." She glanced toward the staircase, where Cici was hustling Derrick and Paul back to their room, whispering to them frantically. "But you understand the point of this visit was to see how you really live."

"But we really don't live like this at all," Lindsay objected. "We really live very nice quiet lives."

Bridget stepped forward, laying a calming hand on Lindsay's arm, smiling graciously. "I know we haven't made a very good first impression, but maybe you'd like to have a cup of coffee while we freshen up and get ourselves organized? Ida Mae," she called, but Ida Mae was already there, marching a tray filled with coffee cups toward the living room.

Lindsay scurried ahead of her, snatching up the wineglasses, empty bottles, and empty snack bowls from the night before. "Nightmare," she muttered to Bridget as she passed, doing her ineffectual best to hide the empties in the folds of her housecoat. "This is a freakin' nightmare." And then she called brightly over her shoulder, "We'll be right back. Make yourselves at home!"

Upstairs, they found Paul and Derrick tossing through their luggage with an air of purpose while Noah, across the hall, assured them, "I ain't putting on no tie for no stupid social worker! You can't make me!"

"Cici told us," Paul assured Lindsay as she passed. "Don't worry, we've got it under control."

"Found it!" declared Derrick, holding up a red tie triumphantly.

"You . . . " Bridget grabbed Derrick's arm and propelled him toward the stairs. "Go downstairs and be charming. You . . ." She pushed Paul toward Noah's room. "Do what you can to make him presentable. No tie!" she called over her shoulder as she hurried past.

Within ten minutes Cici, Bridget, and Lindsay came back down the stairs wearing jeans and sweaters, their hair brushed and their lipstick applied, with smiles that were as hastily applied as their makeup. The two social workers were sipping coffee in the living room, where Derrick's charm was having a good effect on Carrie, but left the older woman utterly unmoved. He had managed to get a fire started in the fireplace from last night's embers, and the dancing glow was beginning to dispel some of the room's gloom.

"Noah will be down in a minute," Lindsay said pleasantly, smoothing her hands on her jeans as she sat down in one of the wing chairs across from the social workers. "Things are always a little hectic around here in the morning."

"But not usually as hectic as this," Cici assured them quickly. "You see we stayed up late . . ."

"Yes, your friend was just explaining that," Carrie said.

"We don't get to see each other very often," Lindsay added.

"Ladies, may I refill your cups?" offered Derrick, half standing.

Mrs. Boynton put her cup deliberately on the coffee table and took up her clipboard, ignoring him. Carrie covered her cup with her hand, smiling her refusal.

Lindsay said, "I'm not shy, if you're pouring."

Mrs. Boynton sat straight in her chair, shoulders square and not touching the back. Her formal tone and stern expression matched her posture as she announced, "The purpose of this visit is to inspect the premises on which the minor child resides, and to assess his living situation for the purpose of judging its suitability. We will be interviewing all members of the household, as well as the child." She turned with a militarylike precision to Derrick. "Do you live in the home?"

Derrick paused in the process of passing Lindsay a cup of coffee. "I live," he replied distinctly, "in Baltimore."

She made a notation on her clipboard.

Carrie said apologetically, "We really just need to confirm a few things."

"Why isn't the child in school?" Mrs. Boynton wanted to know.

"He *is* in school," Lindsay returned, a trifle indignantly. "Three hours a day, six days a week."

Carrie added quickly. "Homeschooling was approved by the department and by the school board, and Lindsay is a certified teacher with twenty years' classroom experience."

The supervisor gave a disapproving "Hmph" and made another notation on her clipboard. She turned a page. "I see here that guardianship is shared by Reverend and Mrs. Stewart Holland. Why doesn't the child live with them?"

Lindsay blinked. "Why—because I'm his teacher. It's more convenient for him to stay here."

"Besides," added Bridget, "we have a bigger house, and the animals, and Noah likes to work outside . . ."

"And because he prefers to stay here," Cici said with an air of simple finality.

For the first time a smile ghosted Mrs. Boynton's lips. It

was not a pretty sight. "One never wants to make the mistake of assuming that what a child prefers is in his best interests, Mrs...." She checked her notes, searching for Cici's name.

"Burke," said Cici coolly. "And it's Ms."

"I wonder," continued Mrs. Boynton, "whether the good reverend approves of your"—she slanted a glance toward Derrick—"lifestyle."

Derrick's eyebrows rose. "Excuse me?" Cici asked, as she raised herself to her full height of five foot, eight inches.

"Noah!" Carrie's face flooded with relief as she looked over Cici's shoulder. "Come in and join us, please."

Noah stood at the entrance to the living room, his expression thunderous. Lori stood a few inches behind him, and it looked as though she had pushed or dragged him all the way. Even as they watched, Lori gave him a little shove from behind, which he returned with a backward thrust of his elbow that just missed her ribs.

He was wearing jeans which, though worn and fashionably frayed in some places, were at least clean. The pale pink cashmere sweater he wore, although tucked and pleated to its best fit, clearly was not his, and neither was the Oxford shirt with the maroon stripe and open French cuffs that were stylishly folded up over the sleeves of the sweater. Noah had, apparently, won the battle of the tie. His hair was wet and slicked back with a comb, and on his feet he wore mud- and manure-stained running shoes without laces. No socks.

Paul appeared behind the two young people with his hands and eyebrows raised in a helpless gesture. Cici, Bridget, and Lindsay smiled at him gratefully.

"Noah," Lindsay said steadily, "you look very nice. Come in and sit down. These ladies would like to talk to you."

Noah just stood there scowling. "This ain't my sweater."

Carrie said, "We were just talking about your schoolwork, Noah. I understand you're doing very well."

He said, "I ain't talking to you."

Mrs. Boynton said briskly, "Young man, come inside this minute and sit down. We have some questions for you. Ladies..." She swept her eyes around until they rested on Derrick. "And gentlemen," she added precisely, "if you'll excuse us."

Derrick departed with obvious relief; the ladies a bit more reluctantly, each one touching Noah's arm or straightening his collar or patting his shoulder as they passed by. They all met up in the hall on the way to the kitchen.

"The old one has lizard eyes," Lori said with a mock shudder. "Never thought I'd feel sorry for that kid."

"She doesn't have any eyebrows, did you notice?" Derrick whispered.

"Not to mention a sense of humor," said Bridget.

"Tell me about it. I'm the one who had to try to make conversation for half an eternity before you came down. Silas Marner was more fun."

"Thanks for getting Noah cleaned up and downstairs, Paul," Bridget said.

"I could only do so much with the raw material," Paul admitted regretfully.

"I must say," Derrick commented in his customary dry way, "you girls do lead colorful lives. Do be sure to invite us back real soon."

Cici returned a weak smile as she pushed open the door

to the kitchen and leaned against it to allow the others to pass. "I think I'm starting to remember why we don't entertain anymore," she said.

∾

Hoping that the aroma of good things baking would have the same effect on cranky social workers that it did on prospective home buyers—which was why Cici had never shown a home without first sprinkling a little vanilla flavoring or cinnamon on a hot burner—Bridget and Ida Mae got busy whipping up a batch of muffins. But before the oven even preheated, Lori—who had volunteered to spy on the proceedings in the living room—came scurrying back to report, "They're coming! You won't believe it—he didn't say a word! They kept asking him questions and he kept not answering until I guess they got tired of wasting their time. I guess he meant it when he said he wasn't going to talk to them."

As one, Cici, Bridget, and Lindsay groaned out loud.

Cici volunteered to take the social workers on a tour of the house while Noah, jerking Paul's cashmere sweater over his head, stalked off to his room. Before the tour even made it up the stairs, he was barreling back down again, wearing his own sweatshirt and coat. "Goin' to the barn," he muttered as he shoved past, and was out the front door.

They looked into all the rooms and made notes. They asked about daily schedules and the division of labor. They refused muffins. They talked to Lori, to Ida Mae, and to each of the women separately. Finally Mrs. Boynton said crisply, "I think we have all we need. Ladies, you'll be hearing from our office."

Bridget, Cici, and Lindsay walked them to the door. Carrie lingered as the older woman went to the car. "I am so sorry," she said, her expression distressed. "But since it was a court case, they had to send a supervisor."

Lindsay asked seriously, "Are we in trouble? I mean ... do you think she'll try to take Noah away?"

Carrie hesitated. "I think there may be some concerns," she admitted. Then she gave them a reassuring smile. "But in the end I'm sure she'll see this is the best possible situation for Noah at the moment. After all, this is a very small county and, well, there simply aren't that many foster homes available." Again a pause before she added, "We might have to rethink the home-schooling, though."

"We promised Noah he wouldn't have to go to public school," Bridget said.

"The public school doesn't have an art program," Lindsay objected.

Cici said, "Carrie, this is the longest he's ever stayed any-where without running away. We're starting to make some real progress. It would be a shame to give up now. Can't you see what you can do about keeping things stable for him a little while longer?"

Carrie smiled and squeezed her hand. "Of course I will. I'm on your side, remember?"

She opened the door and looked back over her shoulder. "It certainly would have helped if he had at least *talked* to us, though," she said.

Lindsay leaned against the door and closed her eyes. "I am going to strangle that kid."

"Not until after breakfast," Bridget said, and linked her arm through hers. "Come on. We have company, remember?"

"You ain't gonna invite them sour biddies to breakfast, are

you?" Ida Mae demanded as she took the breakfast casserole out of the oven.

"Oh, yes, please, tell us you didn't invite the sour biddies," Paul said. He and Derrick, as at home in the Ladybug kitchen as they were in their own, were pouring orange juice into stemmed glasses and arranging them on the kitchen table, which was already set with bright yellow Fiesta ware and tangerine napkins. The hickory wood table, which was arranged in a nook beside the raised kitchen fireplace, was the coziest place in the house.

Lindsay made a face at him in reply to his remark, and he added, "I hope the kitchen table is okay for breakfast. We thought it would be cheerier than the dining room."

Ida Mae grumbled, "I didn't think no such thing. Decent folk use the dining room when they've got company."

Derrick gave her a playful one-armed hug as he passed. "We're not company, Ida Mae. Haven't you figured that out by now?"

She pretended annoyance as she shrugged way from his embrace and set the casserole down with a clunk on the center island beside a colorful bowl of fruit salad and a basket of muffins. "Ya'll're gonna have to serve yourselves from the counter," she told them.

"You're right, Paul," Bridget declared, picking up her plate. "The kitchen table is cheerier. And if there's one thing this house needs right now it's a little cheer."

"It's funny," Cici said, "but as much trouble as he is, and impossible as he can be sometimes, I'd really miss that kid if he were gone. I don't want them to place him somewhere else."

"I guess you never know how much someone really means

to you until you're faced with losing him," Lindsay agreed somberly.

Lori took up her own plate. "Don't take this the wrong way, but I don't understand what you're all so upset about. I thought Noah was only supposed to stay here temporarily, anyway. Isn't that what temporary guardianship means? Maybe he'd be better off with the preacher and his wife."

Cici gave her a look. "Don't you take this the wrong way," she told her daughter, "but go out to the barn and tell Noah to come to breakfast."

"My eggs will get cold!"

"They will if you don't hurry."

With a huffing breath, Lori put down her plate, snatched up a muffin, and left the room.

"Put your coat on!" Cici called after her.

Lindsay absently scooped breakfast casserole onto her bright yellow plate. "Maybe Lori's right. Maybe he would be better off in a traditional home."

"He wouldn't last a day," Bridget said.

"There's nothing traditional about him," Cici said, taking the serving fork from Lindsay's hand and sliding one of the three servings of casserole Lindsay had taken onto her own plate.

"I think the worst part is being disapproved of." Lindsay placed a muffin on her plate and topped it, rather forcefully, with a dollop of butter. "It's not that I care what other people think about me. I just don't want them thinking I'm not good enough."

"It's your own fault," Ida Mae pointed out gruffly. "Anybody that stays in the bed until ten o'clock in the morning and leaves dirty dishes and empty bottles scattered all over the front room deserves what they get. I never been so scandalized in my life. You ought to be ashamed of yourselves, every single one of you."

"I, for one, take full responsibility for my actions and am properly chagrined." Derrick's tone was reassuring as he took her elbow and guided her toward the table, a full plate in his other hand. "Here you are, dear lady, I fixed this just for you. Sit by me."

"I got no time to sit down," Ida Mae objected, her eyes narrowing suspiciously even as she sat and let Derrick unfold a napkin in her lap. "I got things to do."

Bridget and Cici shared a secret smile with Paul. "Can he come live with us?" whispered Bridget.

"You've already got your hands full with one renegade male," Paul reminded her.

"Speaking of which . . ." Cici looked over her shoulder toward the window. "Where are those kids, anyway?"

⁊ʊ

Noah was not in the barn, or the studio, or any other likely place, which suited Lori just fine. The morning air was bitter and she was hungry and she could smell hot muffins and sausage even from here. She was hurrying back toward the house to report that the boy could not be found when she actually caught sight of him, crossing the stubbly back field that led toward the woods. She cupped her hands around her mouth to shout for him, and then changed her mind.

For one thing, he was leading Bambi on a rope beside him. For another, he was wearing his backpack and his red stocking cap, which Bridget was always badgering him to put on when he went outside in the winter, and which he never would. It was all very odd. Curiosity momentarily overcame her hunger, and Lori decided to follow him.

She didn't rush, not that she cared whether he knew she was behind him or not, so that by the time she reached the little structure in the woods he was already inside, prying aside some stones in the fireplace. He didn't notice her at first, and she looked around appreciatively.

It was a good-size round building with a tin roof and a stone floor, open on the sides like a gazebo or an open-air dance pavilion. The freestanding stone fireplace had a chimney that went right through the roof, and there were remnants of rusted-out and crumbling furniture—a table and a wooden chair, an old truck seat, an aluminum patio chair with frayed and missing webbing. It was a rather desolate-looking place on this cold morning in the middle of the winter-bare woods, but there was still enough of an air of romance about it to stir a young woman's imagination.

"Wow," she said. "So this is the folly."

When she spoke, Noah whirled around guiltily, and several of the glass bottles he had been removing from their hiding place behind the fireplace spilled from his hands and clinked on the floor. Lori did not even notice his angry scowl as he began scooping them into his backpack. Bambi trotted over to her, hooves clattering on the stone floor, and she scratched the deer's head absently as she looked around.

"I wonder what they used it for," she said, "way out here in the woods. Do you think anybody lived here? Or maybe it was just a party house. Like the movie stars have in California."

Suddenly she noticed the glass bottles he was stuffing into his backpack. "Say, did you find all those in the garden?" She dropped to her haunches beside him and picked up one of the bottles to examine it. "What are you going to do with them?"

He snatched the bottle out of her hand. "Sell 'em."

"Oh." She regarded him matter-of-factly. "You're running away again, huh?"

He glared at her. "What's it to you?"

She shrugged. "I don't care what you do. But my mother cares a lot, and so does Aunt Bridget, and I think it would break Aunt Lindsay's heart."

His scowl deepened, and he jerked the iPod out of his jeans pocket. "You want to buy this?"

"No thanks. I already have one. Besides, it's rude to sell a gift. What's this?" She tugged at the corner of a rectangular glass plate that was sticking out of his backpack. When he tried to grab it back she turned away, holding the plate up to the light.

"That ain't yours," he demanded. "Give it back."

"Look at that! It's our house." She looked at him. "Where did you get this?"

He regarded her defiantly, and she turned back to the sepia plate. "It must be really old. Look at the dresses the women are wearing. Does Aunt Lindsay know you have this?"

"She's got plenty of them."

"Well, you're only going to break it if you carry it around like that, or scratch it up so badly it won't be worth anything. Don't you have anything you can wrap it in?" She handed it back to him casually and began rummaging around in the backpack.

"Hey, get out of there! Leave my stuff alone!"

He wrestled the pack away from her, but not before she had pulled out several more glass plates, an art box, a T-shirt with holes in it, and a small oil canvas of a fountain in a garden.

Glass bottles rattled in the bottom of the pack as he started stuffing things back in, but Lori picked up the canvas before he could.

"Wait a minute," she said. "I know this place." She looked at him as recognition dawned. "Is this the pool in the back garden?"

He shrugged, his scowl thunderous, but he did not immediately try to retrieve it from her. "That fellow, that Derrick, he said it was good."

Lori said softly, "Wow. So this is what it's supposed to look like." She regarded him curiously. "How did you know...?" And then her eyes fell on the glass plate he was clumsily wrapping in a T-shirt before returning it to the backpack. "Ah," she said, "the photographic plates. They must tell the whole story of this house."

She returned the canvas to him, but he hesitated, looking at the painting, looking at the plates. "Story, huh?"

Bambi wandered up and nudged Lori's shoulder, hard, causing her to almost lose her balance. She caught herself with one hand, and used the other to stroke Bambi's neck as she pushed to her feet. "What are you going to do with Bambi?"

Noah finished repacking his backpack. "Take him with me."

Lori let out a hoot of laughter. "What, on the bus? Don't you think that would be a little conspicuous?"

Noah's cheeks colored dully. "I never said nothing about a bus."

"Well, how far do you think you're going to get on foot, leading a deer on a rope? Boy, talk about not thinking things through!"

"I guess you expect me to just leave him here and let the law come get him," Noah returned angrily. "Well, that just goes to show what a smart-ass city girl knows. You turn a pet deer like that loose in the woods and he wouldn't last a week. He don't know how to live on his own anymore."

"And you do?" Lori shot back.

"I'm not letting the law come get me either!" He grabbed for Bambi's rope, but the sudden movement startled the deer, who was, after all, still a wild animal. A single leap took him out of the building and bounding through the woods.

"Bambi!" Lori cried, and Noah shouted, "Hey!"

They both took off after him at once.

The deer was spotted a few dozen yards into the woods, plucking berries off a spiky bush. Noah made to lunge for him but Lori flung up a staying hand. "You're the one who scared him in the first place!" she whispered angrily.

Lori crept forward, reaching slowly and cautiously for the rope that still dangled around the deer's neck, but she needn't have worried. Bambi lifted his head and regarded her with interest as she closed her hand around the rope, then plucked a few more berries off the bush. He made no objection as she led him back toward Noah.

"Wow," Lori said, pressing her hand over her still pounding heart. "Now I know what Aunt Lindsay meant when she said you don't know how much somebody means to you until you think you're going to lose them. That was scary."

Noah shot her a sharp look as he took the rope. "Stupid deer," he muttered. "You don't know when you're well-off."

"Yeah, well he's not the only one."

Tugging on the rope, Noah pushed his way through the brush back toward the folly.

"Hey," she shouted after him, and took a couple of running

steps to catch up. "What I was going to say, before you started acting like a fool and scared him half to death, is that there might be a way for us to keep Bambi *and* stay out of trouble with the law. All we have to do is apply for a permit to keep wildlife."

His step may have slowed a bit, but he did not stop, or look around, or give any indication at all that he had heard her.

Lori threw up her hands. "Okay," she said. "Run away, don't run away. My breakfast is ruined either way. But put Bambi back in the barn before you leave."

As they reached the folly, she veered off on the path that led back to the house. Noah said, "Hey," and Lori looked back impatiently.

"Did Lindsay really say that? About missing me?"

Lori rolled her eyes. "What an idiot. People who don't even know you are tripping all over themselves to help you, and you don't even notice. You go out of your way to screw up. Well, let me tell you something, kid. A person only gets so many chances in life. Maybe you'd better start taking advantage of yours." She started back down the path.

"Oh by the way," she called over her shoulder, "I'm going to tell Aunt Lindsay you stole her photographic plates, so if you're going to sell them you'd better do it quick."

"Bitch!" he shouted after her.

She returned an expressive hand gesture without looking back, and left him there.

❧

Ida Mae was clearing away the remnants of the lovely breakfast casserole when Lori came into the kitchen. Everyone else was lingering over coffee.

"Sit down," Ida Mae commanded. "I kept your breakfast warm."

"Ida Mae, I love you!" Lori beamed, and tried to kiss her cheek, but Ida Mae shrugged her away.

"Where's Noah?" Cici asked.

"He wasn't in the barn," Lori hedged, taking her seat at the crowded table. "Or the studio."

"Well, where is he?" Bridget wanted to know. "What took you so long?"

Ida Mae came to the table with two breakfast plates held in hot pads. She sat one before Lori, and another in the empty place reserved for Noah. Lori said, "Thank you, Ida Mae, you're the best. Pass the butter, Mom?"

But she looked at Bridget's curious face, and noted the anxiety creeping into Lindsay's eyes, and the expectation in her mother's expression as she passed the butter to Paul, who then passed it to Lori. Lori put down her fork. She took a breath.

"Sorry," Noah said gruffly, unzipping his jacket as he came into the kitchen. "Damn deer got lost. Had to go chasin' him." He took his place at the table and tucked into his breakfast.

"Noah, please don't swear at the table," Cici said.

And Noah, surprisingly, replied, "Yes'm."

Lori buttered her muffin, and didn't say anything at all.

❧

Everyone lingered over hugs by the car when it was time for Paul and Derrick to go. Even Noah, hanging back a little from the women, came to see them off.

"It's going to be like the day after Christmas when you leave," Lindsay said, hugging Paul hard. "Oh, I wish you could stay!"

"I wish you could live here!" Lori exclaimed, embracing Derrick.

Derrick laughed. "Shall I tell you the truth? After only a couple of days, I almost wish I could, too."

"We always talked about buying a B&B," Paul reminded him.

Lori tossed a triumphant look to her mother and said, yet again, "I *told* you it was a good idea."

Amidst the laughter, Paul cupped Lori's chin with his fingers and told her, "You hang in there, precious girl. If you need any more inspirational speeches, you know my number."

"It's on speed dial," Lori assured him, and returned a fierce hug.

Derrick walked over to Noah. "Young man," he said, "we'll talk again."

Noah said, "You coming back?"

"I am. And when I do, I'll expect a completed masterpiece from you. Until then . . ." He offered his hand, and this time Noah shook it.

They promised recipes and photographs and telephone calls and letters, and then the blue Prius was gliding down their drive, leaving the women nothing to do but wave until it was out of sight.

"I got stuff to do," Noah said, and slumped off toward the studio.

Lori sighed as she turned to go inside. "Well, I guess it's back to the real world."

Bridget, Lindsay, and Cici stood in the drive for a moment longer, rubbing their arms to keep warm, looking wistful. "It really *is* like the day after Christmas," Bridget said.

"Funny how one little change in the routine can make everything seem different," Cici agreed.

"It's not that I miss our old life," Lindsay said. "It's just kind of . . . fun to be reminded of it now and then."

"Like drinking a half-caf vanilla mocha latte on the way to work in the morning," Cici said, with a touch of longing.

"Or remembering how the shoe department smells at Macy's," Bridget said wistfully.

"Or getting a pedicure at Francine's."

Then Cici admitted, "There are a few things I miss, but nothing I can't live without."

"Me, either," Lindsay agreed. "But I don't think I realized how much I missed those two characters until now."

Bridget said, "It was sweet of them to invite us to go with them on that cruise to Alaska this fall."

Cici smothered a chuckle. "Like that's ever going to happen."

Bridget sighed elaborately. "I'd hate to think our cruising days are over."

"Not over." Cici slipped her arm through Bridget's. "Just temporarily postponed."

A film of anxiety clouded Lindsay's eyes. "Do you think it's too soon to call Carrie?"

Cici slipped her other arm through Lindsay's. "She'll let us know something as soon as she knows."

Bridget said, "I guess I'd better get Lori to help me to undress the sheep. The forecast calls for fifties this afternoon."

"And burn those coats," Cici advised.

Lindsay smiled wryly. "Like the girl said: back to real life."

"There are worse things," Cici pointed out.

The other two couldn't help agree as they turned, arm in arm, to go inside.

# 11

# In Another Time

*Marilee, 1944*

"Always observe the amenities," her Grandma Addie had told her. "No matter how low life knocks you, you can hold your head up high if you observe the amenities."

As a child, Marilee had thought the amenities might be a flower, or a bird, that had something special to teach, which was why she was supposed to observe it. After all, Jesus had said, "Consider the lilies of the field . . ." and "His eye is on the sparrow . . ." Later, she reckoned it might be something you studied in Earth Science class, like those beautifully colored plants that lived beneath the sea. Now, as a mature young bride and mother-to-be, she understood exactly what the amenities were, and how important it was to observe them. The amenities were gestures of civility performed in this big, often very uncivilized world, small acts of kindness to let others know that their lives were noticed, and their presence valued.

That was why, as her last act before leaving Mrs. Blackwell's Home for the Wives of Our Heroes Serving Abroad, Marilee sat down at the small, elegantly crafted writing table in her room to pen a note of thanks to her landlord of the past two years, and to attach it to a gift-wrapped box of rose-scented talcum that she had purchased on her last trip into town a week ago Saturday.

Emily Blackwell had sent two sons to fight in Europe. One would not be coming home. On the day that Mitch Crane—whom the girls in the house had nicknamed "the Grim Reaper" both because of his long, dour face, and because of the dreadful news he so often brought—stepped out of his black Hudson with the telegram in hand, Emily Blackwell had locked herself in her room and refused to come down to read it. She stayed there for two days. When she emerged, Mitch was still there, and he sat with her in comforting silence, until the pastor arrived. Observing the amenities.

It was then that Emily had decided to open her home to the military wives, many of whom had come from other parts of the state, who worked at the nearby textile mill while they waited for their husbands. The textile mill made the cloth that was used for uniforms. They worked to keep their husbands warm, and they liked to think they worked to bring them home sooner.

When Marilee first arrived at Blackwell House, there had been fifteen young women swarming through the upstairs rooms in their housecoats and slippers, their hair done up in papers, tossing laughter and shouts back and forth. Someone had broken a heel. Someone else had lost a button. Someone needed a bobby pin. And everyone stopped and turned with big welcoming smiles when Mrs. Blackwell brought Marilee up the stairs and introduced her as the "wife of Sergeant Jefferson T. Hodge," and the newest member of their household.

There were three beds in most rooms, four in some, but there were six bathrooms and they never felt cramped. They took all their meals at the big noisy table downstairs and climbed onto the rattletrap old bus that the mill sent for them every morning. After work they all helped in the creamery, making butter and cheeses and buttermilk and thick cream, because what they didn't need for their own table could be sold to help buy household necessities. In the evenings they would leave their doors open upstairs so that they could talk back and forth, sometimes passing around a bottle of nail polish or reading aloud from a magazine article, writing letters to the ones they loved or sharing the letters they had received, until Mrs. Blackwell called lights-out. Sunday afternoons they gathered around the radio in the big front parlor and rolled bandages for the Red Cross.

Suzie Todd had been the first to leave them, when her husband was wounded in a firefight in the French countryside. He was flown to the naval hospital in Norfolk, where Suzie would join him. The other women rushed to her aid, making travel arrangements, helping her pack, loaning or giving her little items they thought would be of use on her journey. Though their words and their faces were full of sympathy, inside they were secretly torn with jealousy, and ashamed of it. Her husband was coming home. For her, the war was over.

Twice Mitch Crane had come to their house in the big black Hudson and stood in their front parlor with a telegram in his hand and a grim look upon his face. All activity stopped upstairs. Silence fell like a caught breath. The girls clung to each other, feeling the sweat that prickled on each other's skin, heartbeats pounding in their ears, straining to make out the words that were murmured in the parlor below. And then listening to Mrs. Blackwell's slow, heavy steps coming up the stairs to the steady frantic inner prayer of *Not me, please don't let it be for me, not me, please* . . . And then she was there, a tall, dignified figure in her spectral black dress, and she gently spoke a name and extended a hand, and there was a sob, a cry, a scream of denial, and everyone else breathed again. Their numbers were diminished by one.

Then Amy McClellan had flown to Guam to join her husband on leave, and had returned home pregnant. That was much the way it had happened for Marilee, only for her and Jeff it had been four glorious weeks in Hawaii, the best time of her life. Neither woman had pretended her pregnancy was an accident. Even though they knew it would mean leaving Blackwell House before their babies were born, they were among the rare and lucky ones who had had the opportunity to seize new life from the hovering shadow of death. They did not waste it.

Amy had gone home to her parents in Indiana to await the birth of her child, and had later written to gush about her baby girl. Her husband was still serving in Europe. But Marilee, who was due in a mere ten weeks, was going to San Diego, where Jeff would be permanently stationed at the end of the month. She was the luckiest woman in the world.

"You're the luckiest woman in the world. You know that, don't you?"

Marilee grinned to hear her own thoughts echoed out loud,

and she turned to see Penny standing at the door of the room, her arms and white cotton sock-clad ankles crossed, leaning against the jamb. Penny, so called because of her bright copper hair, was one of the three women with whom Marilee had shared this room for the past year, and it hadn't taken long for them to become fast friends. Penny's husband Bill was fighting in the South Pacific, too, just like Jeff. But Penny hadn't seen her husband in eighteen months.

"First you get to go gallivanting off to Hawaii on an all-expenses-paid honeymoon courtesy of the United States government," Penny went on, feigning annoyance, "and you stay there just long enough to make sure there's a bun in the oven, mind you, then you come traipsing back here and expect us to welcome you home like nothing ever happened. And if that wasn't bad enough, we barely get used to your snoring again before you're off to San Diego." She sighed elaborately. "Baby. Husband. White picket fence. What did you ever do to deserve all that?"

Marilee pinched off a wilting blossom from the bouquet of black-eyed Susans on the desk and playfully tossed it at Penny. "Comes from clean living and hard praying," she returned. "Besides"—she sealed the envelope on her thank-you note, and tucked it carefully beneath the grosgrain ribbon with which she had wrapped the gift to Mrs. Blackwell—"I don't think there are many picket fences in military housing."

"That makes me feel ever so much better." Penny picked up the tossed blossom and crossed the room to drop it into the wastebasket. "All packed? You didn't forget the stationery, did you?"

The night before, the girls had given her a going-away party, using up almost all the sugar rations for the cake they'd baked, and even opening a purloined bottle of scuppernong wine. Mrs. Blackwell had pretended not to notice. Their going-away gift to her had been a box of scented writing paper delicately decorated with pansies in each corner, and they had made her promise to use it to write to them. Marilee had cried and hugged their necks, one by one, and told them she would never forget them, not ever. And it was true.

"I just wrote my first letter on it." Marilee smiled as she carefully closed the box of stationery and rearranged the lavender ribbon with which it had been wrapped. "A thank-you note to Mrs. Blackwell."

Penny gave her an indulgent look. "You are just the sweetest thing. I don't know what we're going to do around here without you."

Marilee braced herself against the seat of the chair and pushed herself up. She really wasn't all that big yet—in fact, she had worked up until three weeks ago and her employer hadn't even known she was expecting—but she still found her increased girth awkward and hard to get used to. She brushed down the hem of her flower-print maternity jacket as she crossed the room to tuck the stationery atop her open suitcase.

"Well," she said, snapping the locks on the suitcase, "I guess that's it."

"Oh, honey! You're not forgetting this, are you?"

Penny picked up the quilt that was folded neatly at the foot of Marilee's bed, and Marilee laughed as she hugged it to her.

"Grandma's quilt? Not a chance. I just didn't have room for it in my suitcase. I'll have to carry it on the bus. Did I ever tell you the story behind this quilt?"

"Only about a dozen times," Penny assured her affectionately, and slipped her arm through Marilee's. "Earl Crowder is going to be here any minute to drive you to the station. Let's get your things downstairs. Maybe we'll have time for a glass of lemonade."

Marilee looked around the room with something close to regret. "I'm glad everyone else went on to church today. I don't think I could stand saying good-bye again. I sure am going to miss this place."

Penny squeezed her arm. "And we're going to miss you, too. Now, let's get you out of here before we both start bawling again."

They both turned toward the window at the sound of tires crunching on the hard-packed dirt below. "That's probably Earl now." Holding the quilt over one arm, Marilee turned to get her suitcase.

"Honey, don't try to carry that heavy thing. I'll holler down for Earl to come up and get it."

Penny went to the open window and leaned out, but she did not call down. She didn't do anything. In fact, for a long moment, she didn't even move.

Then she straightened up slowly and turned around. The flesh at the corners of her eyes seemed tight, and her bright red-painted lips a garish contrast to a face that had suddenly gone very white. "It's not Earl," she said. "It's Mitch. He's got a telegram."

Marilee felt the baby inside her belly turn over once, slowly, and then was very still. Instinctively she drew her arm over her abdomen, shielding the little one inside with the quilt she still held. She could feel her heart beating.

They listened to the knock on the door, the *clop-clop-clop* of Mrs. Blackwell's sturdy black heels as they crossed the polished pine floors. The door opening. A murmur of voices.

"The girls are at church," Marilee said on an exhaled breath, for of course it had to be for one of them. As much as she loved them, it had to be for one of them. It couldn't be for Penny, her dearest friend, who had stayed behind today to see her off; not Penny, please God, not Penny.

Penny's hand slipped into hers. It felt hot, feverish, even. "It doesn't have to mean . . ." Her voice sounded as though it was filled with dust, cracking and strained. "It could be something else. Telegrams come all the time. It could be something else."

The door closed. Steps crossed the floor again. *Make him go away, it's no one here, please make him go away.*

And then the steps started up the stairs.

Marilee looked at Penny, stricken. She felt small fingers tighten on hers. Penny's blue eyes had turned dark, and she seemed to shrink within her skin.

Heavy black heels on the landing. Fingernails dug into Marilee's palm. And then Mrs. Blackwell was at the door to their room; her stern, reserved features unrevealing, her shoulders straight in black broadcloth, her eyes still.

"Mrs. Hodge," she said gently, "will you come with me, please? There is a telegram for you."

The quilt slipped from Marilee's clutches and pooled around her feet. She heard Penny stifle a sob at her side. Her hand left

Penny's and somehow found its way into the cool, dry grip of Emily Blackwell's.

Marilee walked down the stairs, and took the telegram. Then she sat on the sofa between Mitch Crane and Emily Blackwell, and, with eyes that were dry and a heart that was bleeding, observed the amenities.

# 12

# The Art of Parenting

Spring returned to Ladybug Farm. Baby lettuces formed straight green rows behind the garden fence, punctuated by the feathery tops of carrots and radishes. Spring peas sprang up overnight and began to climb the rope trellises that Bridget and Noah had built for them, their dainty white flowers promising an abundant harvest to come. Bridget set pots of herbs on the stone patio to soak up the sun, and Lindsay worked bonemeal into the soil of the rose garden, underplanting the beds with fragrant thyme and pale gray lamb's ear.

The sheep gradually began to lose their pinkness to a soft thatch of baby white wool, and the pear trees, recovering from the late freeze, unfurled their snowy blossoms like lace parasols. Baby leaves of yellow green and emerald, gray green and lime green, ruby and pink, erupted on near and distant branches, and bluebirds, chickadees, and a magnificent display of yellow finches hopped hungrily back and forth between the nearest trees and Bridget's feeders.

Once again the fireplaces were cleaned, the woodboxes emptied, the hearths swept. They touched up the winter-worn paint on the porches and scrubbed down the outdoor furniture. They raked up the last of winter's debris and planted yellow and purple pansies in the flower beds. And the day before Easter Sunday, Lori donned hip boots borrowed from Farley, elbow-length rubber gloves borrowed from her mother's workshop, and, armed with a shovel and a rake, waded into the murky black depths of the pool in the back garden.

"Bless her heart," Bridget said, watching from the back porch. "She's been at it all morning. You couldn't pay me in gold to do that job."

"Don't you dare feel sorry for her," Cici warned, peeling the striped cover off a wicker love seat. "And don't take her any cookies either."

"Gee, I'm glad you're not my mom."

"Let's keep our eye on the prize," Cici reminded Bridget. "Lori wants to work on a farm, so she's going to get to *work* on a farm."

Bridget grimaced as Lori dug her rake deep into the murk and brought up a glob of dripping black weed, some of which splattered onto her hair and face as she tossed it into a waiting wheelbarrow. She had already carted a half dozen similarly loaded wheelbarrows to the compost pile.

"Well, I can't watch anymore." Bridget turned toward the door. "I'm going to check the mail. Did you—"

The back door opened and Lindsay stood there, looking unsettled. "I just talked to Carrie," she said, and both women immediately stopped what they were doing and turned to her. "I couldn't stand it anymore, so I broke down and called her. She said that Noah's case has been marked 'pending further investigation.'" A worried frown creased her brow. "What do you think that means?"

Cici tried to sound confident. "It sounds like a bureaucratic stamp to me. I'm sure it just means they haven't gotten around to it."

"Sure," Bridget added reassuringly. They probably just haven't finished the paperwork."

"They might have to do some more interviews," Cici suggested. "You know, talk to people around town, and don't forget the Reverend and Mrs. Holland. They're the ones vouching for this living arrangement, so what they say will carry a lot of weight."

"Which is exactly why Noah will be sitting in the front row on Easter Sunday wearing a coat *and* a tie and scrubbed to within an inch of his life," Lindsay assured them. "And," she added, "it's also why I just invited the illustrious pastor and his wife to Easter dinner tomorrow."

Bridget's eyebrows shot up. "I'd better tell Ida Mae. She'll want to polish the silver."

"Like there's any silver left she hasn't polished?" Cici quipped. "But you'd better remind her to drape a tablecloth over the liquor cabinet. Baptists don't approve of drinking."

"I doubt they approve of three single women having two gay men as overnight guests in their home, either," Bridget ventured uncertainly.

"I thought we wouldn't mention that," said Lindsay, but she, too, sounded uneasy.

"The Hollands like us, though. And why shouldn't they? We're nice people."

"And we never miss a service," Bridget added.

"Or turn down a committee," said Lindsay.

"Which reminds me. I promised to bring cinnamon rolls to the sunrise breakfast in the morning," Bridget said, turning toward the house. "And I know Ida Mae is going to want to use the good damask tablecloth if the preacher is coming. Now I've got to find it."

"I think it has a wine stain on it from Christmas," Lindsay called after her.

"We'll tell them it's cranberry sauce!"

As the screen door closed behind her, Cici said seriously, "What you really need to do is have a talk with Noah. You know how he is about authority figures, and he's not all that wild about the Hollands in the first place."

"Don't worry, that's number one on my agenda." She glanced at her watch. "Where is he, anyway? His placement tests are coming up soon and we have a study session scheduled this morning."

"I haven't seen him," Cici said, and admitted, "I've been too busy watching Lori."

"Oh, that poor child." Lindsay winced as she watched Lori trundle another leaking wheelbarrow full of debris toward the compost pile behind the barn. "I hope she doesn't get a disease, fooling around in all that muck."

"It was your idea," Cici reminded her sternly.

"I know. But maybe we should offer to help."

"What is it with you and Bridget?" demanded Cici in exasperation. "You never heard of tough love?"

Lindsay gave a shake of her head. "All right, I promise I won't do your only child any favors. But I think I will go try to find

Noah, if you don't mind. If I'm going to get him whipped into shape by tomorrow, I'd better get started."

❧

"I thought this was a smoke-free workplace."

Noah whirled around guiltily to see Lori standing with her hands on her hips. He jerked the iPod earbuds from his ears and scowled, as he casually stubbed out the cigarette on the side of the barn door, then ground it underfoot—making sure that the evidence was buried in the mud. "You gonna tell on me?" he demanded.

Lori shrugged irritably and took up the handles of the empty wheelbarrow. "I'm not your mama. Besides, I've got better things to do with my time than babysit you."

He followed her around the corner of the barn and across the yard, watching as she picked up the shovel and waded back down into the water.

"Any old catfish in that pond?"

"Why don't you get down in here and see?" She swung a shovel full of debris that barely missed covering his shoes.

Noah pretended nonchalance as he stepped out of the way. "You're going about it all wrong, you know. You need a pump."

"You can't put a pump in here until you clean out all the trash, smarty-pants," Lori said.

"Shows what a girl knows. You put the pump on a rock or something, pump out all the water, then you scoop out the trash. Farley said he'd rent you one for ten dollars."

Lori scowled, wondering how he knew these things. "I heard him. But I'm going to buy my own. We'll need it to run the fountain."

"What fountain?"

"The fountain that's in here somewhere beneath all this garbage."

"What makes you think there's a fountain?"

She didn't reply, but the answer dawned on him, anyway. "Because of that picture of mine?"

She couldn't tell if he was flattered or incredulous, and then it didn't matter because he let out a whoop of laughter. "That was a hundred years ago!"

She glared at him. "So?"

"So, that's dumb, is all. Where're you going to get the money?"

"For what?"

"The pump."

"My dad's Am-Ex."

When he did not respond she looked up and explained patiently, "American Express credit card."

He scowled at her. "I know what it is. All spoiled rich kids have them."

Lori returned his scowl fiercely. "Do I look like a spoiled rich kid to you?"

At that moment Lindsay called, "Noah! You're supposed to be at your desk!"

As Noah turned toward her voice, Lori's feet slipped on the slimy pond bottom and she splashed backward into the murk.

Lori came up, gasping and sputtering and wiping black goo off her face and out of her hair while Lindsay raced toward her and Noah doubled over with laughter.

"No," he said, as Lindsay helped Lori out of the pond, "you sure don't look like a spoiled rich kid to me."

Three showers and one frizzy-haired blow-dry later, Lori felt clean enough to go into town. Her clothes, on the other hand, would have to be destroyed.

She braided her hair to tame the worst of the flyaways, donned clean jeans and a T-shirt, and borrowed her mother's car. It occurred to her that the kid might be right: If she elevated the pump above the level of the debris it might actually make the job easier to pump the water out first, and then clean the bottom of the pond. She did, however, hope he would keep his mouth shut about her intent to buy a pump. She had an unspoken agreement with her mom about acceptable uses of the American Express card: emergencies, yes; books and other school supplies, definitely; clothes, music downloads, shoes, makeup, and miscellaneous necessities of life—debatable. Household improvements, never.

But this was different. This was important.

Walking into Family Hardware was like walking back in time. The town of Blue Valley, a thirty-minute drive from Ladybug Farm, was little more than a village presided over by two tall-steepled churches, Methodist on one corner and Baptist on the other. Smack in the middle of the two of them was Family Hardware and Sundries, where you could buy anything from a penny nail, which actually cost a penny, to an antique chifforobe. In between were lightbulbs, cinnamon sticks in big jars, insect repellents, camping equipment, garden hoses, Norman Rockwell prints, dog collars, baby diapers, and scented candles—and that was just on the front display.

"Good afternoon, Miss Lori," Jonesie, the proprietor, greeted her as she came in. "Don't you look like sunshine today? Everything okay out at your place?"

Lori beamed. She loved the way he always remembered her name, even though she'd only been in a few times before with her mom or Bridget. And she loved the way he said, "your place," as though she belonged there. "Hi, Jonesie. I'm looking for a . . . oh my goodness!"

She just then noticed a wire cage near the window whose floor was lined with sweet-smelling cedar chips and which contained an adorable assortment of baby bunnies in Easter-egg shades of pale pink, blue, and green. She dropped to her knees, cooing with delight, and poked her fingers through the wire. Several bunnies hopped over to investigate.

"They're for Easter, don't you know," he said, coming over to her. "Kids snap them up this time of year. Here, you can hold one." He reached inside, grabbed one of the bunnies by the scruff, and plopped it into her arms.

Lori buried her face in the cedar-scented, bunny-musky fur. "Oh, you're just too cute. Aren't you the sweetest thing?" She looked up at Jonesie. "Why is their fur pink, blue, and green?"

"It's just food coloring. Won't hurt them, and it grows out."

She nuzzled the little ball of fluff one more time. "Why are they making that chirping sound?"

He laughed. "That's not the rabbits. That's the baby chicks. We just got a shipment in this morning."

He gestured toward the opposite window where, amidst an assortment of toasters, hunting jackets, potpourri, and vacuum cleaners, another wire enclosure had been set up. This one was lined with newspaper, and filled with tiny chirping yellow chicks.

"Oh!" she exclaimed, holding on to the bunny as she went to investigate. "Oh, how cute! Why aren't they colored, too?"

"These are Rhode Island Reds," he told her, "prize-winning chickens. Most folks don't put them in Easter baskets . . . although some do, I reckon," he admitted.

She examined the trilling little chickens with greater interest. "Prize-winning, huh? Do they really have shows for chickens?"

"Sure. That's how farmers know what to buy every year. Which chickens produce the most eggs, the best meat, that kind of thing. Now, then"—he smiled at her—"can I wrap up that bunny rabbit for you? He sure does look like he could use a good home with a pretty little thing like you."

"Oh . . ." Reluctantly, she returned the pink bunny to him. "No, I guess not. What I'm looking for is a water pump. And do you know anything about building a fountain?"

❧

"This is stupid," Noah grumbled, not looking up from the answer sheet he was marking. "Taking a test to practice for a test."

"It will help us both know what you need to work harder on for the real placement test," Lindsay explained. "People do it all the time."

While Noah marked his sheet, Lindsay was using a tool to stretch preprimed canvas over a four-foot by four-foot frame. Though she didn't like to admit it, Derrick's comments about her art had stung, and she was determined to rise to the challenge—just as soon as she found something she was passionate enough about to paint. While she waited for inspiration, she stretched canvases. It was a slow and laborious process, as she knelt on the brick floor and pulled the canvas one corner at a time, stapled it, turned the frame, and repeated the process. It occurred to her this might be a good time to let Noah get some practice at stretching canvases.

"Oh yeah? Name one."

"The PSAT, for one." She set her teeth and put all her strength into pulling another inch of fabric across the frame.

"What's that?"

"It's a practice test for the college boards. You'll be eligible to take it next year."

He grunted. "No I won't."

She finished securing another section with a pop of the staple gun and looked up. "Why not?"

"Waste of time. I ain't going to college."

Lindsay sat back on her heels, flexing her hands, and said firmly, "Noah, you're one of the brightest students I've ever had. There's not a reason in the world that you can't go to college."

"Yeah, there is." He continued to study the questions, and mark the answers, as though the subject under discussion were only of the slightest interest to him. "College is for rich kids." And before she could even protest that, he added, "Kids with folks to take care of them."

The speech she had been about to make about scholarships and grants seemed a little hollow at that point and so, in some confusion, she picked up her tools again. "By the way, the Reverend and Mrs. Holland are coming to Easter dinner tomorrow, so I want you to be on your best behavior. And wear a tie."

He didn't answer.

She looked up at him.

"Noah?"

He gave her a brief glance, then looked back to his paper. "What for?"

"*What for* what?"

"Do I have to be nice to them?"

"In the first place," Lindsay explained patiently, "because they've been nothing but nice to you, as you know perfectly well. And in the second place, because if you want to stay here—and you said you did—we need them to put in a good word for us."

Noah slumped down lower over his paper. "Won't do no good," he mumbled.

"What do you mean?"

"I mean it ain't up to them whether I stay or go." He continued to look down at his paper. "And it ain't up to you and it for damn sure ain't up to me. So it don't matter whether I'm nice to them or not."

For a moment Lindsay was taken aback. "But you *will* be nice," she said, and made her voice stern, even though stern was the last thing she felt.

Noah thrust the answer sheet out to her. "Can I go now?"

She got to her feet and took the paper from him, glancing over it as he stood. "If you're sure these are the answers you want to stick with. Remember, you'll have extra homework to do on anything you get wrong, and you still have an hour left. Maybe you'd like to take a little time to look over your work?"

Scowling, he sank back into his chair, and she returned his paper to him.

Slumped down in the chair, one arm over his head and his chin practically resting on the desk, he frowned over the paper for a time. Then he looked up. "I want to ask you something."

"As long as it's not the answer to one of the test questions."

"It's about that ole deer."

Lindsay sighed. "Noah, we've explained that to you. There are laws against keeping wild animals. If we don't find a petting zoo or a game ranch to take him we're going to have to pay a big fine—and the fish and game people will still take him away from us."

He slanted a glance toward her, his eyes only barely visible between the fall of his hair and the curve of his elbow. "Not if you have a license."

Lindsay, turning back to her canvas, glanced at him. "What?"

"That's what the fellow said, isn't it? He was giving you a ticket for keeping wildlife without a license?"

Lindsay shook her head and popped another staple into the canvas. "We're not a zoo, Noah."

"Maybe you could be."

"Maybe you could focus on your work."

"You could at least look it up. You're all the time telling me to look stuff up."

"All right," she said, pulling out the last wrinkle in the canvas and holding it taut as she placed the staple. "I'll look it up. There," she added with satisfaction as she stood the canvas upright and admired her work. "As soon as you finish your practice test, I'll show you how to do this."

He gave another grunt. "Just more work for me to do that I don't get paid for."

"Every artist needs to know how to stretch his own canvases."

"I'm not an artist. I'm never going to be an artist. It's all just a big old waste of time, anyway. Just like this test. Here." He grabbed the paper and once again thrust it at her. "I'm done."

As he pushed up out of his chair she said, "Sit down." She stared at him. "Now, suppose you tell me what this is all about. What do you mean you're not going to be an artist?"

He glared back at her. "I mean you're wasting my time with all of this isosceles triangle crap, and nobody gives a rat's ass about the French Revolution, and by the time I learn how to stretch canvases that social worker lady will have me living somewheres else and they don't teach art in public school. It's stupid. It's all just a big fat stupid waste of time."

He bolted up from his chair and swung toward the door, and before Lindsay could draw a breath to try to stop him, he turned reluctantly back. His face was still tight, but some of the heat had gone out of his eyes, and he spoke as though the words were being dragged out of him. "Look," he said. "I don't mean to make you feel bad. You've been real nice to me—you all have. But it was never permanent. And I don't mean to hurt your feelings or nothing, but folks like you—well, you just don't get it. You think if you're nice to people they'll be nice back, and if you do the right thing good stuff happens, and all you need to get by in the world is a good education and maybe where you come from that's so. I ain't saying it's not. But for kids like me that's not the way things work, don't you get it? Kids like me don't need to know algebra. We don't grow up to paint pictures that hang in fancy city store windows and we don't wear ties and we don't go to college. I've been going along with it the best I could, but it's time to get serious. What you're offering, it ain't for the likes of me. And that's all there is to it."

When he was gone Lindsay felt tears of anger sting her eyes, and she brushed them away impatiently. "Damn it," she whispered. "Damn it."

She wandered around the studio for a moment, kicking a chair leg, balling up a scrap of paper and flinging it into the trashcan. And then she turned to her newly stretched canvas.

Barely thinking about what she was doing, she took it to an easel and sat down at her work space. She squeezed colors at random onto her palette and in big, bold strokes transferred them to the canvas. Cobalt blue, rich scarlet, deep sienna, pthalo green. And now an upward curve of ochre, a slash of sap green, a shadow of umber. Gradually, the face of a boy began to emerge. His hair was dark, his face was intent, and his eyes were filled with passion. She worked until it was almost too dark to see.

# 13

# Easter

The town of Blue Valley, Virginia, was strictly divided along two lines: the Methodist side, and the Baptist side. The division was physical as well as spiritual, since the two churches dominated the main intersection of town, with the Methodist on the right and the Baptist on the left. Twice a year—at Christmas and Easter—the churches joined forces in one grand ceremony for the good of the community.

Soon after they arrived at Ladybug Farm, the ladies had understood the social necessity of developing a nonpartisan alliance, so they had promptly joined both churches. After all, their banker was on the Methodist side, their plumber on the Baptist; their heating and air man was a Methodist, their wood supplier a Baptist, and they couldn't afford to offend any of them. So at five o'clock on Sunday morning, every member of the Ladybug Farm household was dressed in his or her Easter finery and each of them stumbled, bleary-eyed, down the stairs and into the vehicle that would transport them to the site of the original Blue Valley Settler's House of Worship, established 1786—the debate still raged as to whether the settlers had been

Baptist or Methodist—where the two churches joined together to conduct Easter sunrise services.

A low, chill mist lay over the gray landscape as Cici pulled her SUV onto the wide field beside the rows of other, already parked cars. Hundreds of folding chairs had been lined up in front of a twelve- by twelve-foot rock foundation, which was all that remained of the original Blue Valley church. Just inside the square of rocks was a pulpit draped with a white cloth, and behind that, a white-robed choir. In the distance a haze of mountains overlooked the dramatic folds and shadows of the valley. Even in the predawn light, it was breathtaking.

Cici wore a new ivory suit with a flared skirt and a pale blue silk scarf artfully draped into her cleavage, with matching pale blue pumps and a blue linen hat worn low over her brow. Lindsay said she looked like she was going to the Kentucky Derby, but Cici just tossed her head and admired the effect of the hat in the mirror one last time before they left the house. She liked hats, and one of the great things about living in a small town was that everyone dressed up for Easter.

Lindsay herself wore a multilayered skirt of lilac georgette paired with a lace blouse and a spray of artificial lilacs at her throat. Her hair was pulled up into a twist, and although no one could talk her into a hat, she had added ornamental pearl combs. Bridget wore pink, and Lori, with her usual vintage flair, looked like something out of a Renaissance painting. Even Ida Mae honored the occasion with a dress—worn over black stockings and sturdy Oxfords—and Noah had been wrestled into a tie.

After all, Easter only came once a year.

"Whose turn is it this year?" Lindsay asked as she got out of the car. "Methodist or Baptist?"

Each year the respective pastors of the competing churches took turns delivering the holiday sermons—one at Easter, and the other at Christmas. "Methodist, I think," replied Bridget. She adjusted the hem of her pink bouclé skirt and straightened the short matching jacket before reaching back inside the car. "Ida Mae, hand me the cinnamon rolls and I'll take them over to the table."

She hurried off across the lawn to the tables that were set up under green funeral home canopies. And Lori, dressed in a 1960s chiffon and velvet gored skirt and a smart little brocade peplum jacket (for which she had no doubt paid a fortune in California), offered Ida Mae her hand to help her out of the car. Ida Mae brushed it away. "Wow, this is fantastic," Lori said, gazing around. "Is this the church you went to when you were a little girl, Ida Mae?"

Ida Mae scowled at her. "What am I, two hundred years old? Use your brain, child."

Noah looked miserable in a starched white shirt, clean jeans, shined loafers—with socks—and a dark blue tie. "It's cold," he said, hunching his shoulders. "Whoever heard of going to church in the middle of the night, anyhow?"

Cici said mildly, "I told you to wear your blazer."

"That's a sissy coat."

"It's a gentleman's coat," corrected Lindsay.

"Are we going to stay for the Easter egg hunt?" Lori wanted to know, and Noah rolled his eyes.

"That's for little kids," he said.

"Well, they're fun to watch. Sometimes it's nice to remember when you were a little kid."

"I got a ham in the oven," Ida Mae warned.

Lindsay, watching Noah's face, said, "Come on, let's find our seats."

The sun tipped the mountaintop with gold and streaked the sky with cerulean and pink while the choir sang hallelujahs. The good Reverend Mitchell delivered a sermon of warmth and hope while the good Reverend Holland sat on his right, beaming beneficently. Ghost tendrils of mist drifted across the lawn, interlaced with the aroma of coffee as the Ladies Aid Society got busy under the tents. And as the final benediction was declared and the swells of the final hymn faded in echoes across the valley, the gentle rose light of morning burst over the ruins of the old church and the gaily dressed crowd spread across the baby green grass, bonnets nodding like daffodils in the breeze.

Bridget sighed happily as the service ended. "Easter is my favorite holiday of the year."

Cici grinned and slipped her arm through Bridget's. "Every holiday is your favorite."

They made their way toward the canopies and the coffee, high heels catching a little in the soft grass. They waved to Maggie, who was Farley's sister-in-law and the real estate agent who had sold them their house. They called a greeting to their banker and to their plumber, and to Jonesie and his wife. One of the obvious advantages of attending both the Methodist and the Baptist churches was that they knew almost everyone in town.

"Remember when we used to get all dressed up in our little white gloves and patent leather shoes and hats with ribbons and have our pictures taken downtown in our Easter outfits?"

Cici nodded at the memory. "Remember that horrid plastic

Easter basket grass that used to get all over the house? I'd still be vacuuming it up at Christmas."

"Remember those little yellow marshmallow chickens?"

Lindsay broke in. "Remember when we didn't used to say 'remember' all the time?"

Noah said, jerking at his tie, "I'm gonna wait in the car."

Lindsay watched him go, her expression sobering, but she didn't try to stop him. "Did you ever stop to wonder," she said after a moment, "how different your lives might have been—or your children's lives—without Easter baskets and birthday cakes and crazy old Aunt Ruth at Thanksgiving dinner and all the things that come with growing up in a family?"

Bridget slipped her arm from Cici's and draped it around Lindsay's shoulders, giving her a brief understanding hug. "Like a new outfit for the first day of school."

"And someone to make you write thank-you notes," added Cici. "My mother used to make me crazy, insisting I do that, but now I realize it wasn't so much the note that was important as the feeling of connection that came with writing it. It made me remember the people who loved me."

"Exactly," agreed Lindsay quietly. "And who would we be today, any of us, if we had never known the people who loved us?"

Cici glanced over her shoulder to catch sight of Noah, head down and hands in pockets, headed toward the car. Then she caught the flash of color and light that was Lori, dancing in and out of the crowd, laughing and chatting with people she barely knew, her skirt billowing as she sank down to help a child with his Easter basket. She looked back to Lindsay.

"Maybe," she said quietly, "we'd have problems trusting people because we'd never known anything but betrayal."

"And maybe we'd prefer to live in a shack in the woods than in a room with a private bath, because we'd be too afraid to get attached to anything permanent," added Bridget with understanding softening the sorrow in her voice. "Oh, bless his heart."

"And we'd be very, very careful not to make ourselves vulnerable to anyone or anything," said Lindsay, "because we would know how much it hurts to lose something once you start caring about it."

"We can't do anything about his past, honey," Cici reminded her. "All we can do is try to make up for it as best we can now."

Lindsay said simply, "I only hope it's enough."

❧

Priscilla ("but call me Prissy, everyone does") Holland was a diminutive, silver-haired woman with a soft, girlish voice that perfectly suited her frame. She was dwarfed by her husband, a broad, genial man with thinning white hair and a florid face. Though he was a man of few words, his voice boomed when he spoke.

"Oh, I just admire you girls so much," Prissy was saying. "What you've done with this old house, will you just look at that staircase? And don't you just love the big old windows, but however do you manage to keep them clean? I've always wanted to see the inside of the place, but old Mr. Blackwell wasn't very sociable, was he, Stewart?"

"You have a beautiful home, ladies," Reverend Holland responded. "And you're very gracious to have us. Something smells mighty good from that kitchen, too."

But Prissy went on in her soft, happy, breathless way, "And I just can't believe Ida Mae is still here and cooking for you! Isn't that just the most wonderful thing? Christmas just wouldn't be the same without one of her fruitcakes. They always make me think of my grandma. There's something so old-fashioned about a fruitcake at Christmas, isn't there? When I was a little girl I can remember mounds of flour and spices and all that chopped fruit spread out over the big wood kitchen table . . ."

Cici exchanged a look with Bridget over the small woman's head. "Wouldn't you like to see the upstairs? Lindsay, why don't you show the Hollands around while Bridget and I see what we can do to help Ida Mae in the kitchen?"

After a time the sound of Prissy Holland's voice became like sweet background music to which no one really listened but everyone enjoyed. By the time they led their guests to the dining room, the ladies had learned when to interrupt and when to let the music flow into conversational lapses.

The Easter table was spectacular. The wine stain had been removed from the white damask tablecloth through some miracle of baking soda and lemon juice. A three-tiered silver candelabra bearing a dozen snow-white candles sent sparks of light dancing across every glass, plate, spoon, and mirror in the room, and a mild breeze billowed the lace curtains at the open window. The ham, beautifully browned and glistening with honey glaze, rested on a bed of fresh parsley and red spiced apple rings, and was surrounded—in homage to a tradition only Ida Mae understood and would not deign to explain—by bright yellow deviled eggs sprinkled with paprika. Bowls of garden-fresh peas and carrots, roasted new potatoes, and fluffy sweet potato casserole flanked the ham platter, accompanied by buttered corn from the freezer, a pineapple-cheese casserole that was Ida Mae's specialty, and a basket of fragrant homemade rolls. The table was set with Cici's Haviland china and Bridget's Baccarat crystal and starched white linen napkins. At each place setting was a bright yellow daffodil in a silver bud vase, courtesy of Lindsay's collection.

After all, having the preacher to dinner was not something that happened every day.

Noah appeared at the table on time, still dressed in his white shirt and looking unhappy about it, but Lori was nowhere to be found. "It's not like her to be late for a meal." Cici cast an apologetic look at Lindsay, who had spent the entire trip home from sunrise services threatening dire consequences if both of them weren't on their best behavior. "Maybe I'd better—"

"Oh, my, have you ever in your life seen anything so lovely?" intoned Prissy. "Why it's just like a fairy tale. Everything's so gorgeous, and all those flowers! You ladies certainly do have a flair, and will you just look at all that food—"

"Did you all invite somebody else to Easter dinner?" Ida Mae, her church dress covered by a frilly print apron, shouldered her way through the swinging door with a gravy boat in her hand. Her tone held a note of outrage at the mere thought they might have invited guests without telling her. "Because a truck just pulled up."

"A truck?" Cici started toward the window. "I can't imagine—"

Prissy went on, "My mama used to make a Coca-Cola ham every Easter. Have ya'll ever heard of that? It's the sugar in Coca-Cola—"

"*Dear Lord in heaven.*" The voice of her husband boomed off the walls and rattled the china. Prissy stopped speaking. Then, following the big man's lead, they all bowed their heads as he intoned, "We thank Thee for the bounty of this table and for the good hands that prepared it . . ."

Seats were found, and napkins were unfolded. Prissy was saying, "I just can't tell you what a treat this is, to be in your lovely home and sitting down to such a lovely meal. Now, Noah, don't you agree? You are such a lucky young man, aren't you? And you look so handsome today, doesn't he Stewart? Will you have a roll?"

Bridget was gently nudging Noah to straighten his posture when Lori burst through the swinging doors, flushed and a little breathless, juggling a long, flat box in her arms.

"I'm sorry, I didn't know you'd already gone into dinner," she said. "Hi, Reverend Holland, Mrs. Holland. I don't mean to interrupt. That was Jonesie who just left. I asked him to, well, to drop something off."

Lindsay's smile was a little stiff. "Couldn't it wait, Lori?"

Cici eyed the box with some trepidation. "What, exactly, did you ask Jonesie to drop off?"

Lori beamed. "Your Easter surprise!"

As a corner of the box shifted in her arms, Lori dipped quickly to right it, unsettling the lid in the process. When an alarming scratching and chittering issued forth, Cici half rose from her chair.

"Lori, what on earth—"

But even as she spoke the box slipped further, tilting toward the floor. Then the lid slid off and a veritable ocean of tiny yellow cheeping balls of fluff spilled out.

"Chickens!" gasped Bridget.

Like a miniature yellow tide, baby chicks swarmed over

the dining room floor, chirping and bobbing and darting this way and that. Prissy squealed as tiny claws scrambled over her feet. "Whoa! Call the Colonel!" Noah exclaimed, jumping to his feet. Ida Mae came through the swinging doors just then with a pitcher of iced tea, and a stream of chicks escaped into the kitchen before Cici could cry, "Ida Mae, the door!"

As Ida Mae disappeared behind the swinging doors and returned seconds later with a broom, Lori got down on her knees and tried to scoop the chicks back into the box, but they hopped out again as soon as she replaced them. Bridget tried to shoo them into the box with napkins while Ida Mae used the broom to block them from scurrying under the buffet, and Noah, enjoying himself, stuffed baby chicks into his pockets. The Reverend Holland, with his hands planted firmly on either side of his plate as though for security, clucked his tongue and murmured, "My, my," while his wife, with her heels drawn up securely on the chair rung and her eyes big, said nothing at all. "For heaven's sake, Lori, how many are there?" Cici exclaimed.

"A hundred and forty-four." Lori stretched across the floor to scoop up an armful of cheeping fluff. She looked a little desperate. All three women stared at her, momentarily abandoning the reconnaissance effort. "*A hundred and forty-four chickens?*"

"You're gonna need a bigger box," Ida Mae said, flatly.

She thrust the broom into Cici's hand and disappeared into the pantry.

❧

Half an hour later, having tracked down baby chicks under the stove, behind the china cabinet, in the cabinets, and under the table, all were present and accounted for and safely contained inside a deep cardboard box from which they could not escape. Cici and Bridget helped Lori carry the box into the kitchen while Ida Mae stayed behind to pluck feathers from the dining room rug and Lindsay, pretending a savoir faire she could not possibly feel, tried to get Easter dinner back on track.

Cici collapsed into a ladder-back chair, and for the longest moment seemed incapable of doing anything but staring at her daughter. "A hundred and *forty-four*?" she said, again.

"There are two more boxes on the porch."

"But . . . Lori!" Now it was Bridget's turn to stare as she searched for words. "A hundred and forty-four! Chickens!"

"They were twelve dozen for a hundred dollars," Lori said defensively. "We would have paid a lot more if we'd just bought a dozen."

"We?" repeated Cici. "*We?*"

"But . . ." Bridget gestured helplessly. "I don't understand. What . . . why . . . chickens?"

Lori spread her hands in a sincere gesture of apology. "I really didn't mean to ruin Easter dinner, honestly, and I *never* would have brought them inside if I'd realized everyone was at the table, but Jonesie stopped by early—he had to go to his mother-in-law's for dinner—and . . ."

"Lori," Cici said. "The point."

She took a breath, the spark of irrepressible excitement creeping back into her eyes, and declared, "The way to success in business is to reinvest your profit. Donald Trump or someone said that. So we're taking our profit from the sheep and investing it in chickens. Our new business!"

There was absolute silence.

Ida Mae came through the swinging doors with a dustpan

scattered with yellow chicken fluff. A scattering of laughter and Prissy's melodic chatter filtered in from the dining room, signaling that all was not lost on that end, but neither Cici nor Bridget turned her head. "Ya'll gonna eat?" Ida Mae demanded. "Food's getting cold."

They ignored her. "Where are they going to live?" Bridget asked. "What are you going to feed them? Don't baby chicks have to have special food?"

Ida Mae shook the dustpan out in the trash can. "You're gonna need an incubator, least till they get bigger."

Lori looked at her in surprise. "An incubator? Jonesie didn't say anything about that."

"Everybody knows that," Ida Mae returned with a touch of exasperation. "Reckon you could rig one up with a woodbox and some lightbulbs, though."

"Lori, don't you realize these chickens aren't going to stay this size forever?" Cici demanded. "Do you have any idea how much room a hundred and forty-four chickens need?"

"We'll build them a coop," Lori assured her.

"A *coop*? For a hundred and forty-four chickens, we're going to need a commercial chicken house!"

"Not to mention the work," added Bridget. "I don't know how to tell you this, but chickens make a mess!"

"Exactly," returned Lori, pleased. "And do you know how much chicken manure costs?"

"No," admitted Bridget, "but I do know how it *smells.*"

"It's a high-nitrogen fertilizer," Lori explained, "great for the garden. And we get it for free! But that's not even the best part."

"I'm so glad," murmured Cici.

"Cage-free eggs!" Lori declared. "They're over three dollars a dozen in the grocery! All we have to do is hook up with a distributor—"

"Who'll take half the profit."

"Which still leaves us with $1.50 a dozen, and if each chicken gives a dozen eggs a day—"

"Ain't no chicken alive gonna give you a dozen eggs a day," Ida Mae pointed out sourly. "It takes fourteen hours of sunlight a day for a laying hen if you want to get just one egg. It also takes a rooster. You got any roosters in there?"

For the first time, Lori looked nonplussed. She turned to the box. "Well . . . I don't know. But I'm sure . . ."

"Lori, didn't you do any research at all before you spent a hundred dollars on chickens?" Cici could not quite keep the incredulity out of her voice.

Lori's chin went up in a gesture that was remarkably reminiscent of her mother. "Of course I did! For one thing, these aren't just ordinary chickens. They're Rhode Island Reds—show chickens! They've won all kinds of awards. And show chickens, I'll have you know, can go for up to a thousand dollars a piece."

Bridget's eyebrows arched. "Where did you hear that? From Jonesie?"

"No," Lori admitted, looking uncomfortable. "Noah."

Ida Mae sniffed. "Rhode Island Reds are common as dirt. Fine chicken, but if I ever met a man who'd pay a thousand dollars for one I'd sell him my worn-out stockings next."

Cici blew out a breath that was so forceful it ruffled her bangs. "Lori, we've talked about this. You've got to think these things through. You can't just invest in a business idea and *hope* it works out—especially when it involves as much work as this one."

Lindsay pushed open the door and poked her head through. "Ladies," she said through gritted teeth, and rolled her eyes dramatically back toward the dining room, "could you do this later? We have company, you know."

"I'm sorry Aunt Lindsay," Lori said, and she turned away, busying herself with stroking the tiny bobbing chirping heads in the cardboard box as Lindsay closed the door.

"I reckon we could clear out a place for them in the conservatory," Ida Mae grumbled, "at least till you get a coop built. Plenty of daylight in there. I'll go take up the carpets."

Bridget stood and gave Lori's shoulder a sympathetic stroke before she left the room. "Honey," she reminded her gently, "the library is our friend."

When they were alone, Cici pushed herself to her feet with an air of resolve. "Lori," she began.

Lori whirled on her, with her arms flung wide and her eyes flashing. "Okay, Mom, I get it, okay? I'm a total screwup. Nothing I do is right. I don't know anything about farming or old houses or sheep or chickens. The only chance I'll ever have at making a life for myself is to go sit in some boring classroom and bat my eyelashes at some boring professor until he gives me a passing grade in some boring subject so I can be some boring lawyer or something. Got it. I'm not as smart as you. I'm not as talented as you. I can't make things work like you can, and guess what? I'm not perfect like you are! But I don't see anyone else coming up with any better ideas, do you? At least I'm trying! And if you want to know the truth, I think you're afraid to even consider the possibility that one—even *one*—of my ideas might work because then you'd have to admit you were wrong! Well, my new goal in life is to make sure that's exactly what you have to do. You're wrong, okay? You're wrong and I'm going to prove it to you! Maybe not with chickens, maybe not with sheep, but I'll prove it! You just watch me!"

Lori's face was flushed, her breath was quick, and there was a slight catch in her voice with the last words. The room practically rang with the silence that followed her impassioned speech, broken only by the cheeping from the box on the countertop behind her.

At last Cici spoke. "I was just going to say, we'd better bring the other boxes in from the porch before some stray cat wanders up."

It seemed to take a moment for her mother's mild tone to register, and yet another for the heat to fade from Lori's gaze. Finally she glanced away, embarrassed. "Oh."

Cici crossed the room, opened the back door, and let Lori lead the way to the porch. And she waited until Lori was out of hearing distance to murmur, under her breath, "That's my girl."

ॐ

"Well." Cici lowered herself into the rocking chair, next to her friends, and stretched out her legs, grimacing a little as she did so. "One temporary chicken coop-slash-incubator is up and running. One hundred and forty-four tiny little chickens are scattering sawdust all over the sunroom and preparing to keep us up all night with their cheeping. Tomorrow I start building a chicken house. Oh no, don't thank me. It's all part of the service here at what is rapidly becoming Loony-bug Farm."

Following Ida Mae's instructions, Cici had built a large, bottomless wooden box out of one-by-sixes to contain the chicks, drilled holes for ventilation, and added a lid. She then had taken apart several small lamps, threaded the sockets through holes in the lid, and added sixty-watt bulbs to keep the chickens at their ideal temperature throughout the night. It had taken most of the afternoon.

Bridget poured white wine into the glass Cici held out. "Isn't there some kind of law against building chicken habitats on Easter?"

"If there's not, there should be." Cici leaned back in her rocking chair and groaned. "My daughter hates me."

"Which only means you're doing your job."

"Why did I think this would get easier the older Lori got? I'm the worst mother in the world."

"Impossible," Bridget assured her. "I am."

"Remember last year how worried I was about her? All I wanted was for her to come home. And now that's she's home . . ."

Bridget stretched her hand across and patted Cici's arm. "It's the old be-careful-what-you-wish-for syndrome. When Jim and I were first married, I was sure all my life needed to be complete was a baby. Halfway through fifteen hours of labor I was rethinking that, I can tell you. And, as much as I adore both my kids, I rethought it about once a day for the next twenty-five years."

"To top it off, we ruined Easter dinner." Cici glanced over at Lindsay. "I'm awfully sorry. After the way we behaved, the Hollands probably don't think we're qualified to care for ourselves, much less Noah."

Lindsay smiled absently, her gaze distant. "Oh, that's okay. They were good sports about it. And you saw how Prissy was after dinner, wanting to ooh and ahh over the chicks."

"You've got to admit they're awfully cute. They remind me of those little stuffed chicks we used to put in the kids' Easter baskets."

"Maybe that's where I went wrong," mused Cici. "I should have made sure that stupid Easter bunny only left chocolate chickens."

Bridget laughed. "Well, I think Lori and I have come to an agreement—a hundred forty-four chickens are too much. So we agreed to keep two dozen. I called Jonesie and he was really nice about taking the rest of them back. He said he had a feeling he'd be hearing from us."

"I'll just bet he did." Cici sighed. "Thanks for handling that for me, Bridge. I didn't dare try to bring that subject up. But why are we keeping two dozen? Couldn't you have talked her into returning them all?"

Bridget rocked complacently. "It will be nice to have the eggs," she said. "And besides, I like chickens."

"Sometimes I don't know which of you is worse," Cici said, sipping her wine. "In fact, I think you're probably very bad for each other." She glanced over at Lindsay, who was gazing out over the mountains, lost in thought. "Everything okay, Linds?"

"Hmm?" She looked at Cici absently. "Sure, fine. Two dozen. Right. Sounds great."

Bridget and Cici exchanged a look. "You seem preoccupied."

Lindsay turned her attention to the almost untouched glass of wine in her hand, and took a sip. "Did you know all you have to do to get a permit for a wildlife preserve is to apply to the Department of Natural Resources? I talked to Zeb—you know, Farley's cousin—after services this morning."

Cici's eyes went wide. "Wildlife preserve? What are you talking about?"

"I know." Bridget leaned forward, a note of excitement in her voice. "Bambi!"

Lindsay nodded. "You have to be approved, of course, but he said he would talk to his boss and didn't think there would be any problem. Meanwhile he can give us a temporary permit."

"Which means we don't have to go to court!" Bridget exclaimed.

"Well, we do," Lindsay clarified, "but we won't have to pay a fine, and we get to keep Bambi."

Cici stared at the two of them. "Sheep, chickens, deer . . . what's next, skunks and raccoons?" She blew out her breath and gave a short shake of her head. "We already *are* a wildlife preserve. Might as well make it legal."

"Exactly," Lindsay agreed thoughtfully, sipping her wine. "And all it takes is a piece of paper."

"Well, well, well," Bridget said with satisfaction. "Will you look at us? We start out three fancy ladies from the city and we end up running a wildlife preserve. I love the way that sounds."

"Don't get too carried away," Cici warned. "It's just a title. And it's just one deer. Lindsay, I hope you know what you're doing."

"So do I," murmured Lindsay, almost too softly to be heard.

"It just goes to show," Bridget insisted, "you never know where life is going to take you."

"Well, I'll drink to that." Cici held out her glass.

"Right," Lindsay said with a sudden resolve, and she leaned forward to touch her glass to both of theirs. And then she said, "I'm going to adopt Noah."

The three of them remained perfectly motionless, glasses

# May Flowers

*Where we love is home.*

—OLIVER WENDELL HOLMES SR.

# 14

# In Another Time

*Emmy Marie, 1967*

Andrew Jackson Blackwell was forty-five years old, about to be elected District Court judge, and in love with a woman half his age. If it had happened to anyone else, he would have laughed.

The problem was that he did not think of himself as old. He was still as tall and straight shouldered as when he had worn his army uniform. He had a full head of coal black hair and straight white teeth and when he looked in the mirror he saw a boy of twenty-three, toasting the fine long legs of a honey-haired mademoiselle with mischief in her eyes. As his mother told him all too often, life had been too good to him.

She did not know his heart was broken, as hers had been, that he had had to leave his brother behind in an unmarked grave in Germany. She did not know that he had loved only once, briefly and passionately, and had watched his beloved's blood spill between his desperate, rain-soaked fingers onto a cobbled street in France. She did not know that afterward there was a hole inside him, because he worked so hard to cover it up with big plans and glad hands and fine dinners and lots and lots of laughter. And the truth was that until Emmy Marie came along some twenty years later to fill it, even he had almost forgotten the hole existed.

She was fresh out of William & Mary with a degree in art history, of all the useless things, and she had promised her mother she would call Miss Emily before she left Virginia. Emily Blackwell never forgot one of her "girls," as she referred to the young soldiers' wives to whom she had offered a home during the war, and when it turned out one had given birth to a daughter who was named after her, she naturally invited her namesake to come out to the house for a weekend.

She was a blond-haired bundle of charm in a Pucci-print minidress who threw herself into Emily Blackwell's arms and hugged her as though she were a long-lost aunt, and then turned the same exuberant affection on Ida Mae, about whom her mother had told so many stories. Andrew noted her arrival, but he was busy in the vineyard that time of year and barely looked at her until dinner that night, when she enchanted him as effortlessly as she did everyone else at the table.

It was his mother who suggested Emmy might enjoy a tour of the winery, and, although he told himself he was only being the polite host, he found himself enjoying the sound of her laughter on the warm dewy air the next morning, and the faint breeze of her perfume as it mingled with the scent of the vines. He told her how he had fallen in love with the wine country of France during the war, and how its misty valleys and rolling hills had reminded him of home. And how he had wondered why the great wines of the Loire Valley, which was so similar in climate and topography to the Shenandoah Valley, could not be reproduced across the ocean.

She laughed as he told her how he and his French friend Robert DuPoncier had smuggled vine cuttings out of the country under their shirts and had almost gotten caught twice but had evaded the customs officials by pretending to be suffering with food poisoning. He had actually vomited all over one poor fellow's shoes. He told her how Robert, who had worked at wine making in every chateau in the valley in hopes of one day creating his own vintage, had believed in his dream and left his own country for the valleys of Virginia to make it come true. They had grafted and coddled those cuttings, brutally pruning and tenderly nursing, cutting away and preserving, until they had a grape that was uniquely their own. He told her of the hopes they had had for each year's vintage, how some years had been disasters of such proportions that bottles actually exploded in the rack, and how others had produced decent, drinkable wines, and others, as the years went on, were even better until now they were actually beginning to win awards, and Robert, who had given up so much to invest in Andrew's dream, was so proud that Andrew threatened to bottle their latest vintage under the peacock label.

He poured her a glass of last year's red, which had turned out quite fine, and her eyes closed in gentle appreciation as she tasted it. "I can taste Virginia in it," she said in a moment, and she opened her eyes, smiling at him. "It tastes like home."

They took their glasses and sat at the wrought iron table under the shade of an oak, gazing at the mountains, talking with an ease that was rare and refreshing to Andrew. He did not find her as fatuous and boring as he did most young people; in fact when he was with her he forgot her age altogether. She had a composure and a maturity that were beyond her years, and her interests embraced the world. She told him about her childhood in Little Rock, where she had grown up with her mother and her grandparents and cousins of all descriptions, and about college and her ambitions for herself, which were straightforward and filled with modern ideas. She believed a woman could be more than a wife and mother, although certainly she wanted to be both someday. But first she wanted to travel the world, to see the Louvre and the L'Orangerie, and to touch the face of a pyramid and walk the streets of Florence, and sit in St. Mark's Square and gaze for hours upon the horsemen that crowned the Doge's Palace. When she spoke her face became rapt, her gaze dreamy, and Andrew was seized suddenly by a longing as intense as any he had ever known. He wanted to be the one to take her to those places, and show her those things. He wanted to see the world anew through her eyes.

Instead, he did the next best thing, which was to take her there through *his* eyes, and his memories. While they still sat there together, beneath the oak tree, he took her to the castles of Germany and the cathedrals of France, across the canals of Venice in a gondola against a fiery sunset, through the fine hotels of London. And then he told her of Dominique, Robert's sister, and how she had died in his arms on a dark cobbled street and had taken a part of his heart with him. By this time the sky was turning pink behind the mountains, and the wine was long gone, and her hand, small and soft and sweet, was covering his. She leaned forward, her eyes filled with distress, and she said softly, "I'm so sorry."

He looked at her hand, and he took it and turned it gently, ever so gently, palm up in his. He looked at her face, and he thought, *I am going to kiss this exquisite creature.*

It was then that Dominic called to him across the lawn, and as Andrew rose to introduce Emmy to Robert's son, he wasn't sure whether he was sorry or relieved.

After supper he invited Robert and Dominic up to the house, as he often did, but that night the occasion was social, not business. His mother enjoyed the company of the handsome young Dominic, who was apprenticing to take over Robert's position at the winery when or if Robert decided to retire. Emmy seemed to enjoy speaking French with Robert, and was held rapt by the stories he told. Andrew himself was held rapt by the sound of her voice, the glint of lamplight on her hair, the curve of her wrist when she lifted her glass to sip, and her smile, which seemed to be meant only for him.

At some point, he wasn't exactly sure how, the conversation turned to the great tasting rooms of Europe, the lush decor and the muraled walls, and how the Vanderbilts and the Fords and the Rockefellers had decorated their wine cellars similarly, and his mother said, "Well, my dear, I think we must bring someone in to paint a scene for us, don't you think?"

Thanks to the determination and business acumen of Emily Blackwell, the small dairy operation she had started during the war had grown into Blackwell Farms Creamery, purveyor of fine cheeses to restaurants throughout the state, and her kitchen jelly operation now required its own manufacturing plant and shipped Blackwell Farms Fine Jams and Jellies all over the South. But it had taken almost twenty years for her to acknowledge that "Andrew's little winery," as she called it, was

230 ~ Donna Ball

anything more than a hobby. For Andrew, of course, it was his law practice that was the hobby, and wine making his passion. And it always gave Andrew a small thrill of pride whenever she took an interest in anything having to do with the winery. Commissioning a mural for the tasting room was, for her, a very big step indeed.

That was when Emmy shyly volunteered that she had done some mural work and would be honored to design something for their tasting room, if they liked. His mother liked that idea immediately and there was a great deal of discussion about the project, and in the process it was agreed that in addition to the winery, she should also paint a mural here in the living room where everyone could see and enjoy it, and that rather than the traditional vineyard scene Emmy should render two views of the scenic meadow, winter and spring, and that the two bookshelf alcoves that flanked the fireplace would be the perfect place for them.

Andrew did not care what she painted or where she painted it. The project would take weeks. She was staying.

# 15

# Changes

"Don't be ridiculous," Lindsay said, "of course I haven't thought it through." Her voice was high and tight and her hands gripped the steering wheel as though if she relaxed them the car might leave the road of its own accord and sail into the sky. Given her speed and the erratic nature of her driving, that was not, in fact, entirely out of the question. "If I thought about it for even one minute I'd realize how crazy it is."

Bridget, in the backseat, squeezed her eyes closed as Lindsay swerved around a tractor that was chugging along the shoulder with a bale of hay. Cici twisted in the passenger seat and waved apologetically at the tractor driver.

"I mean, here I am, a fifty-year-old woman who's never had children of her own, with no visible means of support, living in a broken-down house with two other women and a twenty-year-old girl, none of whom has a job—"

"Hey."

"Well, she's right," Bridget pointed out.

"Not to mention a dog, a deer, a flock of sheep—"

"And two dozen chickens," added Bridget. Then, in alarm, "Do you *see* that stop sign?"

The force of the brakes locked all three seat belts, but Lindsay went on, oblivious. "I mean, it's crazy, right? What makes me think they'll even consider letting me adopt a teenage boy? A teenage boy, of all things!"

"The pickup has the right of way," Cici broke in.

Lindsay waited until the truck completed its turn, and then accelerated through the intersection. "But it's just like when we bought the house. We didn't think about that, did we?"

She looked over her shoulder to Bridget for confirmation, as Cici instinctively reached for the wheel. "No! No we didn't!"

Lindsay's eyes returned to the road. "We just"—she searched for the word—"*felt* it. And everyone thought we were crazy for doing that, too. But look how that turned out. We were right and everyone else was wrong. Weren't they?" As she spoke, she turned the steering wheel too sharply, and the car's left tires skittered on the shoulder before she regained the pavement.

"Stop the car."

"What?"

"Stop the car," Cici repeated, with force.

Lindsay pulled over to the side of the road and got out, a bit sheepishly, as the two women traded places.

And as Cici pulled carefully back onto the road, Lindsay pressed her head into the headrest. "I *am* crazy," she groaned. "What am I doing?"

Bridget leaned forward to rest a hand on her shoulder. "Right now," she said, "you're just going to talk to Carrie about adopting a great kid who would be the luckiest boy in the world to have you as his mom."

Lindsay reached up and squeezed her fingers. "Thanks for coming with me, both of you."

"This is probably the most important thing you've ever done. Like we'd let you do it alone?"

"Besides," added Bridget, "he's our Noah, too."

"But you're supposed to be building a chicken coop."

"Believe me," Cici said, "I'd rather be here."

Lindsay cleared her throat. "Listen, I know this isn't fair to either of you. I mean, it affects your lives, too. When we moved in together, it was to enjoy our retirement years. No one counted on a teenage boy."

"Or a twenty-year-old college dropout," Cici pointed out.

"Or a flock of sheep or a crazy sheepdog," Bridget had to add.

"Or a deer."

"Or two dozen chickens. I still don't know what you want with two dozen chickens."

"Look," Cici said, glancing over at Lindsay, "I couldn't have raised Lori after Richard left without the two of you. Even now, I sometimes think you're better mothers to her than I am, and I *know* she thinks that more often than I do." They smiled. "It might not take a village to raise a child, but it for damn sure takes a few good friends. We're right beside you in this, Lindsay, and we're in it all the way. You should know that."

Lindsay, smiling, sniffing, and blotting moisture from her eyes with her fingertips, said, "I do. But thanks for saying it."

They reached out to clasp hands, right there in the car, and closed their fingers together briefly before Cici returned her hand to the steering wheel, and her attention to the road.

୬∾

"Ida Mae sent you out here for the chicken boxes half an hour ago." Lori's irritation was plain to see.

Noah straightened up from his slouching position against the barn door, drew on the cigarette in his hand, and deliberately blew smoke in her direction. "You're not the boss of me."

Lori pushed past him into the barn.

"You can tell if you want," he said sullenly, following her. "I don't care."

"Yeah, well that's easy to see."

"What do you mean by that?" Noah demanded.

Shafts of light filtered through the boards of the barn and caught bits of chaff that were stirred up by Lori's feet. She stood for a moment, letting her eyes adjust to the dimness, then spotted the cardboard boxes in an untidy pile where Noah apparently had tossed them yesterday. She started gathering them up.

"Is this going to be another lecture about how I don't know how lucky I am?" Noah pursued. "Because you're a fine one to be talking, if you ask me."

Lori flicked a dark glance his way. "I'm not even going to ask what that's supposed to mean."

"It means you *are* a spoiled rich kid. You got folks that *want* to give you stuff—they're practically throwing four years at a fancy-pants college in your face—and all you can do is screech at your mama about wanting to raise chickens. You're not only spoiled, you're stupid."

Lori hesitated, then stuffed the lid on one of the boxes with particular force. "I'm exploring my options," she told him archly. "I'm allowed to do that."

"Yeah?" He pinched out the cigarette and tossed it away. "Like I said, you're lucky."

Lori lifted the boxes and turned to him. "You know, it wouldn't hurt you to at least act like one of the family. To pretend you appreciate what everyone is doing for you."

He returned, "I ain't one of the family and pretending don't make it so."

Lori elbowed past him with her arms full of boxes. "I really don't have time for this teenage angst," she said. "I was supposed to get those chickens back to Jonesie an hour ago, and Ida Mae's having a fit about them pooping all over the sunroom. But just for your information," she tossed over her shoulder, "the reason no one is home this morning to catch you smoking is because they all went into town to try to beg that social worker to let you stay here. I heard Aunt Lindsay on the phone making the appointment. Of course, the way you acted to her it probably won't make a difference, so good thing you don't want to be part of the family."

He stared at her. "Did they really do that? All three of them?"

"What do you care?" she retorted, and marched on to the house.

ॐ

The Department of Family and Children's Services was housed in a small white clapboard building at the end of Riker Street, between the police department and the library. "Oh, damn," Bridget said as Cici pulled into one of the three visitor parking spaces. "I left that library book I was supposed to return on the kitchen table. It's overdue. Do you think I should run in and apologize?"

"I think the library is like the IRS," Cici said. "They don't care about apologies. Just penalties and fines."

Lindsay got out of the car and smoothed her skirt. She looked from one to the other of them, trying to mute her anxiety. "It's the right thing to do, isn't it? Do I need lipstick?"

"Your lipstick is fine," Bridget assured her. "Everything is going to be fine."

"Relax," Cici added. "Carrie likes you, remember? You—we—are the best thing that ever happened to Noah."

Lindsay straightened a little, and smiled. "That's right. We are, aren't we?"

"And possession is nine-tenths of the law," Bridget reminded her, and they all laughed.

They crossed a small lawn dotted with crepe myrtles, and took the pansy-lined walk to the front door. Just before Cici reached to open it, Lindsay put a hand on each of their wrists. She looked from one to the other of them. "This is the scariest thing I've ever done. Even scarier than the time I had the bad mammogram, remember?"

Bridget said, "We went with you then, too."

Lindsay nodded. "I just wanted to say thank you. Really."

Cici gave her a smile that was filled with reassurance and understanding, and she opened the door.

The reception area was small and utilitarian, with cheap wood paneling on the wall and industrial tile on the floor. The receptionist's desk looked as though it had been reclaimed from a public school, and was piled with untidy manila folders. The entire place had an air of barely managed chaos, even when it was empty, as it was now. Carrie must have seen them drive up, because she came to the door of her office right away and beckoned them in, saving the receptionist the necessity of interrupting her phone call.

"Hi, ladies, come on in. It's good to see you. I didn't expect all three of you to come," she said, closing the frosted panel door and pulling up an extra chair in front of her desk. "I hope this doesn't mean there's a problem?"

"No, not at all," Cici assured her.

"In fact quite the opposite," Lindsay added. "Of a problem, I mean. At least I think so. I hope you will, too."

Carrie's smile was puzzled as she took her seat behind her desk. There was a potted hyacinth in the center of it, and her inbox looked slightly more manageable than the receptionist's had, but the room was depressing overall, with its utilitarian shelves stacked with office supplies and its gray metal filing cabinets. The lone window looked out over the parking lot.

"It's really a coincidence that you called when you did, because I was about to call you. There's been a little complication in the case. That's why it's taking so long. It's nothing to do with you," she assured them quickly. "We're very pleased with the job you've done with Noah. I know that caring for a teenage boy can't be easy, and we appreciate your level of commitment. But there's been a change . . ."

"Yes," blurted Lindsay, her hands twisted together in her lap. "Change. Yes, that's exactly what we want to talk to you about. We want to change our level of commitment."

Carrie blinked. "Oh. Oh, dear. Well, I can certainly understand that. But maybe I'd better explain what's going on. You see, the fact of the matter is that this might soon be out of my jurisdiction altogether. You see . . ."

"No, wait, I think I said that wrong. What I want to do is—"

Bridget laid a calming hand on Lindsay's arm. "You do think we're a good foster home?" she insisted.

She looked surprised. "Well, of course. As far as I'm concerned, Noah has made excellent progress under your care. His schoolwork has improved dramatically, he attends church regularly, certainly he appears to be healthy and as well groomed as one might expect from a boy his age." She smiled a little at that. "Until the incident with the traffic ticket—and that was minor, really—he hasn't been in a bit of trouble. I'm sorry if we made you feel otherwise, but there are rules and standards we have to go by, and the procedures are there for a reason."

A small frown had creased Cici's forehead. "What do you mean, this might soon be out of your jurisdiction?"

Carrie turned to her to reply, but Lindsay interrupted.

"As long as it is still in your jurisdiction, and as long as you do think we're a good foster home . . . what I'm trying to say is, since we've been approved as a suitable temporary home, is there any reason we wouldn't be just as good a permanent home?"

"I'm afraid I don't understand."

Lindsay drew a breath. "I'd like to apply to adopt Noah. Permanently."

The silence that followed seemed to go on for eons, although in fact it was only a couple of seconds. Lindsay rushed to fill it.

"I know I'm a single woman," she said quickly, "and that will work against me. But I do own my own home—kind of"—she glanced at Bridget and Cici—"and I'm a responsible member of the community, and I've got a good credit score, and I've been a teacher for over twenty years—"

"And we can supply a list of character witnesses as long as your arm, if you need us to," volunteered Bridget. "There isn't a person who ever met Lindsay who didn't love her, and some of her students are lawyers and doctors and—and congressmen now! You can't ask for better child-raising skills than that."

"We're all behind this decision," Cici assured her. "Noah will have a place in our home until he reaches adulthood, and we're committed to doing what it takes to see him through college or whatever avenue he decides to pursue. Now, I know we haven't lived here all that long, but you're welcome to do a background check—"

"Ladies, please." Carrie held up both hands, her expression a little overwhelmed. "No one is questioning your suitability. I'm sure it would be a lovely placement for Noah, but . . . oh, dear. I don't know how to say this."

She looked at them helplessly. "The fact of the matter is, Noah isn't available for adoption. That's what I was going to call you about. It seems that the investigation after the court incident uncovered some errors in the paperwork in this office, and I just received the memo over the weekend. Noah isn't an orphan. He has a mother, and she's alive and well and living in Richmond."

❧

"I thought you had to take them chickens back."

Lori was dressed in mud-spattered overalls and clunky work boots, and she was unwinding an orange extension cord across the backyard toward the outlet on the back porch. Rebel stalked the cord from a low crouch and a safe distance, as though it were a snake. "Are you looking for something to do?" she demanded.

"I got stuff to do. Them chickens'll smother in the boxes."

"In the first place, you know perfectly well the correct term is *those* chickens, and you only embarrass yourself and all of us when you talk like a hick."

He scowled at her. "I'll talk whatever way I want to."

"It makes it look like Aunt Lindsay doesn't teach you anything."

"You're nothing but a big-mouth girl. You don't know jack."

Lori noticed with satisfaction that he avoided the double negative with no noticeable effort. "In the second place, the chickens are not going to smother because there are holes in the boxes and Jonesie said they'd be okay in there all day if they had to be." She plugged the cord into the outlet. "And in the third place, I would have been to town and back already except everybody left in such a hurry this morning they forgot to leave me a car key. Why do you keep following me around?"

"How about you give me a ride to town when you go?"

She looked at him suspiciously. "Why should I?"

He thought about that for a moment. "Maybe because you're gonna need some help loading all them cement bags in the car."

"What cement?"

"The cement you need to patch the bottom of the pond before you try to fill it with water again. And the cement it's gonna take to fill in the cracks and holes in the patio all around it."

Her brows drew together, but the expression was more one of uneasiness than annoyance. "That's not a patio. It's a path."

"Whatever."

She glanced up at him as she plugged the extension cord into the outlet on the side of the house. "What do you want to go to town for, anyway?"

"There's a fellow there, buys old glass and junk."

"Do you mean the antique store at the edge of town? Are you still trying to sell those glass bottles?"

"I found them didn't I?"

"Well, he'll recognize the pictures of the house if you try to sell Aunt Lindsay's photographic plates, and the first person he'll call to buy them is her."

He scowled. "I ain't selling anything that's not mine. She said I could borrow them to draw from and I gave them back. And if you say different I'll call you a liar."

"Oh, yeah, that's the way to get a ride into town." She started back toward the pond.

"How come you're going to so much trouble to get this thing running again, anyway?"

For a moment it seemed she wouldn't answer. And then she said, with a nonchalance in her tone that wasn't entirely convincing, "Mostly because nobody thinks I can."

"I can help."

She gave him a disparaging look. "I don't need your help, thank you."

"Oh yeah? What do you know about mixing cement?"

Frowning, Lori traced the orange cord back to the pond, and to the pump that was waiting there. "I don't have any cement."

"Maybe you could trade the chickens for some. And another thing. You're going to want to—"

She plugged in the pump and jumped back as a geyser of filthy water shot six feet in the air. She stood watching in dismay as Noah finished, "Hook up a garden hose to that pump before you plug it in."

Lori ducked down and jerked the plug out of the extension

cord as she watched the geyser sink, and then disappear. She sat back on her heels, eyeing Noah suspiciously. "Why do you want to help?"

He shrugged, hands in pockets. "Clear to see you can't do it by yourself. Besides . . ." His eyes shifted away from hers. "I ain't gonna be here that much longer. It'd be kind of nice to think there was something around here that I'd done. Something that'd be here for a while."

Lori regarded him skeptically. "Oh yeah? So where are you going now?"

"Don't matter. Maybe wherever the social worker sends me. Maybe somewheres else. But they ain't gonna let me stay here."

"They would if you asked them to."

He gave a derisive snort. "Shows what you know. Nobody gives a damn what I have to say."

"You're such an idiot. Haven't you ever heard the phrase 'in the best interest of the child'? You hear it all the time on Court TV. That means the only thing the social workers are supposed to care about is what you have to say. If you'd just stand up straight, and be polite, and stop saying 'ain't,' and tell them where you want to live, they'd have to listen to you."

He scowled at her. "That's crazy."

"It's true."

The scowl deepened. "You want me to help you build this thing or not?"

She squinted up at him, the sun in her eyes. "You're just a kid. You'll screw it up."

"You're just a girl. You'll screw it up worse."

Her eyes narrowed further. "I'm the one with the Am-Ex card."

"Yeah, well." He rocked back on his heels. "I can make it look like the picture."

She studied him for a time. "Can you really?"

"I drew it, didn't I?"

She thought about it another minute, and then stood, brushing off her hands. "Okay, you can help," she decided. "But I'm in charge. Is that clear?"

"Sure." He grinned. "Now, how is it you mix cement again?"

She glared at him. "Just shut up and get the garden hose."

❧

Carrie explained earnestly, "It's really not so hard to understand how something like this might have happened, although I'm awfully sorry it did. Noah and his father only moved here ten years or so ago, and he told everyone his wife was dead. We had no reason to suspect otherwise. And Noah never really came into the system formally—through proper channels, I mean. When his dad died last winter, you ladies were kind enough to take him in, and the Reverend Holland asked us to expedite the paperwork, so . . ." She spread her hands helplessly and leaned back in her chair. "We did. It's not an excuse, and I suppose the fault does lie with this office to a certain extent, but this is a small town and it's not the first time we've cut through a little red tape for the well-being of a child."

Cici said, "We're not blaming anyone. It's just . . ." She gave a shake of her head, as though trying to clear a fog. "How can his mother be *alive*?"

"Are you sure you have the right woman?"

Lindsay just looked stunned.

Carrie smiled sympathetically. "We're sure. The state office has been working on this, and they were finally able to contact her last week. I really don't know the details, but it's definitely the right woman."

She sorted through some papers on her desk until she came up with the right one, then slipped on a pair of black-framed glasses. "According to our records, Noah Clete was born in Charlottesville to Amanda and Robert Clete. Shortly after his birth, the mother, Amanda, left her husband. The child lived with his maternal grandmother until her death four years later. That was when Robert Clete moved with Noah to this county. He worked as a handyman off and on and . . . well, you know the rest."

Lindsay nodded slowly. "His father was an alcoholic whose only contact with Noah was to beat him. He couldn't be bothered to make sure he went to school or had warm clothes or regular meals. He—"

Bridget laid a quieting hand atop Lindsay's. "I don't understand," she said firmly, "why no one tried to find his mother—or even knew about her—until now."

Cici, who had opened her mouth to speak, closed it again and gave Bridget an approving nod.

"Well, that's just it, isn't it?" Carrie replied apologetically. "No one knew about her. No abandonment charges were ever filed, there was no child support to pursue, no reason for the state to get involved . . . and when the grandmother died, the child went back to live with his father, which was, for all intents and purposes, as it should have been." She removed the glasses. "Noah was so young when they moved here I doubt he would have even known where he was from if we had interviewed him. And I'm sure he believes his mother died when he was a baby, just like everyone else did."

"And the mother?" demanded Cici. "What's her excuse? She's been living in Richmond all this time and she never once thought to inquire about her son?"

"Apparently," Carrie said, "when the grandmother died and Robert took over custody, he moved around a good bit before he settled here. She simply lost track. She looked for Noah, but she couldn't find him." She glanced again at her notes. "She's only been in Richmond a few years. She's a resident counselor at a privately owned halfway house for recovering substance abusers."

Lindsay blew out a long slow breath. "Wow," she said. And again, "Wow." The expression on her face was reminiscent of someone who had just run into a plate glass window. "What do you know about that?" she said. "Noah ends up with a mother after all—even if it's not me. Things sure have a way of working themselves out." Then she looked back at Carrie. "I guess someone should tell him."

Carrie held up a staying hand. "I wish you'd hold off on that for a day or two. Amanda, his mother, will be here Wednesday, and I thought the best thing to do would be for all of us to meet, and try to figure out the best way to explain things to Noah. This will be a shock, and he's bound to have questions. It might be best if his mother was actually here to answer them."

Lindsay released another breath, which seemed almost to deflate her. She sagged a little in her chair, and there were lines around her mouth and her eyes that had not been there when she walked into the office. "Do you, um, do you think she'll want to take him back with her on Wednesday? That's not a lot of time to, well, prepare."

"I think we can come up with a better plan than that," Carrie said gently. "I haven't actually spoken to the woman, you know, but I'm sure she'll understand it will take Noah a little time to adjust to the news. There's no need to have his things packed until after we've all talked."

And that was it. They agreed to come back to the office on Wednesday morning at nine. They agreed that nothing would be said to Noah about his change in circumstances. They gathered up their things, they murmured thanks, they left the office. And no one said much of anything on the way home.

# 16

# Making Adjustments

Although lunch was usually an informal affair, with everyone grabbing whatever they could whenever they had time to eat it, Ida Mae was a little stricter with the young people's diets. Promptly at noon she called Noah and Lori in to feast on ham sandwiches made from thick homemade bread, with deviled eggs and bread-and-butter pickles on the side.

"I love the week after Easter," Lori declared, letting the screen door bang behind her. "Ham sandwiches every day!"

"Take off those muddy boots before you come tramping through my kitchen," Ida Mae told her, casting a critical eye over the rest of her outfit. "Those overalls don't look fit to bring to the table, either." She raised her voice as Noah appeared at the door. "If you bang that door again, young man, I'll take a strip out of your hide."

Lori kicked off her boots and left them by the door as Noah closed the screen door with exaggerated care. "I'll change after lunch," she told Ida Mae. "I have to go into town as soon as Mom gets back with the car keys."

Ida Mae grumbled about people running hither and yon,

wasting time and gasoline, as Lori slid into her place and took a bite out of her sandwich. "Isn't there anything to drink besides milk?" Noah complained. "I hate milk."

"You'll drink it and be grateful for it," Ida Mae returned. "Did you wash your hands?"

"Outside," he assured her around a mouthful of sandwich.

Ignoring them, Lori reached for the book that had been lying on the table and flipped it open. "Say, there's some stuff in here about Blackwell Farms. That's what this place used to be called!"

Ida Mae set her own plate on the table, and lowered herself into a chair. "Does your mama allow you to read at the table?"

"Only at lunch," murmured Lori absently, turning pages. "Look!" She held up the book, open to a photograph, and turned it to each of them. "A picture of this house, way back in the sixties. We're famous!"

Neither one of them seemed very interested, and Lori returned to her reading. "It says here they used to make cheese in that very dairy where Aunt Lindsay has her art studio, and they aged it in caves. Imagine that! I didn't know there were any caves around here."

Noah gave a derisive snort. "Everybody knows about the tourist caves down the road. Where're you from, anyhow?"

Lori looked at him, uncomprehending, for a moment, and then made a dismissive face. "Oh, you must mean the Luray Caverns. I don't think the Blackwells aged cheese there. Where did they age the cheese, Ida Mae? It would have to be on this property somewhere, wouldn't it?"

Ida Mae, chewing, didn't reply.

"Well, I guess it makes sense though," Lori commented, mostly to herself, as she turned back to the book. "Where there are caverns, there'd have to be caves."

"Soldiers stored ammunition there during the Civil War," Ida Mae said.

Lori looked up excitedly. "Here? In our cheese caves?"

And Noah said, "No kidding? Betcha there's some old cannonballs and stuff still lying around. Might be worth looking around for."

"Won't do you no good," returned Ida Mae smugly. "They ain't around here."

"But I thought you said—" Lori broke off at the sound of tires on the drive. "Oh good, they're back." She finished the last bite of her sandwich and washed it down with milk. "Thanks, Ida Mae, that was delicious." She hurried from the table, taking the book with her.

"Hey, Mom." She met the three women in the front entrance, her hand out. "I need the car keys."

Cici fumbled distractedly in her purse and came up with the keys. "Have a good time," she said as she handed them over.

Lori gave her a confused look and started to say something, but Bridget interrupted. "Oh, honey, if you're going out, do you mind taking that book back to the library for me? It's overdue." She too started searching in her purse. "I have the fine here somewhere."

"Hey, Teach." Noah came in from the kitchen. "We having school today or what?"

For the longest time, Lindsay said nothing. Then she smiled. "Actually, Noah," she said brightly, "I have some good news for you."

Both Bridget and Cici looked at her sharply.

"That idea you had about applying for a license to keep wild-life," she went on, "was a good one. I talked to the game warden and it looks as though we're going to be able to keep Bambi after all."

"Hey," said Noah, his face brightening.

Lori lifted an eyebrow at him. "*Your* idea?"

"So," Lindsay went on, "in honor of that, I thought we'd take the day off. Everyone else gets spring holidays, and, besides, I have some things I need to get done today."

"You got no argument from me," said Noah, heading for the door.

The three of them watched him go. Then Cici said, "Well, I'd better change into my chicken coop–building clothes."

"Yes," said Lindsay, turning away from the door as though with an effort. "I'll help you. Build the thing, that is. Whatever."

"Me, too," said Bridget.

Lori said, "You guys are acting weird."

But no one seemed to hear her, and the three of them went upstairs.

Lori, shrugging, started to follow them, and then something caught her eye. She looked at the display on the entrance wall: the framed collage of historic newspaper scraps, the charcoal drawing of the house that Noah had given Lindsay for Christmas, an old-fashioned invitation, the faded scrap of paper with a child's drawing on it that Lindsay had found in the guest room woodbin. She frowned, and opened the book, flipping through pages until she found it. She looked. And looked again.

"Holy cow," she said. She turned toward the stairs and started to call "Hey!" but she stopped herself. Then she looked back at the book. "Holy cow," she repeated, and the amazement on her face slowly turned into a big and satisfied smile.

She hurried to the door and saw Noah crossing the lawn. "Hey, kid!" she called. "You still want that ride into town?"

❧

"I think this is a good thing," Lindsay pronounced. The certainty in her voice seemed a little forced. "Of course it is."

"No doubt about it. How big do you think a chicken coop is supposed to be, anyway?"

"I think it depends on the number of chickens, Cici," Bridget said.

"They should each have their own nest."

Cici stared at Lindsay. "This isn't the Hilton, you know. Besides, they're only three inches tall. If we make it too big, they won't be able to keep warm at night."

They had decided on a sunny spot behind the barn, and had brought a measuring tape, level, string, and dowels to mark the spot. Bridget handed over the tape to Cici. "Of course it's a good thing. Every child should have a chance to know his mother."

"I think the most important thing is to have a yard that's big enough for them all to roam around in. We'll have to enclose it in chicken wire."

An hour later, as she took her turn wrestling the posthole diggers into the ground while Cici ran the power saw on an extension cord from the barn, Lindsay added, "I just hope she'll encourage him to keep up with his art."

"He could be going to a wonderful new life," Bridget offered. She was panting as she dragged a two-by-four fence post across the ground. "Who knows what this could mean for him?"

"Definitely the best thing that could have happened." Sweat rolled down Lindsay's face and she grunted with effort as she stabbed the blades of the tool into the ground again.

Two hours later the three women examined the framework of what was roughly a six-by-eight-foot structure. The back was dramatically lower than the front; the left side seemed longer than the right; and the whole resembled a lopsided doghouse more than a building meant to house fowl.

"Did you leave room for windows?" Lindsay asked critically, tilting her head to one side.

Cici whipped off the sweatband that held back her perspiration-darkened hair and mopped her face with it. "Chickens don't need windows. If they want fresh air, they can walk through the door."

"You can't leave the door open at night," Lindsay said in alarm. "Foxes will come in!"

"That's why we're building a fence," explained Cici patiently.

"Oh. Right."

Bridget circled the entire structure, from front to back, before venturing an opinion. "I don't see how we're going to get in to collect the eggs. It seems a little . . . short."

"They're chickens, not giraffes," returned Cici testily. "You'll just have to bend down."

"You don't think it seems . . . I don't know. Lopsided?"

"Someone"—Cici looked meaningfully at Bridget, who had been in charge of marking the boards before they were cut— "might have measured wrong."

They regarded their handiwork for a moment longer. Then Bridget ventured, "Cici, do you have any idea how to build a chicken coop?"

"Not a clue."

And so began the process of tearing down, re-measuring, and starting again. By five o'clock they were sweaty, bug-bitten, and sunburned. Four fence posts were set into the ground, and the chicken coop consisted of a square of two-by-fours arranged on the ground. The women stepped back to survey their work and agreed as one that it would not hurt the chickens to spend one more night in the sunroom.

Lori and Noah had returned from town, and were making a great deal of noise unloading something on the other side of the house. As the women started wearily toward home, Lindsay's eyes turned toward the sound of their voices. "I know it's the best thing that could possibly have happened," she said. "But..."

Suddenly both her friends put their arms around her waist.

And Cici added, "We hate it, too."

❧

As the days lengthened, and spring settled firmly into place, twilight lingered until after eight o'clock. The ladies sat on the porch and watched as the lacework of emerald leaves patterning the lavender sky turned to black. Then, illuminated only by the faint glow of stars, they sat and rocked, weighed down by exhaustion and their own thoughts.

"There should be a law against people our age working this hard," Bridget said, stifling a groan as she stretched out her legs.

"You should never take on a physical job like that when you're angry."

Lindsay glanced at Cici. "I thought working hard was supposed to make you feel better when you're upset."

"Nope. It just makes you tired."

They were silent for a while. "She's right, you know," Bridget said. "Whenever I'm upset I start cleaning the house, and the more I clean the more I find to do until it's really just a vicious cycle."

"I used to go to the gym," Lindsay admitted, "and work that treadmill until the trainers started giving me dirty looks because people were waiting to use the equipment."

"It's what women do. Instead of picking fights in bars or whipping out small caliber handguns when someone cuts them off in traffic."

Bridget rubbed her shoulder. "I don't know. I think we might need to take another look at our coping mechanisms."

"Those kids sure are working hard, whatever they're up to," Lindsay commented.

Lori and Noah had barely paused long enough to gulp their dinner, then returned to work until daylight faded.

"I don't know what Lori used to bribe Noah into helping her. But it must have been good."

"I think he suspects something is going on. He was awfully quiet at dinner."

"He was exhausted," Cici said.

"Noah never does anything halfway," Bridget said fondly. And the smile in her voice faded as she added, "I'm going to miss him so much."

They were quiet for a moment. Dusky clouds settled over

the mountains, silhouetted against a deep purple sky. A cricket shrilled in a nearby bush, and was joined in a moment by his mate. The chorus, breaking the silence, sounded like a cacophony.

Then Lindsay said softly, "You know what's funny? I never wanted children. Not even once, not even a little bit. I mean, I loved teaching and I loved the kids I taught, but as far as wanting one of my own—I just didn't have the urge. I always felt as though other women—other mothers—thought I was strange, or in denial, or maybe something was wrong with me. But there wasn't. I just wasn't interested."

"I never thought you were strange."

"Me either. I thought you were smart."

"Motherhood isn't something that just happens to you," Cici said. "It's a choice you make every day, to put someone else's happiness and well-being ahead of your own, to teach the hard lessons, to do the right thing even when you're not sure what the right thing is . . . and to forgive yourself, over and over again, for doing everything wrong."

"Half the time your kids end up hating you for at least five of their teenage years," added Bridget, "but you count yourself a success if they don't end up pregnant or in jail. And don't ever expect anything so mundane as a thank-you."

"If any of us really knew what we were getting into when we decided to have kids, I don't think we would've signed up."

Bridget smiled to herself in the dark. "I would've."

Lindsay said, "I know this is the best thing. It just . . . doesn't seem fair."

"No," agreed Cici softly. "It doesn't."

They sat and rocked, wrapped in their thoughts. The sky gave up the last of its light and swallowed the mountains. The balmy evening melted into a cooler breeze tinged with the dampness of dew and the scent of woodsmoke. Somewhere behind the house, Rebel started to bark.

After a time Bridget sighed and said, "I should go in. But I'm too tired to get up."

"I told Noah he was having a history test tomorrow," Lindsay said. "I'd better go write it." Her voice had a catch in it. "Not that it will matter, I guess, by Wednesday. I really should give him the rest of the week off."

"What in the world is the matter with that dog?"

"Oh, Cici, he's probably chasing deer," Lindsay said. "You'd think after living with one for all this time, he'd catch on."

"He knows the difference between his own deer and strangers," Bridget pointed out with only the slightest note of pride in her voice. "And it's his job to keep them out of the garden."

"Well, can't someone tell him we've got a fence around the garden for that?"

Upstairs, there was the sound of a window opening, and then Noah's voice. "Hey, dog!" he shouted. "Shut up!"

"Hey, Noah! History test!" But there was a small smile in Lindsay's voice as she called out to him.

The window closed.

Cici glanced across at her, smiling. "You would have made a great mother, Linds."

"Maybe I'll sit just a little longer. It's so nice out, isn't it?"

"Kind of late in the year for anyone to build a fire," Bridget commented.

"Warm, too."

"Maybe Farley's burning trash."

"Probably."

"Is it supposed to rain tonight?" Lindsay wondered. "Look at that mist."

All of them turned toward the foggy bank of mist that was drifting in patches and threads across the yard. Cici stood slowly, moving toward it to get a better look. "That's not mist," she said in an odd, constricted tone.

She moved suddenly, rushing to the rail, peering around the corner of the house. "It's smoke!" she cried. "Call 911! Get everyone out of the house! The barn is on fire!"

# 17

# It Never Rains But . . .

Morning dawned gray and flat over Ladybug Farm. No spectacular watercolor sunrise painted the sky, no shafts of golden light etched unfurling leaves, no diamond dewdrops sparkled on the grass. The air was heavy and still and tasted like wet soot. The lawn was churned up by the tracks of heavy fire trucks and spattered with dark, oily puddles. The lilac bushes had been crushed by the weight of the fire hose and emitted a cloyingly sweet perfume, which, mixed with the rank, sharp taste of smoke in the air, was close to nauseating. A bird shrilled suddenly in a nearby tree and then, as though embarrassed by the inappropriateness of his song, ceased abruptly.

Cici had been sitting on the back steps in her pajamas for the last hour, her arms wrapped around her knees for warmth, waiting for enough light to survey the damage. No one had gotten much sleep after the volunteer fire department left. Cici herself had gotten out of bed every hour or so to look out the window, making certain the fire had not flared up again. She could hear the other women moving around during the night, no doubt doing the same thing. And at three a.m. Lori had crept into bed beside her. Cici wrapped her arms around her and held her tight. Her daughter's hair smelled like smoke.

She got up and crossed to the remnants of the barn, the untied laces of her battered gym shoes dragging in the mud. Rebel, unusually subdued, sniffed along behind her, his normally pristine white legs and underbelly black with sooty mud. She paused to untie Bambi from the tree to which he had been secured during the night, repressing a shudder of horror as she remembered the moment when Noah had dashed into the deer's pen to lead him away from the flaming barn. He had actually taken the animal into the house while the fire was being extinguished. And she hadn't cared.

The massive skeleton of the barn, black and charred against the pewter sky, looked like something out of a horror movie, a gothic remnant of some dark and tragic past. Tendrils of smoke still curled from beams that had collapsed on the ground. The arched ribs stood naked against the sky and the tin roof was scorched and buckled. The rock foundation, six feet high, protected nothing but a pile of smoldering debris, and from the center of it all came a high-pitched squealing, hissing sound as water sank into the hot timbers and evaporated into steam.

After a time Cici realized that Lindsay, dressed in her terry robe and sneakers, was standing beside her. She gratefully accepted a cup of coffee, and held it in both hands to warm them.

"Well," Lindsay said quietly. "This certainly puts things into perspective, doesn't it?"

Cici nodded slowly. "If it had spread to the house . . ."

"But it didn't." Bridget had come up quietly behind them, already dressed in jeans and a sweatshirt, her hair tied back, ready for work. But a look at her face revealed that she had not yet been to bed. "And thank God none of the animals were inside. If this had happened in the winter, or even last month, when we were keeping the sheep in at night . . ." She buried her expression with a sip of coffee, unable to finish the thought.

"There's blessings in everything." Ida Mae, too, was dressed for the day in sturdy work boots and a cotton dress over her twill pants, the whole topped with a fleece sweatshirt. She carried the coffeepot wrapped in a towel, and topped off the ladies' cups as she spoke. "If you all had finished that chicken coop like you was supposed to, them baby chicks woulda smothered to death from the smoke. I reckon I'll be putting up with sawdust and chicken crap all over the conservatory for a while longer. Miss Emily must be turning in her grave."

Cici's voice was heavy with despair and disbelief. "How in the world are we supposed to build a barn when we can't even build a chicken coop?"

The screen door closed and Lori crossed the lawn in a pink sleep shirt printed with a big-eyed kitten and matching capri leggings, stepping carefully around the puddles in her bare feet. Her hair was a mass of tangled coppery curls, and her face was pale and puffy from lack of sleep. She walked up to her mother and put her head on her shoulder, and Cici held her close. Noah followed in a moment, also in bare feet, but wearing jeans and the same wrinkled, soot-smudged T-shirt he had worn the night before. He paused to offer Bambi a carrot he had brought from the kitchen, and then he stood a little outside the circle, surveying the wreck of the barn in the same glum fashion as the others.

Lori asked, "Did they ever figure out what started it?"

Cici shook her head. "The fire marshal said he couldn't officially say until he wrote up his report. The best theory was that a spark from the power tools we were using yesterday started smoldering in the hay. But there were paint cans stored here, and gasoline for the lawn mower, and those hundred-year-old timbers . . ."

"They weren't a hundred years old."

Everyone looked at Ida Mae. "The barn wasn't even built until the sixties sometime."

"Which explains why it wasn't in the mural."

"Well, it sure is a mess now," Noah said.

Bridget made an obvious effort to sound positive. "At least we have insurance."

Cici glanced at her. "About that . . ."

"What do you mean?"

"Are you kidding me? We do have insurance—don't we?"

Cici held up a hand to stop the onslaught. "Yes, of course we have insurance. But if you recall, we decided not to insure the outbuildings separately—they were all so old, and there were so many of them, and half of them were falling down, so we just went with the standard 'separate outbuildings' clause, which for most people means a garage. In other words, we're insured for a fraction of what it will take to rebuild. And we have a five-thousand-dollar deductible."

Lindsay released a long, exhausted breath. "Well, there you go. It never rains but it pours."

The other two merely nodded, glumly, and sipped their coffee.

"You're not getting anything done standing here crying over it," declared Ida Mae gruffly. "Come on in the house and get some breakfast."

"My mouth tastes like it's full of ashes," Lori said. "I don't think I can eat anything."

"That'll be a first," replied Ida Mae, turning back toward the house.

"You kids be careful out here in your bare feet." Cici turned to follow. "There are pieces of hot wood scattered around."

"Breakfast will be ready in a few minutes," Bridget added.

Noah was poking around the edges of the barn's skeleton, absently shoving away pieces of debris, when Lori, dispirited, turned to follow the others inside. She saw Noah squat down to pick something up, and she asked in passing, without much real interest, "What's that?"

Panic crossed his eyes, and he moved quickly, straightening up, turning away from her, and tucking the object into his jeans pocket. He didn't reply, and he didn't look at her. But it didn't matter, because Lori had already seen what he had found.

It was a cigarette butt.

ॐ

They were unenthusiastically picking at breakfast when the sound of Farley's tractor chugging up the drive drew them all outside again.

"Figured you'd need some help cleaning up," he said, shouting to be heard over the sound of the engine. Being their nearest neighbor, Farley had arrived the previous night almost at the same time as the fire engines, and had stood to the side watching the effort with approving nods until the last hose was wound and stored and the taillights disappeared down the drive. Then, in his usual taciturn fashion, he had tipped his hat to them, climbed back into his pickup truck, and returned home.

Cici tilted her head up at him with an apologetic expression. "Thanks, Farley, that's good of you. But we can't afford to pay much."

"That's okay." He spat politely into the ever-ready soda can. "I ain't planning to do much."

But what he did in a matter of an hour was more than they could have accomplished by themselves with a week's work. Using the plow blade on the tractor, he pushed the fallen timbers and charred debris out of the skeleton of the barn and into a pile at the edge of the yard, where Noah was assigned to duty with the garden hose, making certain that the last sparks were fully extinguished. The fact that the pathetic beginnings of the chicken coop were demolished in the process was a small price to pay.

"You all take a shovel and pile some dirt up around the edges of that trash," he advised, "and she ought to be okay. Gonna have to get a bulldozer in to take down the shell, though." He held out his hand. "Ten dollar."

And, because they knew that was all he would accept for his labor no matter how hard they argued, that was what they paid.

The phone rang all morning as neighbors, acquaintances, and the merely curious checked in. A fire, even a barn fire, was an alarming event in the small community, and the news spread like the fog of smoke that still drifted over the valley. "I'm afraid they're going to start a charity drive for us," Bridget said after the fifth or sixth call. "I keep trying to explain that we didn't lose anything valuable, but everyone wants to help."

"You shouldn't discourage them," Cici said. "Maybe someone will donate a bulldozer." She stood on the back porch, with her work gloves on and her hair tied up in a scarf, and shook her head helplessly as she gazed at the ruin. "I don't know where to begin."

Noah, working as though driven by demons, was digging a trench around the pile of smoldering trash that Farley had piled up. Flakes of black ash still drifted from it, and greasy mud surrounded it. There was not a patch of skin on his body that was still white. Lori was using the garden hose to spray down the parts of the structure that were still standing—an unnecessary precaution whose only function was to make her feel useful.

"God, I'm so tired of being poor," Lindsay said. She came around the corner with a hoe, her voice and her posture heavy with defeat.

"We're not poor," Bridget returned sharply. "We've got food in the freezer and wine in the pantry and—and chickens in the sunroom. We've got broccoli and carrots and sweet peas and lettuce coming up out of the ground, for Pete's sake, and we are not poor!"

Cici managed a faint, crooked grin. "Now if we just had a cow for milk."

"And a barn to keep it in," Lindsay pointed out glumly. "Let's face it, girls, we're a bit over our heads, here."

Cici glanced at her. "And you're just now figuring that out?"

"God, I just don't see why this had to happen now, on top of everything else. We've got that meeting with Carrie tomorrow and I can barely even remember why. It just doesn't seem real, any of it."

"I know what you mean," agreed Cici. "But let's just focus on one disaster at a time."

"I can't even decide which one to focus on."

"I'm going to suggest the burnt barn. At least that's something we can do something about."

And Lindsay replied, "Like what?"

"Okay, okay." Bridget had a determined look on her face. "We've dealt with crises before. We might not have the resources the Blackwells did when they built this place, but we're doing okay. We can handle this."

In a moment, Lindsay took a deep breath and squared her shoulders. "You're right. We've been through all this before. We're in it for the long haul, and we knew it wouldn't be easy. What else is new? Come on, let's see what we can do with this mess."

Cici watched as Lori crossed to turn off the spigot, then, leaving the garden hose stretched across the ground, wandered over and sat on the stump of the hickory tree they had cut down last year. Her expression, even from the distance, was noticeably bleak.

Cici said, "You guys go ahead. I'll be there in a minute, okay?" She crossed the yard toward her daughter, and then sat down beside her on the stump and waited.

"Nothing bad has ever happened to me before," Lori said. Her gaze, sad and a little unfocused, remained on the smoldering skeleton of the barn. "I mean, I thought it had. But not really."

She looked at her mother. "Last night was really scary. Some-one could have been hurt. The animals could have burned to death. The fire could have spread to the house, and we all could have been trapped inside. I don't think you realize how impor-tant it is to feel safe until suddenly you don't anymore."

Cici had to swallow hard before she could speak. "No mother ever wants her child to learn that the world is not a safe place. I've worked so hard trying to make sure nothing bad ever did happen to you."

"I know," Lori said softly. "But I'm not a child anymore." She took a breath. "Even though I've been acting like one. All of that nonsense with sheep and chickens and jam and expensive B&Bs . . . they had nothing to do with real life. *This* is real life." She gave a small shake of her head. "I should have stayed in Cal-ifornia with Dad, where the only thing I'd have to think about was whether I'd put on enough sunscreen before I went to the pool. I don't belong here. I'm no good at this. I've just been wast-ing my time and making your life harder."

She started to stand, but Cici put a hand on her knee.

"The only way I got through college," Cici said, "was by tak-ing remedial algebra courses. Even then I barely passed. I had to take the real estate exam twice. It was the math. It's always been hard for me. Of course, there was a lot of math in my line of work, and over the years it got easier, but it's still a struggle. Even yesterday, building the chicken coop—we had to tear down everything we'd done, not because Bridget measured wrong but because I multiplied the fractions wrong. And I've been doing this for over twenty years."

Lori was silent for a while. "Uncle Paul talked to you, didn't he?"

Cici squeezed her knee. "He loves you, sweetheart. So do I. And I don't ever want you to think you're not good enough because you're comparing yourself to someone else—even if that someone is me. Mothers *have* to pretend to be perfect, don't you see that? If we didn't, anarchy would rule the world. But most of the time we're just doing the best we can, and trying to get better at it every day."

Lori tried to smile. "It's hard, when you don't know where you fit in. Everyone else is good at something—Aunt Lindsay with her teaching and Aunt Bridget with her cooking and you building things and even the kid"—she jerked her head toward Noah—"at drawing. But me?" She shrugged. "All I've got is a bunch of dopey ideas."

A note of motherly indignation tinged Cici's voice. "You're twenty years old! You have plenty of time to discover what it is you were meant to do in this world. And it doesn't have to be just one thing, either. Leonardo da Vinci started out with nothing but a bunch of 'dopey ideas,' so did Benjamin Franklin and Thomas Edison and Winston Churchill and—and, well, Al Gore, for heaven's sake! And look what *they* ended up contributing to the world!"

Lori slanted her an upwards grin. "The Internet?"

Cici put an arm around her shoulders and hugged her tight. "And please don't ever let me hear you say again that you've made my life harder. You've made my life—and everyone else's—richer by coming here. You've brought us adventure and inspiration and hope. You've reminded us how to think outside the box. You've made certain no two days are ever the same, and okay, so some of those days have been a little more exciting than we'd like, and maybe a little adventure goes a long way when you get to be our age, but . . ." She took Lori's face in her hand and turned it toward her, regarding her seriously. "I am so glad you are here. And I'm sorry if I've tried to make you into something you're not, or hold you up to a standard that doesn't fit. You are a smart, imaginative, ambitious young woman, and I believe you can make your mark on the world with or without a college degree. Only you know what's best for you. And whatever you choose, I'll support you."

Lori turned and wrapped her arms around her mother, hugging her fiercely. Cici returned the embrace until she felt tears stinging her eyes, and then she pushed away, swallowing the moisture in her throat, smoothing the damp curls away from Lori's face. "Come on," she said, "let's give the others a hand."

❧

Noah was using a wide snow shovel to scrape debris out of the corners of the barn that Farley's big plow had been unable to reach. Lori went behind him with the wheelbarrow, and when it was full, she carted it off to the trash pile where the women had taken over the digging of the trench. For almost an hour they worked in silence, then Lori observed in surprise, "Hey. There's a stone floor under here. I never knew that. Let me see that shovel."

Noah glared at her through bloodshot eyes and a face that was streaked with soot. He looked for a moment as though he would not comply and then, abruptly, handed it over.

"Did you tell your mom?" he demanded.

Lori scraped away a layer of dirt and ash from the floor, exposing another section of mortared stone. "Tell her what?"

"You know what."

Lori looked up, regarding him frankly for a moment. "It's not my job to tell her."

His expression grew belligerent. "Nobody knows what started that fire."

And Lori agreed mildly, "That's right. Nobody does."

"And nobody can prove a damn thing."

The sound of the shovel raking over stone was the only reply as Lori cleared another four-foot section that was dusted with ash. And then the shovel struck something sharp sticking out of the ground. She thrust it back toward Noah and dropped to her knees, brushing the ground with her gloved hands until she uncovered a metal ring. "Hey, look at this. It's like something they used to tie horses to."

She tried to lift the ring, but it wouldn't budge. She tried again, straining her shoulders, to no avail. "Bring that shovel back over here," she said. "It's buried or something."

"So what if it is? We're supposed to be cleaning out this junk." But reluctantly, he returned with the shovel, and even helped her dig out the layers of packed dirt around the ring.

Less than ten minutes later they both stepped back, gazing at the six-foot panel of solid wood set into the stone floor, with the iron ring affixed to it in the center. "Will you look at that?" said Lori in amazement. "It's a door! A trapdoor! I wonder what's down there?"

"Spiders," replied Noah.

"Mom, come here!" Lori called. "You won't believe what we found! Aunt Lindsay, Aunt Bridget, come look at this!"

By the time the women arrived, Noah and Lori had used the metal ring to swing the door upward on a pair of powerful hinges. A couple of spiders did, in fact, scurry out, along with a surge of cool, damp air, but once they were gone, nothing more frightening was revealed inside than a set of sturdy stone steps.

"It's like a castle dungeon," said Bridget in awe. Her voice echoed as she leaned over the opening.

"Or a treasure cave," agreed Lindsay, wide-eyed.

"What do you suppose it is?" Cici wondered.

"Maybe where they used to hide out from the Indians," Noah suggested.

"Or where they hid the Confederate Treasury." Bridget's voice barely contained her excitement.

Lindsay shot a dry glance her way. "With our luck, it will be in Confederate bills."

༄

"Lori, run to the house and get some flashlights," commanded Cici impatiently. "Hurry!"

And so, in an instant, the gray aftermath of disaster was transformed into a morning of adventure and possibility as, one flashlight beam at a time, they made their way down the stairs and into the vast cellar below.

"Smells like somebody puked down here," observed Noah.

They stood close together at the bottom of the stairs, the slow sweeping beams of their light crossing and occasionally glinting off the round curves of something metal. Their voices echoed.

"Sour," agreed Lindsay.

"More like moldy bread," said Bridget.

"Oh, my goodness, I think I know what this place is," Lori said excitedly. "It's the cave where they used to age the cheese!"

Cici swept her light along the wall near the stairs, and found a switch. There was a buzzing and flickering overhead, and, one by one, a bank of fluorescent lights sequenced into life. They found themselves standing in a vast concrete room with a steel door at the far end, surrounded by giant, dusty steel vats with tubes and pipes connected to them.

Bridget gave a little shudder, her eyes wide as she looked around. "It's like Frankenstein's laboratory!"

"Nope," said Cici. "It's not a cheese cave either." Smiling, she flicked off her flashlight. "It looks to me as though Noah and Lori have discovered what remains of the old Blackwell Farms winery."

❧

They bombarded Ida Mae with questions at lunch. Why hadn't Ida Mae ever mentioned the winery beneath the barn? Why was it hidden away like that? Where did the steel door, which they had tried with all their strength to open, lead? Why had all that equipment been abandoned like that? How long had the place been closed up? And why had it been kept such a secret?

Ida Mae, complacently serving up homemade vegetable soup and fresh buttermilk cornbread, replied, "Weren't no secret. You just never asked before."

"I swear, you are *the* most exasperating woman!" Cici exclaimed. "All this time, a part of this county's history has been sitting down there and you never said a word."

"And not one single bottle of 1967 Shiraz with the original label," Lindsay felt compelled to point out, a trifle fatalistically.

"Ida Mae is right, you know. We knew about the winery before we bought the house, but it never occurred to us to wonder where it was."

"I wonder if the equipment is worth anything."

"Maybe." Cici tasted her soup. "We could do some research, try to sell it on eBay or something."

"What I don't understand," Lori said, "is why they put a winery in the cellar of a barn."

Ida Mae gave her a disparaging look. "You ever hear of Prohibition?"

Cici put down her spoon, her eyes growing bright with interest. So did Bridget and Lindsay. "Do you mean . . ."

Ida Mae nodded smugly. "Everybody thinks the Blackwells made their money in phosphates, but that was just the start. It was bootleg whiskey that built their fortune. Hear tell that door you found used to be in the floor of the chicken house, the last place the law would go looking for a speakeasy—or a distillery."

She sat down at the kitchen table and sampled her soup. "Good soup," she commented, "if I do say so myself."

"Ida Mae!" Lori practically squealed. "Is that all you have to say? Tell us more!"

"Ain't nothing more to tell."

"Are you serious?" Bridget demanded. "There used to be a speakeasy in the cellar of our barn and you say there's nothing more to tell?"

"What about the door?" Noah, who had been pretending disinterest in the entire conversation, spoke up for the first time. "Was that some kind of secret escape route in case of raids?"

Ida Mae chewed a morsel of cornbread for an inordinately long period of time. "The door," she said at last, "was put in when they decided to make wine down there. Couldn't exactly carry all them grapes and barrels and stuff down the stairs, so they cut a door in the hill down by the orchard. All they had to do was drive the trucks up and unload."

"I know the hill she's talking about!" Bridget exclaimed. "Where the raspberries are planted, right?" And then she frowned. "But I never saw a door there."

"It would be all overgrown now," Cici said. "That's probably why we couldn't get it open, too. Ida Mae—"

"Will you all stop pestering me about stuff that happened way back in the old days?" the older woman demanded. "Can't a person have a bite to eat in peace?"

"We don't mean to pester you, Ida Mae," Bridget said, sounding a little hurt. "But you could be a little more generous with your information, you know. You know everything there is to know about this house and the people who used to live here, but every time we ask a question you brush us off. All we want you to do is tell us your stories. Why won't you do that?"

Ida Mae dabbed a drip of soup from her chin, crumpled her napkin, and replied flatly, "Because those stories are mine. I can tell them or not tell them. This is your house now. Get your own stories." And with that, she gathered up her dishes and took them to the sink, effectively closing the subject.

They gathered on the porch at dusk, but this time they did not even make it to the rockers. They sat on the front steps to remove their ruined work gloves and filthy boots, and they were too tired, for a moment, to go further.

Finding the winery—and later, uncovering the briar and vine-encumbered door that was cut into the hillside—had provided a welcome distraction from the drudgery of the cleanup, but eventually the inevitable could be postponed no longer. Lori had practically fallen asleep over dinner, and Noah had gone to his room directly afterward. Cici, Lindsay, and Bridget had returned to work until daylight died.

"You know," said Bridget, resting her chin wearily in her hands, "I just realized something. I am really old."

"I definitely can't keep up this pace," admitted Cici. "Especially on no sleep."

"I've got to wash my hair," Lindsay said, but made no move to get up. "I'll never get the smell of smoke out of it. I'm going to look like crap in the morning."

They were silent for a time, trying to wrap their minds around the fact that a crisis of a much different kind awaited them in town tomorrow. On another evening, they would have talked about the upcoming meeting, expressed their feelings, tried to prepare themselves for it. Now they could barely imagine it.

"One crisis at a time," Bridget murmured.

Cici wearily rubbed the back of her neck. "Sounds like a slogan for the Ladybug Farm twelve-step program."

"This is not going to make us look very good in the eyes of Social Services."

Cici gave Lindsay a puzzled look. "Why? It's not like we planned the fire."

"I know. But it makes it look as though . . . I don't know. As though our lives are out of control."

"Right now I feel as though our lives *are* out of control."

"It's not an interview," Bridget had to remind them unhappily. "It really doesn't matter what we look like in the eyes of Social Services, does it?"

And the other two, wearily, had to agree.

"By the way," Cici said with an effort, after a moment, "Ida Mae said the fire marshal called while we were out cleaning up this afternoon. The reports are in, and it looks as though the fire started with that electrical outlet we were using yesterday for the power tools."

Bridget gasped and sat up straight. "Oh, no! I was supposed to put all the tools away and I did, only—I left the extension cord plugged in. I thought we would be back at it this morning, so I just wound it up and—"

But before she was halfway through, Cici started shaking her head. "No, no, it's okay, it doesn't matter. It wasn't your fault. It was old wiring, that's all, and probably chewed on by mice . . . It might have overheated while we were using it, but how could we know that? It's no one's fault."

"I guess not."

"Funny how things work out," she said after a moment. "If the barn hadn't burned, we never would have known the winery was even there."

"I'm not sure it's much of a trade-off," Cici said.

"It might be," Lindsay offered, rousing herself with an effort, "if we can sell the equipment."

"Maybe for enough to rebuild the barn."

"Maybe," agreed Cici. "But I'm really too tired to even think about it now."

"One crisis at a time."

Cici sighed. "Right."

And, one by one, they pushed themselves to their feet and went to prepare for what awaited them tomorrow.

# 18

# In Another Time

*Emmy Marie, 1967*

It was only six weeks, but six weeks can be a lifetime. She set to work with her sketchbook and her paints and an air of fierce concentration that endeared her to Andrew in a way he couldn't entirely explain. They walked at sunset through the vines, and they talked. They had picnics in the vineyard, and talked. And as much as they talked, they laughed. And then one day he kissed her flushed, upturned face, and she kissed him back. They sank to the couch in the sun-dappled folly, shedding their clothes like impatient teenagers, and they made love.

With her, he did not feel like a forty-five-year-old man chasing a twenty-three-year-old girl. With her, he simply felt happy.

It was an extraordinary summer. Although he was running unopposed for the fall election, there were dinners and barbecues and speeches; the law practice still demanded token attention, if for no other reason than good public relations. He worked in the winery, he carried a briefcase, he shook hands and made speeches. But he led two lives, and the only one that mattered began and ended in a folly in the woods where a face dearer than life awaited him.

In the midst of all else, Blackwell Farms Winery was about to bottle its finest Shiraz yet. It was so fine, indeed, that Andrew and Robert still argued whether to bring it out under its own unique label. In the end it was Emmy's opinion that won out, as of course it would. Andrew was impressed by how much she had learned from Robert and Dominic during the days she spent in the winery with them, and she was beginning to develop a respectable palate. When she tasted the subject of the dispute, she did so with care and reverence, and stood gazing thoughtfully at the glass for a moment before declaring softly, "A wine fit for kings. And it definitely deserves its own label."

Dominic, who had taken his father's side in the dispute, laughed and tugged at one of her curls in the familiar way of young people. "There you have it, Mr. Blackwell, you're outvoted. And by the royal princess of the vines, no less!"

Emmy started to make a face at him, and suddenly her eyes went wide and she set down the glass on the tasting table. "Wait!" she said excitedly. "I have it. I have the perfect label for your wine."

She scrambled through drop cloths and under scaffolding until she found her sketch pad and the nub of a pencil, and she quickly sketched out a rough likeness of a heraldic crest featuring a winged horse. "The horse is supposed to be a symbol of supremacy or something," she explained as she drew. "At least that's what my mother said. I think this was our family crest a long time ago. Mother actually has a quilt with this design sewn into it, which has been handed down for generations. Of course it's all patched and worn-out now, but . . . here." She tore the sheet out of the pad and handed it to him. "What do you think?"

He smiled as he looked at it. The sketch was quick and amateurish, but he wouldn't have cared if it had been done in crayon. "Well, what do you know about that? The princess of the vines is actual royalty after all."

She struck a pose and an affected accent. "Perhaps not royalty, my dear man, but definitely of the peerage."

He laughed and tucked the sketch into his pocket. "I would be foolish indeed then, to turn down such a commission—if, of course, you're sure your ancestors won't mind. Can you do a full color sketch for the printer?"

Because of course he would not deny her anything.

He showed the sketch to his mother that night after supper, and told her of their plans for the new label, but she did not seem much impressed—either by the design, or by their guest's lighthearted claim to highborn ancestry. She tossed the little paper away, which was a shame, because Andrew would have liked to have kept it.

❧

He thought he was living the best time of his life. The Shiraz was going to put Blackwell Farms on the wine-making map. He was going to be elected a District Court judge. And every day he came home to that beautiful face, sometimes smeared with paint, sometimes deep in concentration, and always making him feel he could spend hours simply gazing at it.

He planned a party in the winery for the end of the month, to show off the new mural, promote the winery, and honor the artist. His mother loved the idea, and so did Ida Mae, and the two of them buzzed around the house like hummingbirds in a field of poppies. Emmy started the much smaller murals in the living room, and when they were finished, she would go. He could not, of course, let her go. He began to fantasize about taking her to Paris, after the election, of course, and staying there for a month or so, just the two of them in a little hotel on the Rue Sancerre, where the morning sun came through the windows and painted the room gold, and then he began to fantasize about what she would say if he were to ask her, and he tried to imagine how he would ask her. He thought it would be at the party, when the paintings were finished. He would take her off alone, and he would tell her his plans, and he would watch her eyes light up with delight, and he would live on her joy the way other people lived on food and wine.

It happened one afternoon when he came in to find her stretched out in an awkward position in one of the alcoves. There were canvas drop cloths on the floor and paints all around, and she had snagged her hair on a rough board while prepping the area for the first coat of paint and could not get free. So he crawled in with her and tried to unwind the curl and as he did her hair ribbon came loose and her hair tumbled around her face and then she was free and she came up laughing with her breath spilling into his pores and her lips almost brushing his and he stole a kiss with her face held hot between his hands, sweet and hot, the two of them tangled together on the floor in a moment of shameless rapture, and when they broke apart his mother was just leaving the room.

Emmy was embarrassed, but he was amused, until the following day when she told him that she had a job waiting for her in Boston—wasn't that exciting?—and she wouldn't meet his eyes when she said it. He grasped her hands and the words rushed out of him before he could stop them: "Come with me to Paris instead."

There was a flare of something in her eyes—Anger? Hope? Desperation?—which was replaced almost immediately with another expression, one he had never seen before, something cool and calculating and distant. "And then what, Andy?" she said. "After Paris, then what? Will you bring me back here and put me in one of the servants' rooms? Or maybe you'll find me a little apartment in Charlottesville and visit me on weekends."

He didn't recognize the woman who was speaking to him. He did not know what to reply. All he could manage was a hoarse, "It doesn't have to be like that. Don't make it sound like that."

Was that regret or pity he saw in her eyes? She said, softly, "What would it be like, Andy? What would it be like for us? Would it be happily ever after? Would it be marriage?"

Over and over, for the rest of his life, he would wonder what might have happened had he answered her then. Had he not hesitated. Had he found the words. But even as he drew a breath, not even knowing what he was going to say, she shook her head.

"No," she said, and her smile was strained and far away. "I didn't think so. Face it, lover, it was fun, but that's all it was. I knew that, even if you didn't. This is 1967, and I've got a life. Now, if you don't mind, I'd like to get back to it."

She picked up her palette, and her brushes, and turned away from him. And within the week, she was gone.

❧

And that was how he came to be standing in his living room alone while laughter and music from his own party spilled across the lawn from the winery a few hundred yards away, a forty-five-year-old man about to be elected District Court judge, in love with a girl half his age. He was sipping the newly labeled Shiraz, which was much too young to be drunk, and barely tasting it.

After a moment he heard a step in the hall, followed by the subtle flowery scent of the perfume his mother always wore. She stood beside him for a moment, studying the muraled alcoves that flanked the fireplace with a critical eye. Then she said, "I prefer the one in the winery, don't you?"

He said simply, "Yes."

"I can't imagine what happened. Clearly, she has talent. But the quality here is not nearly up to the standard of the mural in the tasting room. Everyone is raving about it. This one . . . I can't say, precisely, but it looks rushed, don't you think? She even left out the building."

She waited for a reply, and he could feel the sharpness of her gaze upon him, but he did not respond, with either look or word, and finally she shrugged. "Ah, well. I suppose she was anxious to move on."

He stared into his wine. "I suppose."

"I would never say anything to her, of course. But it's rather embarrassing, really. I think I'll have the alcoves boxed in. They've always been wasted space, anyway. What do you think?"

"I think that's fine, Mother."

"She certainly was a charming child," his mother went on. "Delightful to have around, for a while. But all that youth and energy . . ." She sighed. "I rather imagine it would try the nerves after a time. Don't you agree?"

He raised his head to look at her, and their eyes held for a long time. She revealed nothing but a cool smile.

And then she said, "Do come out soon, dear. Your guests are also voters."

When she was gone, he took up the bottle to refill his glass, but instead he simply stood there, staring at the label. He stared at it for a long time. And then, without warning, he threw the bottle across the room, where it crashed on the floor, and spilled wine pooled on the polished boards like blood.

🦢

No one at Blackwell Farms ever knew about the baby girl born to Emmy Marie Hodge eight months later. Emily sent Christmas cards to her mother, Marilee, for a few years, but eventually lost touch.

Within a week after the party, Andrew had the mural in the winery painted over, and no one ever asked why. Andrew was elected District Court judge, and he spent the rest of his life fulfilling that position. The 1967 Shiraz won awards, but midway through the run, Andrew discontinued the label. And, once the alcoves in the living room were enclosed, it should have been an easy enough matter to forget that Emmy Marie Hodge had ever existed.

But it wasn't.

# 19

# Hard Choices

They dressed in their Sunday best for the meeting the next morning, and as they got out of the car in front of the unpretentious little building they were self-conscious about it.

"We look like we should be sitting at the defendant's table in a courtroom," Bridget said, straightening the skirt of her navy silk suit. She cast an uncomfortable glance toward a harried mother in tattered shorts who crossed the street in front of them toward the Health Department, carrying a crying toddler. "Wait," she said. "I'm leaving my jacket in the car."

"I wish I hadn't worn heels," Lindsay said. "I never wear heels. And these French cuffs are too much."

Cici was wearing tailored gray slacks in a stylish pinstripe and a burgundy satin blouse underneath the matching, nipped-waist jacket. Her heels were even higher than Lindsay's. She experimented with taking her jacket off, as Bridget had done, but Lindsay shook her head adamantly. "You look like you just got back from a night of clubbing. That blouse is too much."

"It's the blouse I always wear with this suit," Cici protested.

"Button the jacket."

"We have way too many nice clothes for our current lifestyle."

"Maybe we can sell them to pay for a new barn," Cici replied dryly, checking her hair in the side view mirror.

"I always overdress when I feel insecure," Lindsay said uneasily. "Why do women do that?"

"It's a power thing," Cici assured her.

"I don't feel very powerful."

"Do you have a red lipstick?"

"Don't you dare," Lindsay commanded as Bridget began to search through her purse.

Cici glanced at her watch, and blew out a breath. "Well," she said. She slung the strap of her purse over her shoulder, and looked at the other two. "I guess we should go in."

This time the waiting room was not empty when they came in. A pregnant, acne-faced young girl sat beside a very large woman in a cotton shift, and a rail-thin boy with a shaved head and a butterfly tattoo on his forearm was sprawled out in one of the plastic bucket chairs across from them, absorbed in a handheld video game. All three of them stared as the women crossed to the receptionist's desk and were told to go right in.

Their high heels clacked with an embarrassingly loud rhythm on the linoleum as they crossed the room to Carrie's door, knocked timidly, and stepped inside. Carrie rose from behind her desk to greet them. "Good morning, ladies, please come in."

Four chairs were drawn up in a semicircle before the desk. One of them was occupied by a slight woman with dishwater-blond hair, caught at the nape with an elastic band. She turned to look at them curiously as they entered. She was plain looking and painfully thin, with deep purple shadows under her eyes and lips that were cracked beneath her faded lipstick. She wore a long-sleeved turtleneck sweater, despite the warmth of the morning, and a full cotton skirt with sandals. Her hands were wound tightly around a brown vinyl clutch bag whose finish was scratched and worn, and if the ladies had felt overdressed when they stepped out of the car, they felt like runway models pinned by a spotlight now.

"I was so sorry to hear about the fire at your place," Carrie was saying, and Lindsay, Bridget, and Cici dragged their attention away from the other woman long enough to assure her all was well, it had been nothing, really, no one was hurt, nothing of value was lost, and they were all doing just fine.

The thin woman rose uncertainly as Carrie made the introductions. "Mandy Clete, this is Bridget Tindale . . ." Her hand was cold and her fingers fragile as Bridget shook her hand. "Cici Burke . . ." She murmured a "nice to meet you." "And Lindsay Wright." Lindsay shook her hand. "Ladies, this is Noah's mother."

Somehow, they hadn't expected it all to be that simple. There should have been more drama, perhaps a late-breaking development, significant delays. Perhaps they had half expected to walk into the office and discover there had been a mistake in identity, or to be informed that the woman had not shown up after all. After fifteen years of abandonment, it shouldn't have been that simple.

"Cormier," the woman corrected in a small, shy voice. "I go by Cormier now. It's my maiden. And"—she raised her chin a little and her voice strengthened—"I want to thank you all for taking care of my boy."

Carrie said in her dulcet Louisiana drawl, "Let's all sit down, shall we? Can I get anyone coffee? No? Well, then, I thought it would be nice if we all spent some time getting to know each other, and then we'll talk about the best way to help Noah make the transition. I'm sure you have a lot of questions."

It was Lindsay who spoke up first. "Well, yes, I have a few questions. For starters, how could you abandon a helpless infant to a brutal alcoholic even you were too afraid to stay with?"

"Lindsay!" Cici laid a calming hand on Lindsay's arm.

Carrie said, "Really, Lindsay, I don't think it's appropriate—"

But Mandy, shaking off her initial shock, said, "No—no, it's okay. You have a right to ask. I know how it looks, but—I didn't abandon him. I left him with my mother until I could get a job and take care of him. I sent money when I could. But . . ." Her hands tightened around the small brown purse. "I couldn't even afford an apartment on what I made waitressing, much less take care of a baby, and . . . well, I moved around a lot. My mama was a good woman, a good mother. She raised me by herself and I never knew a moment's want. I never expected her to die before she was even fifty. It was her heart, and it was so sudden. I thought he would be fine with her. I thought he'd be safe."

Bridget spoke next, and her voice was much gentler than Lindsay's had been. "I don't mean to pry, but . . . when your mother died, didn't you know your husband would get custody of the child? Couldn't you have come back for him?"

Mandy chewed her bottom lip, her knuckles whitening on the scrap of brown vinyl in her lap. She said, without looking up, "I could have. But I didn't know about it until almost three years later." And then, with a visible effort, she flexed her fingers, straightened her shoulders, and met Bridget's eyes. "I made some very bad choices," she said steadily. "I was looking for an easy way out of the pain I was in. I don't even know where I was when my mother died. There were times during those years when I forgot I had a son, and when I did remember I did my best to forget again because the last thing I wanted was to have something else to worry about, something else to take care of."

She breathed in and breathed out. It made a trembly sound, but her voice was steady and the courage in her deep brown eyes was unwavering. "You're nice ladies," she said. "Look at you. You've had nice lives. You can't understand how a mother could simply lose track of her only child. That's good. I don't want you to understand it. It's a terrible thing, to have to go where I've been and do what I've done and know what I know. Because I lost track of more than my child. There are whole years that I don't remember. And by the time I did remember . . . it was too late. I didn't know where to begin looking for him. And the truth is, I didn't feel as though I deserved to find him. And then"—a faint, wavering smile at Carrie—"a miracle happened. And here I am."

The silence in the room was stifling. Cici looked at Carrie, widening her eyes slightly in helpless question, and Bridget murmured, "I'm . . . so sorry . . ." But it trailed off, as though she was not quite sure what she was sorry for.

Carrie said, "Mandy has been the drug recovery counselor at Safe Haven halfway house in Richmond for almost five years now. She works with troubled teens every day."

"Noah is not a troubled teen," Lindsay said acridly.

"No one suggested he was," Cici intervened before Lindsay could draw another breath. She turned to Mandy. "Look," she said, "I know you think this is none of our business, but we've all grown very fond of Noah and—well, of course we want the best for him. Do you really think . . ." Again she looked helplessly at Carrie. "Are you sure a drug rehabilitation halfway house is the best place to raise a teenage boy?"

"I already have an apartment lined up," Mandy assured her. "We can move in this weekend."

Bridget said, floundering in confusion, "But—Noah loves the outdoors so. Gardening, and building and planting things . . . he even has a pet deer. Living in the city will be hard for him."

"Young people are incredibly adaptable," Carrie assured her. "A great deal more than we give them credit for."

"And I hope you'll let him visit now and then," Mandy said quickly. "Carrie and I were talking before you came in, and I thought that might make it a little easier for him, knowing that he could come back."

"He's just started to think of the farm as home." There was a note of pleading in Bridget's voice. "Surely you could give him a little more time to adjust to the idea of moving away."

Before Carrie could answer Lindsay spoke abruptly. "He's an artist." Her jaw was set and her voice was tight. "He has as much passion for it as anyone I've ever known, and he could have a real future with the right training."

Mandy's face softened. "My mama used to draw. That must be where he gets it from."

"His IQ is close to 150. Did you know that?" Lindsay went on. The slight increase in the pace of her breathing was visible in the rise and fall of her chest. "Despite the absolutely terrific start in life you gave him . . ." The scorn in her voice shocked even her friends, who stared at her. "He's managed to overcome the lack of even the most basic education and, in less than six months, surpass his own grade level. Is there a good school in your neighborhood, Ms. Cormier? One with an arts program? And what about college? How much thought have you given to that? Or have you been too busy thinking about what's best for you to give any consideration to what's best for Noah?"

"Lindsay, please!" exclaimed Bridget, horrified.

Cici apologized, "This has really been a stressful week for us. I'm sure Lindsay didn't mean . . ."

"I know what I meant!" Lindsay snapped.

Carrie placed both hands palm down on the desk, as though readying herself to stand. "I think this might be a good time to take a break."

Some of the fire went out of Lindsay's eyes as she took a deep breath. "I'm sorry," she said with a shake of her head, "but this isn't right. It's just not right."

"Maybe there's a compromise," Cici said, touching Lindsay's arm soothingly. "Why don't you let Noah finish out the school year with us, and spend the summer at the farm while you get settled in your new apartment? He could get to know you gradually over the summer, and by the time school starts in the fall you would be ready to have him move in with you." As she spoke, Mandy was shaking her head, slowly at first and then with more and more force.

Carrie spoke up. "That's not a bad plan," she said. "It might be the best thing for everyone."

"No," Mandy said. "No."

"Why not?" Lindsay insisted, obviously struggling to keep the edge out of her voice. "What difference can a few months possibly make?"

"I don't have a few months!" Mandy cried. The look in her eyes was desperate and wild, and the next words seemed to be torn from her. "I have cancer! I'm dying."

❧

Noah said, "Hey."

Lori did not look up from the laptop computer on her desk. She had several books open beside it and was frowning over the contents of her screen. "Hay is for horses," she replied. "What do you want?"

He stepped inside her room. The bed was rumpled, magazines were stacked untidily on the antique nightstand, dirty clothes were scattered on the floor. She had a stereo system with big puffy earphones and a forty-two-inch flat screen television set with a VCR and DVD player/recorder combination. DVDs and CDs in colorful cases were scattered on the floor in front of the equipment. Noah had a television and DVD player in his room, too, which he thought had come from Bridget, who didn't want them in her room, but most of the movies he had been provided with were either chick flicks or Disney, and after the initial novelty had worn off, he didn't watch it much.

He said, "Here's that picture you wanted." He put a sheet of heavy drawing paper on her desk. "I did it in pencil so it wouldn't smear, like you said."

"Say." She turned away from her work and picked up the sheet. "That's pretty good. Thanks."

"And here's the book back." He returned the book that she had renewed at the library. "What're you going to do with that picture, anyhow?"

"Well," she said, and there was a note of carefully repressed excitement in her voice as she tucked the drawing carefully inside a manila folder, "I was going to give it to Mom, and Aunt Bridget and Aunt Lindsay, for Mother's Day—"

"Mother's Day?" he repeated, surprised.

"I was going to say it was from both of us," she defended. "After all, it was my idea, even if you did draw it."

"But they're not your mama." He frowned. "The other two, I mean. How come you give them a present?"

"They may not be my *actual* mother," she explained, "or mothers, as the case may be, but they're *like* my mothers. My folks got divorced when I was little," she added matter-of-factly, "and my mom had to work a lot, so they kind of helped raise me. You don't have to be related to be a family, you know."

He didn't answer; he just stood there, frowning over the concept, so she shrugged. "Anyway, like I said, I was going to frame your drawing for Mother's Day, because I thought they'd get a kick out of it, you know, but now I have a better idea. A *much* better idea," she added determinedly, and turned back to her computer. "Of course it would go a lot faster if I had actual access to the Internet from my home computer, instead of having to drive half an hour each way just to Google one thing. Anyway . . ." She hit Save on the computer and closed the laptop. "I guess I can put this off until I can get back to the library. So, are you ready to finish the fountain?"

He was still frowning, but this expression was different from his usual demeanor of sullen discontent. It seemed more thoughtful, and even sad. He didn't reply right away, and Lori started to repeat herself. Then he said, "You're gonna have to finish it by yourself."

Lori sat back in her chair and threw her hands up in

exasperation. "Oh, terrific! That's just terrific. I knew I couldn't count on you. Didn't I call it? 'You're just a kid,' I said, 'you'll screw it up.' Well, thank you very much for proving me right!"

He was quick to defend himself. "I didn't screw it up! I mixed the cement, I patched the holes, I showed you how to set the rocks, didn't I?"

"Yeah, but you're the one who knows what the pattern around the base is supposed to look like, and how am I going to move that heavy statue by myself? Typical, just typical. This family is in real trouble and I'm working my butt off to try to help, and what are you doing? Bailing, that's what! You ought to be ashamed of yourself." She turned away in disgust. "I don't know why I'm even wasting my breath on you."

The silence that followed was so lengthy that Lori abandoned her annoyance to slide a glance toward him. He just stood there, looking sad, and that was when she noticed for the first time that he held his backpack by one strap in his hand. After a moment he reached into it, pulled out an eight-by-ten canvas, and looked at it for a moment before handing it to her in a single abrupt gesture. "Here," he said. "This'll show you what it's supposed to look like."

She looked at the painting of the fountain, and then at him, curiously, until his brows drew together sharply and he added, "Even a stupid girl ought to be able to figure it out from that."

She laid the painting aside. "Gee, thanks a lot. That'll make me feel ever so much better when I'm dragging rocks in from the field and trying to lift a two-hundred-pound statue by myself."

"Yeah, well, you're the one that signed up for it, not me."

He turned to go and had reached the door before he looked

back. "Hey," he said. He waited until she looked at him, and then he seemed almost as though he didn't know what to say. His jaw was set but his expression was uncomfortable and it seemed a long time before he said, simply, "Thanks for not telling."

Lori just looked at him. Finally, she shrugged, and said, "Whatever."

He glanced at the floor, around the room, seemed to be searching for something else to say. But he settled on, "Okay. Well, see you."

Again Lori said, "Whatever," as he left the room.

She opened her laptop and didn't think about him again for the rest of the morning.

❧

For the longest time, no one spoke. Carrie sat back in her chair, her expression tight. Bridget's fingers went to her lips, a quick intake of breath flaring her nostrils. Cici's hand closed tightly over Lindsay's and she felt the trembling there.

Mandy's chin rose a fraction. "I've made mistakes," she said steadily, "and I've paid for them. But I've been given a second chance. And the one mistake I refuse to make . . ." Her breath caught, and quavered in her throat, and then, with an effort, became strong again. "The one mistake I refuse to make," she repeated, "is to waste this chance. I'm going to get to know my son before I die."

"Oh . . . I'm so sorry," Bridget whispered. Her fingers fluttered to her lap.

Carrie turned a somber gaze on Mandy. "This changes things," she told her quietly. "You should have told me."

"It doesn't change anything," the other woman replied.

Her knuckles whitened. "He's still my son. You can't keep him from me."

Cici felt Lindsay's surge of breath and she clamped down on her friend's hand, hard. Then she said, "Ms. Cormier ... Mandy ... please forgive me for asking, but—what is your prognosis?"

"There are new protocols being developed every day," she insisted, meeting their eyes bravely. "I've been in remission before. I can fight this thing."

It sounded like a speech she had given many times before. But there was something in her voice that was not quite convincing, and she must have seen that reflected in their eyes. In a moment she dropped her own gaze and said softly, "It's spread to my liver. The doctors say less than a year."

And this time when she looked at them there was desperation in her gaze. "That's why I have to have my boy with me now, don't you see? I don't have much time. There's so much I've missed ... and I don't have much time."

Lindsay said, "But you're sick and—I'm sorry, but you're going to get sicker. How can you take care of a teenage boy? Or are you expecting him to take care of you?"

"Lindsay . . ." Cici cautioned. But Lindsay jerked her hand away and gave a single shake of her head, warning both of her friends with the gesture that she would brook no interference.

"All these years he's believed his mother was dead," Lindsay went on, holding the other woman's gaze steadily. "Now he's going to learn that you abandoned him on purpose, and no matter what you tell him, don't you see, for the rest of his life he'll always think that it was because he wasn't good enough for you to love." And despite the cloud of hurt and denial that gathered in the other woman's eyes, she pushed on. "And now, after fifteen years, you come back to claim him—only so that he can watch you die? How can you do that? How *can* you?"

Mandy stammered, "That's not what I . . . that's not how—"

"I know that's not what you meant to do," Lindsay said earnestly, leaning forward in her chair. "I know you didn't mean for your life to turn out this way and I am sorry, truly I am, but I'm begging you, think about this. Think about what you're doing to this child you've never met. He could be—so much. He deserves so much. This isn't right. It just isn't right."

"What do you know about what's right?" Mandy burst out angrily. "I walked away from my own baby to keep him safe and now, just when I've found him again, I'm dying! Don't you talk to me about what's right!"

"This is not going to change that!" Lindsay cried. "Don't you see—"

Carrie interrupted, with a quiet authority that belied her youth, "Thank you, Lindsay. I think you've said enough."

She turned to Mandy. "There are some things we have to discuss," she said gently. "No one means to make this harder on you than it has to be, but, given the state of your health, have you thought about who will take care of Noah if you no longer can? He is still a minor, you know. Perhaps you should consider leaving him in foster care and arranging a visitation schedule . . ."

Mandy pressed her fingertips to her temples, shaking her head slowly. "How dare you?" she said quietly. Then she looked straight at Lindsay. "How dare you set yourself up as judge of what's best for my child? How dare you judge me?" A breath, a final shake of her head. "No. He's my boy and you can't keep him from me."

"No one is trying to keep him from you," Carrie assured her. "All we're trying to do is—"

"He's my child," Mandy insisted. "I know my rights." Two high spots of color stained her cheeks and her dark eyes took on a feverish hue. She rose abruptly, clutching her purse. "I've come for my son. You have his bags packed and ready to go today. I'll be back for him at three o'clock." She turned to Carrie. "Do I have to bring the sheriff with me?" she demanded.

Carrie said coolly, "That won't be necessary."

"Three o'clock," she repeated. "I'll be back."

And with that, she left the office, closing the door hard behind her.

Cici said, "This isn't happening." She stared at Carrie. "You really can't be sending a fifteen-year-old boy away from the only stable home he's ever known to care for a terminally ill woman he's never even met."

"She is his mother," Carrie said, trying to hide her own distress behind the authority in her tone. "The law is very clear—"

"Then the law is wrong. It's just wrong."

"This will change him forever," Lindsay said. Her eyes had a bleak, unfocused look. "It will change the possibility of who he might have been."

"Maybe," Carrie agreed gently. "We have no right to judge, here, and we can't play God. Every child has a right to know his mother."

Cici said, "This is not how the system is supposed to work. What about what's best for Noah?"

And Bridget added, "Okay, you're right, maybe he does have a right to know his mother is alive, and maybe he does deserve to get to know her . . . but to send him away to live with her—under these circumstances—surely he'd be better off in foster care, even if it's not with us."

"That will have to be decided by the Department of Family and Children's Services in Richmond. I'll file a report with them, of course, and they will follow up . . ."

"And that could take months," Cici said.

"Months," repeated Lindsay. She stood. Her friends followed suit.

"Ladies," Carrie said, coming around the desk. Her face was soft with genuine regret. "I know this doesn't seem fair, and I am so sorry it happened. But there's really nothing more we can do. I'll talk to Mandy again, and maybe we can come up with some kind of support plan . . . but in the meantime, the kindest thing you can do for Noah is to prepare him for the news. We'll be by to pick him up this afternoon."

They were barely out the door before Lindsay snatched her phone out of her purse and flipped it open.

"What are you doing?" Cici said.

"Lawyers," she responded crisply. She scrolled down her address book as she walked. "The whole damn world is run by lawyers. Well, I know a few lawyers and I'm not afraid to put them to work." She pushed a button and clamped the phone to her ear.

Bridget said uncertainly, "Do you mean . . . take this to court?" She had to quicken her steps to keep up with Lindsay's angry stride. "Can we do that?"

"Lawyers can do whatever they want." She took the phone away from her ear, scowling, and redialed.

Cici said carefully, "That would be one way to go, I guess. Once a jury heard all the sordid details of his mother's background—and there have got to be plenty, no matter what she's done with her life now—they would never grant her custody of Noah. Of course, Noah would have to hear all the details, too."

And Bridget added hesitantly, "These things take an awfully long time. She might not survive the trial."

"Either way," Cici added, "with no other living relatives, and without any real wrongdoing, I don't think the court would intervene while the case is pending. Noah would still be living with her."

Lindsay suddenly threw the telephone, hard, down on the sidewalk. "No service!" she exclaimed furiously. "God damn it!"

The other two stopped, startled, and Lindsay turned away from them. She drew a breath and pushed her hands through her hair. And in a moment she said, wearily, "I'm not going to take it to court, am I? I'm not going to torment this poor woman who only wants a chance to make things right, and I'm not going to humiliate a fifteen-year-old boy in a court of law and turn his last days with his mother into a nightmare, and I'm not going to file a complaint with Social Services in Richmond. I'm going to let him go."

Bridget reached down and retrieved Lindsay's phone. Cici slipped her arm around her waist. "Let's go home," she said.

# 20

# Coming Home

Ida Mae was on a stepladder, using an extension pole brush to sweep cobwebs from the living room window casings, when they came in. "For heaven's sake, Ida Mae, get down from there," Bridget exclaimed, rushing toward her. "What are you thinking?"

"I'm thinking it's about time somebody swept up these cobwebs is what I'm thinking." But she did accept the assistance of Bridget's hand on her elbow as she climbed stiffly down from the stepladder. "Looks like nobody lives here but ghosts. Time to take that chandelier down and wash it, too. You can't hardly see for the dust."

"Why don't you get one of the kids to help you with that?"

Ida Mae sniffed derisively. "Oh, they always got plenty better to do."

"I hope they're not fooling around out at the barn," Cici said. "I told them to stay away from there."

"Little Miss Fancy-Pants ain't come out of her room all day, and the boy took off right after you did."

"That was over three hours ago."

"You haven't seen him since?"

Lindsay looked sharply at Ida Mae. "What do you mean, 'took off'? Where did he go?"

"He ain't in the habit of telling me what his plans are, now is he? There's soup on the stove for lunch, if you want it." She started folding up the stepladder.

Cici went to the bottom of the stairs. "Lori!" A muffled reply came from behind a closed door, and she called, "Will you come down here please?"

While they waited for Lori to appear, the three women shared a worried look. "He's probably just roaming around the woods somewhere," Bridget said. "You know how he likes to go off by himself."

"I should check the folly," Lindsay said.

"Maybe he's in the studio," suggested Cici.

"No he's not," Ida Mae said, passing them with the clattering ladder. "He took off down the driveway with his backpack."

Lindsay's hand went to her throat.

Lori came down the stairs two at a time. "What's up?"

"Do you know where Noah is?"

She seemed surprised. "I haven't seen him since early this morning, Mom. Why? What's he done now?"

"Did he say anything to you?" Lindsay demanded urgently. "Anything that might give you an idea . . ."

Ida Mae paused on her way to the pantry with the ladder and looked back curiously. "You don't think that young'un has run off, do you?"

Sudden comprehension dawned on Lori's face. "Oh no," she said softly. "*That's* what he meant." She looked at her mother, her expression anxious and apologetic. "I wasn't really paying attention. I would have tried to stop him if I'd known, honestly I would . . . but this morning, when he came to talk to me, I think he was trying to tell me good-bye."

There was nothing but the sound of someone's sharply indrawn breath, and for a moment no one moved. Then Cici said briskly, "Okay, first, let's search the property, just to be sure. Lori, check all the outbuildings, and Lindsay, you check the folly. He wasn't on the highway. We just came that way. I'll start calling the neighbors. After all, he couldn't have gone far. He doesn't have any money."

Lori said in distress, "Mom . . . he does."

They all stared at her.

"He's been saving these antique bottles and stuff that he found on the property," Lori explained. "The other day I gave him a ride into town and he sold them to that fellow at the junk shop. I don't know how much he got for them, but it was at least fifty dollars."

Lindsay looked at Cici. "You can get a bus ticket to Charlottesville for that," she said.

Bridget took up her car keys. "I'll go," she said.

Lindsay turned for the door as she did. "I'll check with Reverend Holland."

Cici said, "Lori—"

"I've just got to get my shoes." She raced up the stairs.

೨ꝏ

Noah was not at the folly. He was not in the studio or the workshop or the cellar or the old winery under the barn. He was not in the sunroom with the baby chicks or wading in the stream with the dog or sitting in the sun on the rock in the woods behind the house where he sometimes liked to sit and sketch. The motorcycle was still in its shed, gas tank empty. But the extra ration of apples that had been left in Bambi's pen was not a good sign.

The neighbors had not seen him, and neither had the Hollands. He had not, to the recollection of the ticket attendant at the bus station, been on the bus that had departed at eleven a.m., nor had he purchased a ticket for the one that was to leave at eleven p.m. Of course, if he had hitched a ride to Charlottesville, he might already be on a train.

They met back at the house, exhausted, distraught, and virtually out of ideas. They stood in the foyer, uncertain whether to continue the search by foot or by telephone, or to get back into their cars.

"Lori, did he say anything, anything at all that might give you an idea where he might be going?" Bridget insisted.

Lori shook her head helplessly. "We had a fight. It was a stupid fight. But we're always fighting. Mom, I'm so sorry!"

Cici put her arm around her shoulders in a brief squeeze. "It's not your fault, honey. No one thinks that."

Lindsay said, "We should check the highway one more time. And one of us should go to Charlottesville, to start asking questions there. I've got some photographs of him in my digital camera. All I have to do is run them off on the computer—"

"We can't do this by ourselves. We have to call the sheriff."

Bridget nodded in agreement. "We should call Carrie." She looked anxiously at her watch. "It's almost three o'clock."

"You don't suppose he overheard something, do you?"

Lori drew a deep breath. "Mom," she said, "there's something I think you ought to know."

And then, from behind them, Noah said, "What're ya'll looking for?"

With a cry, they rushed him. He was dusty and sweaty and his battered sneakers had left muddy footprints across the floor. Lindsay grabbed his shoulders and looked for a moment as though she would shake him, but embraced him instead. When she released him she had to turn away quickly and wipe the tears with both hands before he could notice.

Bridget took Lindsay's place, hugging him. "Where have you been? You scared us to death!"

Lori said, "We've been looking everywhere!"

"Don't you ever do anything like that again, do you hear me?" Cici demanded, as she pulled him away from Bridget and hugged him hard.

Noah looked embarrassed by all the attention, but, for the first time, also a little pleased. He shrugged away uncomfortably. "I had some stuff to take care of," he said. "Didn't mean to cause all this fuss."

Lori stood with her hands on her hips, scowling at him. "Well, you did. What have you been up to, anyway? We thought you'd run away!"

He looked from her to the others, all of them gathered around looking anxious and relieved and waiting for him to say something. Ida Mae came in from the kitchen silently, sweeping up his muddy footprints, but even she had an obvious ear cocked toward the conversation. Noah shuffled his feet, looked at the ground. Then he looked from one to the other of them reluctantly. "I thought about it. Running away, I mean. Figured it would be for the best. But then I got to thinking, what kind of jerk would walk out on a bunch of women in trouble, all by yourselves like you are . . ." Just then, he flicked a quick glance toward Lori, who looked surprised. "So here." He dug into his pocket and produced a roll of bills, which he presented to Lindsay. "Here's what I owe you for the ticket, plus some extra. There'll be more," he promised. "But that's all I could raise today."

Lindsay took the money, regarding it as though it had sacred powers. She looked up at him in confusion. "But—how . . . ?"

"I sold some stuff," he replied with a shrug. "That fancy iPod was nice, but I got too much to do to be fooling with it." There was a small sound of protest from Bridget, but he went on. "And Jonesie gave me twenty-five dollars apiece for some of my paintings," he added with an unmistakable note of pride. "He thinks he can sell them to tourists out of his store. He said that job of his is still open, too, but I've got to have your permission before he'll hire me." He was speaking faster now. "Two afternoons and a half day on Saturday, unloading trucks and stocking shelves. I turn sixteen in six months, and I can get a legal license, so getting back and forth to work won't be a problem and I can keep up with my chores here and my schoolwork, too. And he said he'll give me a discount on hardware—I had to talk him into that one, though—which I figure we're gonna need, rebuilding the barn. It's gonna take a while," he admitted, "but I found a place that sells salvage lumber, and we should be able to get her back up again for a couple of thousand if we do all the work ourselves."

Cici had her hand at her mouth and was blinking hard. Lindsay's eyes were lowered; she was looking much too intently at the roll of money in her hand.

"No point in carrying on so," Noah went on, but his brows drew together sharply to hide his distress, and it was with obvious determination that he added, "I figured it was only right I should pay for the barn since"—he squared his shoulders—"it was on the account of me that it burned down."

All the women stared at him, but he did not flinch.

"I was smoking behind the barn," he said. "I know I told you I wouldn't and it was wrong, and I ain't gonna do it again, and I'm gonna work until every last nail is paid for and that's a promise. If you want me to, that is," he added, and for the first time he let his anxiety show. "If you'll let me stay."

"Oh, Noah," Bridget said fervently, "we want you to stay more than anything else in the world."

"This is your home for as long as you want it," Cici assured him. "That's a promise."

Lindsay, for a moment, didn't seem to be able to say anything at all. She simply stared at the roll of bills clutched in her hand. At last she managed, "Noah, you didn't start that fire. The fire marshal said it was overheated wiring."

For a moment relief flashed in his eyes, and his shoulders sagged visibly. Then he stiffened with determination. "I still want to pay my share."

Lindsay said, with an effort, "Noah, we need to talk about something."

His shoulders sagged again. "I know you're mad at me," he said. "I don't blame you for wanting to kick me out."

She was shaking her head. "No. It's not that. I don't want to kick you out. I want you to stay. I want it so badly that—"

Outside in the yard a car door slammed, and Rebel began

his raucous barking. Lori rushed to the window. "It's the social workers again," she reported. "Only there's a different one this time." She rushed to the door. "I'll get Rebel."

Noah looked at them in confusion. "What're they doing here again? Did ya'll call them to find me?"

Cici, Bridget, and Lindsay exchanged a desperate, helpless look. They could hear Lori outside, greeting the visitors and shouting Rebel away. Ida Mae went to the door.

Lindsay forcefully relaxed her features, and it was as though the very act of doing so forced a measure of calm to steal over her. "Noah," she said, laying a hand lightly upon his arm, "hang around for a minute, will you? There's someone we want you to meet."

Ida Mae escorted the two women inside. Carrie looked nervous, although she greeted them with her usual grace. Mandy looked frail and strained and timid, with her dark eyes and her black sweater and her hands clutching her purse. She looked around the big house, with its cobwebs and its dusty chandelier, as though she had never seen anything so fine.

"Oh my," she said softly. "What a lovely home."

Then her gaze fell on Noah, and her expression softened. For a moment, she was almost beautiful. "Hello, Noah," she said.

Lindsay's voice was strong and pleasant as she said, "Noah, you remember Miss Lincoln from the Department of Family and Children's Services." Only the slightest hesitation before she added, "And this is—"

But Noah stepped forward. "I know who you are," he said, and everyone stared at him. "You're another do-gooder that thinks they know what's best for me. Well, I'll answer all your stupid questions and I'll take all your tests, and I'll use my manners and speak good English, if that's what it takes. But if you really want to know what's in the best interest of the child"—he slid a glance toward Lori, who had just come in the front door— "it seems to me the person to ask would be the child hisself. I mean, himself. And since I'm him—I mean, he—I can save you some time. I'm doing just fine where I'm at. Why do you want to mess with it?"

For a moment everyone seemed too stunned to react. And then Mandy smiled slowly. "Well now," she said, "that does seem like a foolish thing to do, doesn't it? But I wonder if you wouldn't mind sitting down and talking with me for a while, anyway. I'll try not to ask too many stupid questions."

She glanced around, and there seemed to be a note of pleading in her eyes as she said, "Is there somewhere we could be alone—just for a little while?"

Lindsay began, "Um, we really haven't had a chance to talk about our meeting this morning . . ."

Mandy repeated, "Alone? Please?"

"Yes, of course." Bridget was the one to move. She showed Mandy to the living room. Noah accompanied them with an air of resolute determination, and Bridget pulled the pocket doors closed behind her as she left.

Lori folded her arms across her chest with a smug smile. "I'm the one who taught him to stand up for himself like that. He did pretty well, didn't he?" Then her smile faded. "I know I probably should have told you about"—she cast a wary glance at Carrie—"the other thing, but I promised I wouldn't. And it seemed important to keep my word."

"It's always important to keep your word," Cici assured her. But even as she spoke to Lori her attention was on Carrie. "You did the right thing. Why don't you go get a sandwich or something? You must be starved."

"I don't mind if I do. Ida Mae, is there any of that pie left from yesterday? Can you believe that kid walked all the way to town and back?"

"I'll bring out some coffee," Ida Mae said, following Lori to the kitchen. "And some pie, if she leaves any."

Cici gestured toward the front door as they departed, and the women moved silently out to the porch.

"Carrie," Lindsay said, keeping her voice low but urgent, "we didn't get a chance to tell Noah about his mother. I don't understand what's going on."

"Shouldn't you be in there with them?" Bridget added, casting a worried glance over her shoulder.

"Has something happened?" Cici asked. "She seemed different from when we left her."

Carrie gave a slow uncertain shake of her head. "I don't know. We had a long talk on the way out here. She didn't seem as sure about her decision as she was before. She asked a lot of questions. But there are so many emotions involved. This is the first time she's seen her son in fifteen years and . . ." Again she shook her head. "I don't know."

"Is there anything we should be doing?" Lindsay asked.

Carrie replied simply, "Wait."

And so they sat on the porch, and waited. They waited for over an hour, their ears tuned to any sound from the other side of the screen door. Ida Mae brought a tray with coffee and strawberry pie. They sipped the coffee but mostly just pushed the pie around on their plates. They didn't talk much. When they heard the pocket doors to the living room slide open, they all stood and hurried inside.

Mandy paused outside the living room door. "Well, Noah," she said, and extended her hand, "you're a nice young man. Really nice. It was good to meet you."

He replied, "Yes, ma'am. Likewise." And he actually shook her hand. Then he said, "So. Do you think I'll be staying here, or what?"

She hesitated before answering, for what seemed like an eternity. The smile she gave him trembled slightly at one corner, but she said, "I don't see why not."

The grin that broke across Noah's face seemed to be a thing of itself, unrestrained and alive. He struggled to get it under control but was not entirely successful. "That's good," he said simply, "'cause I've got stuff to do."

"Good-bye, Noah," Mandy said softly.

He replied nonchalantly, "Bye, ma'am." Then he turned toward the kitchen.

Lori, on her way upstairs, had come around the corner in time to hear the verdict. As she came abreast of Noah she winked at him and held up her hand for a high five. He slapped it, sharing a grin, and they passed without speaking.

As Mandy started to move toward them, Lindsay's hand was clamped down so hard on Bridget's that she couldn't feel her own fingers. She let go, and made herself breathe, and tried to flex her fingers. Her mouth was too dry to speak.

Carrie was the first to move forward, and she went to put her arm around Mandy's shoulders in sympathy. "So you've made your decision," she said gently.

Now that Noah was gone, Mandy let go of the forced smile, the brave shoulders, the cheerful eyes. Her demeanor sagged and she looked tired, and haggard, and heavy with grief. But she also looked peaceful.

"I remember being fifteen," she said, and a faint wistful expression crossed her face as she spoke. She looked at Lindsay. "Being carefree, and hopeful, and waking up every day feeling like anything was possible. I wouldn't take these years from him for anything in the world."

Lindsay found her voice. "Do you mean . . ."

Mandy said, "I didn't tell him about me. About who I was, I mean. I let him go on thinking I was a social worker. I just wanted to . . . know him a little, you know?" She looked at Carrie for understanding. "I wanted to know that he was okay. I wanted to know who he was turning out to be. I wanted to know about his life. He told me about his drawing, about how he wants to hang his pictures in a fine gallery in Washington, and about his pet deer, and his garden, and what he's studying in school . . . my, he's smart isn't he?" Almost unbidden, a flare of motherly pride came into her eyes. "He told me you're a good teacher," she said to Lindsay. And to the others, "He told me a lot of things."

Cici said hoarsely. "Does this mean—are you going to leave him with us?"

They could see her throat constrict as she swallowed. And she replied quietly, "Sometimes a mother has to make hard decisions."

Lindsay said, "The things I said to you before . . . they were cruel. I'm sorry."

"They were true, though," Mandy said. "That's why I didn't

want to hear them, I guess." And she managed a weary smile. "I know you're nice people. I knew that from the minute I heard about you, and I knew it more when I met you. That's why I'm trusting you to raise my child."

Lindsay could not make a sound. She simply nodded.

Mandy glanced at Carrie, then back to the others. "Ms. Lincoln here said you wanted to adopt Noah. I can't let you do that, not while I'm living. But she said there was a paper I could sign that would put you in charge of him, and make it legal and permanent, and that's what I'd like to do. If you'd let me come see him from time to time," she added, "that would be a blessing. And maybe, when he's older, and we've gotten to know each other . . . well."

She dropped her eyes, acknowledging the futility of completing that thought, then looked at the three women again. Tears shimmered on her lashes. "I want him to grow up believing in a mother who loved him so much she would die before she hurt him. Please . . ." Her voice broke there. "Help me do that."

༚

Ida Mae cleared her throat behind them. "You gonna want any more coffee?"

The women stepped apart. Mandy turned away to wipe her eyes. Cici said, "Please, will you sit and have some coffee, or pie, or—"

Mandy shook her head. "No, thanks. I want to start back." She stopped, her attention caught by the art on the opposite wall. "Oh, that's nice."

"Noah did it." Lindsay walked with her to the framed drawing of the house, which hung in the center of the display.

She smiled as she touched the frame, and let her fingers linger. Then her eyes began to wander over the rest of the collection.

"They're things we found in the house," Lindsay explained. "It kind of tells a story."

Mandy stopped before the child's drawing that Lindsay had found in the woodbin, and she tilted her head a little, studying it. "That's odd," she said. "That drawing. My grandma had a quilt with something just like it right in the center. She used to wrap me up in it when I spent the night with her, and it smelled so nice. Like home." She smiled reminiscently. "I haven't thought about that quilt in years."

Ida Mae, who had been passing on her way to the porch to gather up the coffee things, stopped and looked at Mandy. She didn't just look. She stared. And then she said, in a very odd voice, "Child, who was your granny?"

"She was a Hodge," Mandy replied, though her expression was a bit puzzled. "Marilee Hodge."

Ida Mae's expression softened. "Well, I'll be," she said. And her gaze traveled to the window, but no one could see what had caught her attention there. She looked back at Mandy and repeated, "I'll be."

Then she walked back to the kitchen, and she forgot the coffee tray.

The women walked with Mandy to the car, and then Lindsay said suddenly, "Wait."

She ran across the yard to the studio, and returned in a moment with a thin square package wrapped in brown paper. She handed it to Mandy. "It's a painting I did of Noah," she said simply. "It belongs with you."

Mandy hesitated, and then took it carefully. She gazed upon

the paper wrapping as though she could see through it, and gentle wonder touched her face. "I—thank you." She looked up at Lindsay, and repeated, "Thank you."

And Lindsay replied quietly, "Thank you."

She looked at the other two, and seemed to want to say more. But in the end she simply got into Carrie's car, and they drove away.

# 21

# Mother's Day

Two dozen baby chicks were finally transferred from their cozy quarters in the sunroom to the spacious accommodation of a brand-new chicken coop. On one of her increasingly frequent trips to the library, Lori had found plans for a regulation-size henhouse, complete with box nests and a door tall enough to allow for egg collection. Using scrap lumber and a roof made of tin, which they salvaged from the barn fire, it took the five of them less than two days to erect the structure and fence in the chicken yard.

Ida Mae, however, spent almost a week sanitizing the sunroom and fussing over the mess they had made.

Cici contracted with Deke Sanders, of Sanders Grading, Hauling, and Septic Repair, for a half day's dozer work. Since he had worked most of the previous summer on their septic system and was a fellow member of the Methodist church, he was willing to wait for his payment. He pulled down the remains of the barn in a matter of a few hours, leaving the stone foundation ready for rebuilding.

Noah passed his tenth-grade placement test with a score

that impressed even Lindsay. As a reward, and because he seemed so determined to do it, they all agreed to allow Noah to start his part-time job with Jonesie on Saturdays only. Lori, surprisingly enough, agreed to drive him back and forth. He talked a lot about Melanie, Jonesie's fourteen-year-old daughter, who sometimes ran the cash register on Saturdays, and whenever he did, worry lines appeared between Lindsay's brows. With his first paycheck he bought nails and hinges for the new barn.

Lori spent every spare moment either at the library or working on her computer with complicated graphics and spreadsheet programs. To Bridget's delight she began to accumulate quite a collection of actual books, but whenever anyone tried to look at them she quickly hid the titles. Her research was not Lori's only secret. Although it was obvious she was making considerable progress with the pool and fountain project, for the last couple of weeks she had erected an elaborate screen of beanpole stakes and old blankets around the work site, and she and Noah conducted the final stages of construction in absolute seclusion.

On the second Sunday in May the ladies came down for breakfast and were greeted by garden roses in a cut glass vase on the table, orange juice and sugared strawberries at each place setting, and, through the open kitchen windows, the breeze of a balmy May morning and the musical sound of splashing water.

"Happy Mother's Day!" Lori exclaimed. In her hands she held a beautifully glazed pecan coffee cake on a footed cake platter, and she had surrounded it with rose petals.

"Don't worry," Noah assured them as they exclaimed over the

cake and the table, "she didn't make it. She bought it yesterday at the bakery in town."

Lori gave him a dark look as she set the cake on the table, which he ignored. "Come on," he insisted. "Let's show them."

"They have to have breakfast first," Lori argued. "Everyone knows you have breakfast first, then presents."

Ida Mae came in, tying her apron. "What's all this fuss? You kids have been banging around in here for an hour."

"Happy Mother's Day, Ida Mae!" Lori said happily. "You just sit down and relax. We're making breakfast this morning."

"Not in my kitchen, you're not!" she returned in real alarm.

"Presents," said Cici quickly, hoping to distract Lori. "Did you say something about presents?"

"Come on," Noah said, barely able to disguise his excitement as he held open the back door. "It's this way."

"Oh, okay!" Lori pushed ahead of him to lead the way. "Maybe just this once, presents before breakfast."

The ladies walked in their slippers and robes across the dewy grass, and they could see the spray of the fountain as soon as they rounded the corner onto the flagstone path.

"Oh, Lori!" exclaimed Lindsay. "You did it! You got the fountain running again."

"Not exactly by herself," Noah interjected.

"So that's what you two have been working on so hard these last few days!" Bridget said, pretending surprise.

"But that's not the best part," Lori insisted. She grasped her mother's hand and pulled her along. "Wait until you see."

The rose garden, just coming into full bloom with its showy pink and yellow and scarlet velvet blossoms, formed a partial screen as the path wound around and opened, at last, onto the pool and fountain area. All three women stopped, and caught their breath, pressing their hands together in a moment of sheer delight.

"Oh my goodness," said Lindsay softly. "I can't believe you did this."

"Lori . . . Noah . . ." Bridget shook her head in wonder. "It's just like I imagined."

Cici stared at Lori. "You did this? With your own hands?"

"I helped," Noah reminded her, a trifle belligerently.

"Not that much," Lori shot back, then relented. "Okay, he helped." And finally she modified it to, "We did it together."

This prompted Noah to admit, "She did a pretty good job, for a girl."

The pool was ten feet in radius and highlighted in the center by a fountain that sprayed a delicate bell of water three feet into the air. Deep purple water lilies drifted across the surface, which was punctuated by delicate sprays of green and lavender water grasses. The circumference was trimmed with a perfectly even and highly polished surround of river stone, and around it a six-foot flagstone sitting area had been cleared. At one end was the statue of a little girl with a flower basket that Lindsay and Cici had moved to the rose garden last year, now returned to its rightful place. At another was a hand-crafted wooden bench, stained and sealed against the weather. And all around the sitting area were carefully mulched plantings of colorful primrose, variegated coleus, pink begonias, and even a small weeping willow tree. It was a secret garden in the midst of a rose garden.

"Well, will you look at that." Ida Mae, curious, had come up behind them. "It's just like it was in the old days."

"Almost," Noah corrected. "The willow tree, she needs to grow some. And we don't know what happened to that bench that was under it, so we had to build a new one."

Cici stared. "You built that?"

"It wasn't easy neither, since you wouldn't let me use your power tools," Noah pointed out, a little accusingly.

"So I did the cutting," said Lori cheerfully, "with a jigsaw I borrowed from Farley. We had to do it while you weren't around," she added.

Cici's hand went to her heart. "You—used a jigsaw?"

"Look." Noah grinned as he gestured to the bench. "We fancied it up some for you."

The ladies walked over to the bench. Cici still looked stunned as she tried to get the picture of her daughter with a power saw out of her head. Lindsay reached the bench first and burst into delighted laughter. In a moment the others followed suit.

On the seat of the bench Noah had painted three large red and black ladybugs.

Noah and Lori wanted to show them the reflecting pool, which had also been cleaned and restored—although, Lori assured them, without nearly as much trouble—and which was actually reflecting a swatch of blue sky and the corner of a puffy cloud. The secret, according to Noah, which he had learned from some of the guys at the hardware store, was painting the bottom with pitch.

But by far the best idea of the morning was when Bridget suggested that they all enjoy a breakfast of fruit and coffee cake out in the fresh air around their beautifully restored fountain—which of course, made it impossible for Lori to cook the breakfast feast she had planned. Afterward, they all went to church services, and Noah wore a tie.

Two dozen long-stemmed roses arrived from Bridget's children, along with handmade construction paper greeting cards from the grandchildren, and after lunch her son and daughter placed a conference call and they talked for half an hour. Ida Mae made a strawberry shortcake using angel food cake layered with fresh strawberries so sweet and juicy they soaked all the way through. They ate it sitting on the front porch in the lacework shade of the poplar tree, watching the hummingbirds dart back and forth.

"This," declared Cici, setting her plate aside, "has been an absolutely perfect Mother's Day."

"I couldn't agree more," sighed Bridget contentedly.

"Me, either," agreed Lindsay. "In fact, I think I'll spend the rest of it sitting by our gorgeous new fountain, reading that novel I've been promising myself I'd get to all spring. That's something I've wanted to do ever since we bought this place. You two couldn't have given us a better present."

Noah, who was sitting on the steps, scraped his plate clean. "Maybe I'll just get me another piece of cake."

"You could offer to bring someone else one," Lori pointed out, and he gave her a scornful look as he passed.

"You know where the kitchen is."

Lori glared after him for a moment. "Just when I think there's hope for him . . ."

Then she shrugged it off and turned to them. Her eyes held the carefully guarded excitement of a secret that had been kept too long. "Everybody," she said, getting to her feet, "wait right here. There's one more present. I wanted to wait until you had time to relax and appreciate it."

"Oh, Lori, really, you've done too much already . . ." Bridget started to protest.

But Cici smiled broadly, leaning back in her rocker and stretching out her legs, "I'm totally relaxed."

"If it's more cake," Lindsay said, "bring it on."

"Wait right there," Lori called over her shoulder as she hurried inside.

When she was gone, Lindsay said fondly, "I think the two of them are enjoying this more than we are. They're great kids, both of them."

Cici smiled. "Did you ever think, when we moved in here last year, that it would all turn out like this?"

"Did you ever think," countered Bridget, "under any circumstances at all, that we would be spending our retirement years raising a teenage boy?"

"What, are you kidding? I'm still trying to get my mind around the chickens."

"We should get a cow," Bridget mused. "If we're going to live on a farm, we should have a cow."

Cici returned a steady look. "Do you know what I like best about this house?"

"That it doesn't have a cow?"

"Right."

Lindsay's smile was wistful. "I sent Mandy some photographs of Noah. For Mother's Day, you know."

Bridget looked at her solemnly. "It was her decision, Lindsay."

"I hope so," Lindsay said. "I hope it was the right one."

"Are you disappointed about the adoption?"

The women spoke softly, so as not to be overheard, and occasionally they cast cautious glances over their shoulders toward the house. Lindsay shook her head. "All I wanted was to protect him, and give him a fair start in life. The directed guardianship does that just as well."

"This is a huge responsibility," Bridget said, unnecessarily.

"Tell me about it," Lindsay sighed. And then she added, frowning a little, "I think that Melanie Jones is a little fast. We'll have to keep an eye on her."

They all laughed.

Lori came clattering down the stairs and through the screen door. She had three dark blue presentation folders in her hand, and she stood before them, clearing her throat purposefully, until she had their full attention.

"This," she informed them importantly, and passed a folder to each of them, "is for you."

Exclamations of "Oh my goodness!" and "Look at that!" and "What is it?" greeted the receipt of each folder. On the cover was a full color drawing of what appeared to be a heraldic crest, consisting of a shield that was red on the left and black on the right, overset by a winged horse with its hooves raised as though for combat. Across the top was a banner that read, "Ladybug Farm." And, below the crest, in bold flowing script: "Winery and Gourmet Foods." And below that, in a slightly smaller font: "Special Events and Catering upon Request."

"Wait a minute," Lindsay said, studying the drawing. "This is like that sketch I found in the woodbin." She looked up at Lori in amazement. "That's exactly what it is! How in the world—"

Lori's smile was pleased. "It's also the original label for the Blackwell Farms Shiraz during the sixties," she announced. "I found it in that book you asked me to take back to the library, Aunt Bridget, and Noah drew a copy for me. Only"—she pointed to the banner on Lindsay's folder—"it originally said 'Blackwell Farms,' of course."

"How clever! So that's what you've been spending all your time at the library on! What is this?" Cici fanned through the pages of the folder. "A history of the farm?"

"Actually," replied Lori, leaning back against the porch rail and folding her arms, "it's your business plan."

The pleasure on their faces faded slowly into uncertainty as their eyes dropped again to their folders.

"Winery?" said Cici.

"Gourmet foods and special events?" The doubt in Lindsay's voice was clear.

"Catering." Bridget's tone was thoughtful. "Now there's something I never considered."

"Look," Lori said, when she had their attention again, "you're not the first ones to try to figure out how to make this place pay for itself, you know. I've been reading everything I could find on Blackwell Farms, and what I found out is that they were famous for using everything they had, and for being the best at whatever they tried. They didn't just have a dairy, they had a gourmet Stilton that rivaled the best in England. They didn't just make preserves to sell on the side of the road, they shipped them to all the best hotels in Washington. And as for their wines—well you already know about those. The important thing is that they did more than one thing, and they made every thing they did special. You can do the same thing."

Cici spoke carefully, not wanting to hurt her daughter's feelings. "Honey, I admit I don't know much about the subject, but I do know that establishing a profitable winery isn't something you can do overnight. It takes years, sometimes generations, to bottle a decent wine."

"Right," declared Lori, and her eyes took on a glint of excitement, "if you start from scratch. If you don't have the vinifera, or the right soil, or even the equipment."

Cici mouthed the word *vinifera*? to Lindsay in amazement, but Lindsay merely shook her head, and kept her fascinated attention on Lori.

"Uncle Paul explained all that to me when he was here," Lori explained casually, "but I wanted to make sure I knew what we were getting into, so one morning while you all were in town I had this fellow come out from the county extension office to look at our vines. Turns out, his dad was the original vigneron for Blackwell Farms. Can you believe it? And he used to work in a real winery in New York himself, plus he remembered when old Mr. Blackwell built this one, so he knew just everything about it. Did you know, by the way, that this area of Virginia is a close climatological match for the Loire region of France?"

"Thomas Jefferson brought the first vines to Virginia from France," Lindsay murmured, and Lori beamed at her.

"Right! It was his dream that Virginia would become one of the foremost wine producers in the world. It could have, too, but got derailed by that little Revolutionary War thing. So anyway," she went on, "the extension agent said most of our Shiraz vines are still pure, and should produce for another couple of years with proper care. Of course, we need to start grafting and replanting now so that we'll have mature vines to take the place of the current ones, and we really need to expand the orchard by at least six acres over the next two years. But it's all there in your folder."

By now even Cici was gazing at her with rapt attention, too caught up even to ask questions.

"As long as he was here," Lori went on, "and since he did know something about wineries—his name is Dominic something, by the way, nice fellow, and he said you should give him a call if you had questions—I asked him to look at all that equipment down in the old winery. He said it was state-of-the-art for the time, and all it really needed was to be cleaned and polished and it would be ready to go. It doesn't even matter that all that stuff is over forty years old. In the wine-making business, old is good. In Italy, some of the finest wineries still crush their grapes by hand—or foot, as the case may be.

"But the best part is," she continued, "with the winery already set up like it is, and the vines still producing, you can actually use the equipment to secure a small business loan for start-up costs. You'll have to hire a vigneron to run the place, of course, and laborers for the vineyard, but that won't be until Year Two. You'll age and warehouse the wine here, just like the Blackwells did, but there will be bottling, shipping, and marketing costs— but we're talking Years Three and Four—before you start making a profit. It's all there in the folder. The main thing you have to worry about right now is restoring the vineyard, caring for the vines, and bringing in some new stock. With luck and good weather, you'll have everything in place for first harvest by next fall."

330 ~ Donna Ball

They just stared at her, lips parted, breaths caught on questions they couldn't quite form, looking like first-year students at a fourth-year lecture. Then Bridget cleared her throat, dropped her gaze to the folder in her lap, and said, "Um, catering. Fine foods?"

"Exactly," replied Lori with a wide, pleased grin. "That's exactly what I was talking about. Since you won't make a profit for three to four years, you're going to have to look to other sources, just like the Blackwells did. Not all the grapes are good enough for wine—it's in the folder—so you'll use those to make your wine jams, Aunt Bridget, just like we talked about. All you need is a commercial kitchen license and clearance from the health department, and with the way you and Ida Mae run this kitchen I don't think there will be a problem with that."

Bridget's eyebrows went up in amazement. "That's all we need? I thought it would be harder."

"You can have specialty labels printed up on the Internet for three cents apiece, and your choice of adorable glass jars and lids for under a dollar each. You'll have to invest in an industrial jar sealer, but even so, if you market directly to the public you're looking at a profit of six dollars a jar, easy, and it goes up when the jams are part of a gift basket."

Bridget's eyes lit up. "Gift baskets?"

"It's all in the folder."

Bridget started searching through the folder, and Lori addressed the other two. "I know we talked about a bed-and-breakfast, and you're right—too much work, too little profit. But have you ever thought about renting out the garden for weddings, anniversaries, things like that? If you offered catering as well, you could make as much in one weekend as a B&B could in a whole season."

Lindsay's eyes went wide, and she looked at Cici. "Miriam Wilson spent eight thousand dollars to rent a hotel ballroom for her daughter's reception, and God knows what she spent on the wedding itself."

"And the rehearsal dinner." Bridget looked up from her folder. "Do you remember the rehearsal dinner I did for Katie?"

"And you did that for free!" Cici said.

"All we'd have to do is get the word out to Paul and Derrick," Lindsay said, "and we'd have more business than we could handle—for jams and weddings!"

Lori smiled. "All it took was a little research. And oh, by the way, don't worry about hiring a marketing director. I'm enrolled for the fall in the business school at UVA, and after that I'll transfer to Cornell for my degree in enology and viticulture. I should be ready to take over the business by the time you're ready with your first vintage."

"Enology?" repeated Bridget blankly.

"Viticulture?" said Lindsay, sharing Bridget's puzzled look.

Cici rose slowly and crossed the floor to Lori, where she wrapped her arms around her daughter and hugged her hard. "Thank you," she whispered, "for my Mother's Day present."

Lori returned her embrace, only a little embarrassed. "You ask for a business plan, you get a business plan."

"I don't mean that." Cici's eyes glistened, and her nose was red, and she tucked a strand of Lori's hair behind her ear fussily as she smiled. "I mean you."

Lori hugged her again, grinning, and replied, "You're welcome."

As they broke apart, laughing, Lori added, "And another thing. I'd try to hold on to that boy, if I were you. He may not look like much now, but he's a quick study, and I think he's got potential. He can be a lot of help to you in the vineyard while I'm away at college."

They assured her gravely that they would do their best to hold on to Noah.

"So, I guess I'll leave you alone to look over your folders," Lori said. "If you have any questions, I'll be sitting on the hill behind the house, trying to get a signal on my phone so I can search the web for bargains on shipping materials. By the way . . ." She paused at the steps and held up a finger. "The Internet? Wave of the future."

❧

And so they wandered off their separate ways: Lindsay to the fountain, Bridget to the kitchen, Cici to a nap in her room. But one by one they were drawn to open the folders and to glance through them, first in a desultory fashion, and then with more interest, and then with great intensity. Cici came down the stairs with her calculator. "Girls, you won't believe this, but I just went over the cost analysis page and we might really be able to afford this." They sat at the table. They turned pages. Lindsay said at last, with great hesitancy and no small amount of wonder, "This could actually work."

"Of course there are a lot of variables."

"Just like with any other business."

Bridget said, "I never wanted to be a businesswoman."

"I never wanted to be a farmer," Cici put in.

And Lindsay added, "I never wanted to be a mother."

They looked at each other for a moment, thinking about it. Then Cici closed her folder, leaned back in her chair, and announced in a voice that indicated she could not quite believe it herself, "Ladies, it looks like we are opening a winery."

# 22

# Stories

After supper, they drifted onto the porch again, sipping chardonnay and marveling over the possibility that, in a few short years, the wine in their glasses might come from their own vineyard.

"I've never actually tasted a Virginia wine, have you?" Bridget said.

"I think I did, once, at a restaurant in Georgetown," Cici replied.

"They probably don't sell it in grocery stores," added Lindsay.

Bridget held up her glass, turning it so that it caught the spark of a brilliant sunset. "We'll have to get our wine on the menu at a White House dinner. Our future would be set."

"That sounds like a job for the marketing director," Lindsay said. "And given her ambition, I wouldn't be a bit surprised if we all weren't *drinking* our wine at a White House dinner before too long."

Cici allowed herself a smile of secret pride.

The screen door opened and Lori came out. "Did I hear my name?"

Lindsay looked at her. "Enology?"

And Bridget said, "Viticulture?"

"It's the study of wine making," Cici said. When they all turned to look at her, she shrugged. "I looked it up in the dictionary. You don't have to have the Internet to get answers, you know."

"But you do have to have Internet access to run a website," Bridget said with a certain amount of determination, "which I'm going to need in order to sell my wine jams and gift baskets online."

"Go, Aunt Bridget." Lori grinned and plopped down on the steps with her back against the rail, drawing up her knees.

"Well," agreed Cici reluctantly, "the satellite dish installer did say that if we cut down some trees we would have a pretty clear view of the southern sky. And a website would be helpful registering people for wedding weekends."

"Welcome to the double zeroes, Mom."

"Not to mention," added Lindsay, and an odd note of shyness came into her voice as she glanced down at her glass, "drumming up interest in art shows."

They all turned to her curiously, and she tried to minimize her words with a shrug. "I wasn't going to say anything, but I sent Derrick a photograph of that portrait I did . . ." Her eyes met Cici's and Bridget's meaningfully. "You know the one. I just wanted an opinion, you know. He'd already told me that the painting I did for Bridget of Rebel looked like it belonged on an L.L. Bean catalog cover, so I knew I could at least count on him to be honest."

"I love the L.L. Bean catalog covers!"

Lindsay ignored Bridget's outburst. "So anyway," she said with a breath, "he called to say that he liked it ... Well, actually, what he said was that this was what he expected from me ..." No one could be sure whether the rosy glow on her cheeks was from the sunset, or repressed pleasure. "Gallery quality, I believe were his words, and if I could do a dozen more in that vein he'd like to do a show."

There were squeals of delight and exclamations of excitement, and Lori got up and hugged her impulsively, and Lindsay, laughing, held up a hand in protest. "Well, it's not like I've actually finished anything yet," she said. "But I do have some ideas, and the best part is you know what Derrick charges people for the art in his gallery. With any luck, we might have that barn paid for sooner than we thought!"

The screen door banged again and Noah came out. He sat himself down in the space Lori had just vacated and regarded them all earnestly. "Who do I talk to about getting a learner's permit?" he demanded.

Cici paused with her glass halfway to her lips. "Um, the Department of Motor Vehicles?"

"I mean in this family. That social worker, Miss Lincoln, she said you all are my legal guardians now until I'm eighteen and you make all the decisions about my welfare. So what I want to know is which one of you makes the decisions about driving?"

Lori rolled her eyes. "Just give me some notice and I'll get off the road."

"Noah, you don't have a car," Lindsay pointed out.

"I've got a motorcycle."

"It doesn't have insurance. Or gas."

"I've got a job."

Lindsay looked at Bridget. Bridget looked at Cici. Cici looked at the sunset.

Lindsay said, "You know, Noah, we usually keep the evenings to ourselves. As quiet time, you know. Maybe we can talk about this in the morning."

Noah insisted, "But I've got to have transportation to get back and forth to work. And think how much time I could save you, running errands and hauling stuff and—"

Lindsay held up a quieting hand. "Later, Noah," she said firmly. And then she added, "In the meantime, though, there might be some good news. I know you wanted to move to the folly." As he drew a breath, she quelled it with, "That's not going to happen. However, we're all sensitive to the fact that you're outnumbered five to one in this house full of women." She glanced to the others for confirmation, which she received with sober nods. "So I've been thinking about a compromise. The studio has heat, and plumbing, and if you were willing to do the work yourself we wouldn't object to your turning the loft into a kind of apartment."

He considered that for a moment. "Thanks, but I guess I'll keep my room for now. Especially since that girl will be going off to college this fall. It don't seem right to leave you all in the house by yourselves."

And before they could even recover from that, the screen door opened one more time, and the most astonishing thing of all happened. Ida Mae came out onto the porch, and she had a glass of sherry in her hand.

"Young man," she commanded, "run inside and fetch me that rocking chair from the front hall. I've got a mind to set awhile."

Immediately, Cici, Bridget, and Lindsay scurried to their feet, offering Ida Mae their chairs, but she waited calmly until Noah returned with Bridget's mother's antique sewing rocker, which usually sat in a place of honor by the walnut drop leaf table in the foyer. They all stared as Ida Mae sank into it, took a sip of her sherry, and smacked her lips.

"Sit yourselves down," she commanded. "I've got something to tell you."

Slowly, the women sank into their chairs, the alarm on their faces clear. Even Lori took her post on the steps with her back against the railing, and everyone looked at Ida Mae.

Noah started to go back inside, but the older woman said sharply, "You too, young fella. This concerns you."

"Me?"

She gave him a decisive nod, and, looking uneasy, he took a place on the opposite side of the steps.

"Ida Mae, is everything all right?"

"You're not going to quit are you?"

"Has there been bad news?"

Ida Mae rocked, and sipped. And in a moment she said, "I've got a story to tell. It's about you, young fella, and where you came from. It's about your folks."

Noah looked uncomfortable. "I don't need to hear nothing from you about my folks. My pa was a no-account drunk who burned hisself up and that's all there is to it." He looked as though he might get up again, but she stopped him with a look.

"Maybe he was, maybe he wasn't. I don't know about your pa and don't give a rat's big fat behind. What I've got to tell you is about your mama, and her folks, and a story that goes all the way back to the Old Country."

Everyone stared at her.

"What do you know about my mama?" Noah said, a little curiously, a lot cautiously.

Ida Mae rocked, and sipped. A contented, reminiscent look spread over her face. "Your great-grandma and me, we stayed together, right here in this house. That was during the war, and I was just a slip of a thing. We all worked at the mill down the road, and prayed for our boys to come home. They used to call me Penny back then, on account of my hair, as bright as a copper penny, just like that girl-child there. And the mill, it closed down in fifty-three. But I remember your great-grandma. She was like a sister to me. And your great-grandpa, why, he was a hero in the war. He saved twelve men on that transport before it went down, and they gave him some kind of medal, I don't remember what it's called, after he was dead."

"*My* great-grandpa?" Noah said, astonished. "Mine?"

She nodded firmly. "That's a fact. Wasn't I standing right there at the top of the stairs when the telegram came? And I'll tell you something else. Your granny, you probably don't remember her, but she was a painter, too, just like you. Matter of fact . . ." Ida Mae sipped the sherry, smacked her lips again, and slid a sly look around to the three women. "She's the one that painted those pictures in the alcoves in yonder."

Lori clapped her hands in delight, but Bridget gave Ida Mae a frown of gentle reprimand. "Ida Mae, you said you didn't know anything about those paintings."

"I told you I didn't know everything," Ida Mae corrected smugly, "and I don't. And what I do know, I got a right to keep to myself. But I figure a young'un ought to know where he came from. So I'm here to tell the story."

Cici regarded her skeptically. "This wouldn't be the same kind of story as the one about the Yankee coming through the window, would it?"

Lori said excitedly, "What Yankee?"

And Noah's eyes lit up. "The same ones that hid the ammunition in the caves?"

Now Bridget, Cici, and Lindsay looked thoroughly confused, and Ida Mae rocked back, enjoying herself. "Well now, there's stories, and there's stories. The one about the Yankee getting shot in the parlor . . . well, I guess that's what you might call a little on the exaggerated side. Kind of gives the house some color, you know? But now this other story, the one I'm about to tell you about your folks, it has Yankees, and it has Indians, and it has sailing ships, and every word of it is true, just like it was told to me by your granny's mama."

Already Noah's shoulders were straighter, his head held taller. He said, "I remember my granny, kind of. She used to bake apple cookies. And she had this blanket with a horse on it that I always liked to sleep under."

Ida Mae said, "That was a quilt. And that's the story I'm going to tell you about. There's all kinds of ways to make pictures, you know, and back in the olden times, women did it with their needle and threads. I wouldn't be a bit surprised if that's how you come by your way with drawing things."

Lindsay's fingers went to her lips. "Quilt?" she whispered. The other two women simply stared at Ida Mae as the connection was made.

Ida Mae went on complacently. "The fact is, your folks were some of the first settlers in these parts. It was your great-great-great-great grandpappy, and he was what you call an emissary of the king, who the king himself sent over here to Virginia on a sailing ship to civilize the land."

"The king?" Lori repeated, her eyes big. "He knew the king?"

Noah hushed her with an impatient gesture and leaned in close.

"So I hear tell. Now he brought his young bride with him, because everybody knows you can't civilize anything without a wife, and before they could do much more than fling up a log cabin, the wild Indians attacked his homestead, and burned him out, and he had a newborn baby..."

The ladies stopped rocking, and lost interest in their wine. Noah barely took a breath, so intently was he listening, and Lori changed her position, to better see Ida Mae's face.

Cici grasped Lindsay's hand and squeezed. Bridget leaned forward in her rocker. The day turned slowly to dusk as the ghosts of those who had gone before them marched proudly across the landscape of their imaginations and Ida Mae spun out the story. Ladybug Farm came alive with the retelling, and a boy called Noah, who once had been lost, finally found his way home.

# In Another Time

*1720*

The mother who sewed the cloak, embroidering it with the finest of silk threads imported from India and twice wound, did not know that it was destined to endure three centuries. But it did.

The son, the husband, and the father who wore the cloak did not know that his tale would be legend, passed down from mother to daughter, daughter to son, son to daughter for generations uncounted. But it was.

He stayed beside his young wife throughout the night as the smoke of battle grew ever closer and she labored to bring forth their child. And when at last he could linger no longer, when the enemy must be faced for the sake of all he held dear, he gave his wife and his newborn child to the care of his faithful servant, and charged him with taking them to safety.

He wrapped the infant in his cloak to protect it from the chill dawn, and he spent a long time looking into his baby's eyes before returning her, with the greatest of tenderness, to her mother. He drew his sword. He did not know if he would return. And so at the last moment, he turned back, and knelt beside the woman he loved, and the child he did not know.

"Remember," he whispered to the tiny, sleeping creature who, at that moment, held all the future in its small curled hands. "Remember me. Remember who you are."

And so she did.